# Lessons of a
# Lowcountry
# Summer

## Also by Rochelle Alers

*Secrets Never Told*

*Four Degrees of Heat*
with Brenda L. Thomas, Crystal Lacey Winslow &
ReShonda Tate Billingsley

Published by Pocket Books

# Lessons of a Lowcountry Summer

## Rochelle Alers

POCKET BOOKS
New York  London  Toronto  Sydney

This book is a work of fiction. Names, characters, places and incidents are products of the author's imagination or are used fictitiously. Any resemblance to actual events or locales or persons, living or dead, is entirely coincidental.

 POCKET BOOKS, a division of Simon & Schuster, Inc. 1230 Avenue of the Americas, New York, NY 10020

Copyright © 2004 by Rochelle Alers

ISBN-13: 978-1-4165-2697-1
ISBN-10:    1-4165-2697-8

This Pocket Books paperback edition May 2006

10  9  8  7  6  5  4  3  2  1

POCKET and colophon are registered trademarks of Simon & Schuster, Inc.

Cover design by Julienne G. Ha
Cover photo © Stuart Westmorland/Corbis
Author photo by Devito Studios, LTD

Manufactured in the United States of America

For information regarding special discounts for bulk purchases, please contact Simon & Schuster Special Sales at 1-800-456-6798 or business@simonandschuster.com

To Vivian Stephens—for the endless chats.

*I belong to my love, and his desire is for me.*

—*The Song of Songs* 7:11
*The New Jerusalem Bible*

# Lessons of a Lowcountry Summer

# ⭐ Part One

## HOPE SUTTON

*One is not born a woman, one becomes one.*
*—Simone de Beauvoir*

# One

*Every night we make love, every hour we are parting.*
—Anna Swir

Dear Dr. Hope,

Last year I married a man who is the father of my four-year-old son. My husband also has a ten-year-old daughter from a prior relationship. He is a supportive partner, and a loving and affectionate father, but his daughter's mother is making my life a living hell. A month after we were married, she began dropping off her daughter at our house every weekend and during school holiday recesses with the excuse that she wants her to get to know her brother better. The girl is disrespectful to me, but only when her father is not around, and rebels by refusing to bathe or change her clothes. I have spoken to my husband about her behavior, and he says she's just going through a phase. It may be a phase, but it is putting a strain on my marriage. After

*a rather heated argument, I threatened to leave*
*him because I am tired of being used by a*
*woman who is not above using her daughter*
*to disrupt our household.*

                              *Stressed out in San Antonio.*

Hope Sutton stared at the letter, seeing, yet not
registering, the words; she'd answered the same query
thousands of times since she had become an advice
columnist for a leading New York City daily. She had
been a high school psychologist with a small private
practice when she had begun her "Dr. Hope's Straight
Talk" column for the newspaper's weekend edition.
What had been a temporary assignment had become a
publishing success for her. Four years later, her daily
syndicated column appeared in more than eighteen
hundred papers nationwide.

At thirty-eight, her gift for analyzing interpersonal
conflicts had earned her the sobriquet "the female
Dr. Phil." Her in-your-face approach to tackling life's
problems in her syndicated column had become her
trademark. Her dulcet voice, if she decided to accept a
position with an Atlanta talk radio station, would be
broadcasted throughout the South and Northeast.

"He's not a supportive partner," she said softly.

"Who's not a supportive partner?"

Hope shifted her gaze from the letter resting on
a stack of others on the desk beside her laptop.
Hope smiled at her significant other as he closed the
distance between them. He was dressed for bed in a
pair of silk pajama pants that rode low on his hips.
Kendall Clarke leaned down and brushed his mouth
over her parted lips. She kissed him deeply, enjoying
the feel of the crisp hair above his top lip.

"A woman's husband who refuses to back her up."

His fingers circled her neck. "You know I always have your back."

"My back *and* my front," she teased.

"You've got that right. Aren't you ready to go to bed?" His deep voice rumbled in his chest. It was after eleven.

"Yes." Her throaty voice dropped an octave.

The word was barely out of her mouth before Kendall swept her up into his strong embrace. He shifted her weight and carried her into a bedroom in his Brooklyn Heights duplex. Hope tightened her grip on his neck and rested her head on his shoulder. She hadn't wanted to believe it, but she had fallen in love. It had been three years since a mutual friend introduced her to KC, and at first glance she had dismissed him as someone she would never consider dating. Not only did he *not* look like her type but he was also an accountant. She'd thought watching moss grow on a rock would be more stimulating than interacting with a man who found balance sheets and investment portfolios the pinnacle of excitement.

All of that had changed once she'd taken the advice she dished out to her readers whenever they complained of not being able to find a "good black man," and decided to give him *one* try. She'd discovered that KC was an astute businessman, disease and drug-free, not a baby daddy, and did not have a string of crazy chicken head ex-girlfriends harassing him. It no longer mattered that he was shorter than average, balding, and matched her weight pound for pound. He was sensitive, generous and had impeccable manners.

The coup de grace had come when he'd picked up her five-nine, one-hundred-seventy-pound body with the ease of a running back carrying a football the length of the field, removed her clothes in under a minute, and made love to her in a way that had left her screaming for someone to dial nine-one-one to stop his sensual assault.

He lowered her to the king-size bed, his body following. Supporting his weight on his arms, he pressed his groin to her middle. His dark gaze lingered on her mouth before it inched up to her eyes.

"I love you, Hope."

She closed her eyes. "And I love you, too, KC."

He touched her cheek. "Open your eyes, baby." She complied. "Why do you always close your eyes whenever you tell me you love me?"

Kendall ran his forefinger down the length of her short, straight nose. The light from the bedside table lamp threw a shaft of light across her face, illuminating the warm orange and gold undertones in her flawless mahogany skin.

"I wasn't aware that I do."

"Well, you do," he countered softly. "Can't you tell me that you love me without shutting me out?"

She gave him a direct stare. "I love you, Kendall. Is that better?"

He laughed, displaying a mouth filled with large, perfectly aligned teeth. Tiny lines fanned out around his eyes. "Yes, baby."

Hope smiled as Kendall slowly and methodically unbuttoned her man-tailored shirt, pushing if off her shoulders. His gaze lingered on the swell of flesh rising above the cups of a white lace bra. Reaching around to her back, he unhooked the bra and removed it. She raised her hips as he eased her leggings and panties down her legs. Seconds later, his pajama pants joined her discarded clothes at the foot of the large bed.

Hope closed her eyes as Kendall parted her knees with one of his and eased his penis into her. They sighed in unison when her body closed around his. Curving her arms under his shoulders, she held him as he moved in and out, establishing a rhythm that never failed to bring her to a climax. Just when she felt as if she were falling over a precipice, he changed tempo, pulling her back. This was what she loved about making love with him. He always took his time, making certain she received as much pleasure as she gave. She raised her knees until they almost touched her shoulders, allowing him deeper penetration. Her soft moans overlapped Kendall's as they climaxed together.

Sated, Kendall rolled over and lay beside Hope. "Marry me, baby."

Hope went completely still—so still that she could hear her heart beating inside her chest. She closed her eyes and cursed Kendall's timing. If he had proposed three days before, she would have accepted without hesitation. Three days ago she hadn't been engaged in talks to host a late-night radio talk segment at Atlanta's top radio station. Taking the job would mean relocating from New York to Georgia.

"Hope?"

She reached for his hand, lacing their fingers together. His hand was soft, and as smooth as hers. Hope smiled. Kendall could figure an amortization schedule in his head, yet he was completely helpless with a hammer and nail. "Yes, KC?"

He turned his head and stared at her profile. Her

expression was impassive. "I asked if you would marry me."

"I heard you."

Pulling his hand away, he rose on an elbow. "Yes or no?"

Hope looked at him and smiled. Kendall's expectant expression reminded her of her nieces and nephews whenever she visited them with a shopping bag filled with colorfully wrapped packages.

"I don't know."

"You don't know?"

Pushing into a sitting position, she reached down and pulled a sheet up over her naked body. "Don't make it sound like that."

"Like what?" The two words exploded from him.

"Like I've rejected you."

Kendall waved a hand. "What the hell else is it, if it isn't a rejection?"

Hope combed both hands through her hair and stared at the man beside her. A flush of color had suffused his gold-brown face; his toned pectorals rose and fell heavily with each breath.

"I didn't want to say anything until I knew for certain if I was willing to relocate."

His eyes literally bulged from their sockets. "Relocate where?"

"Atlanta." Her voice was soft. It was her therapist voice.

Shaking his head, Kendall fell back to the pillows. "Who or what is in Atlanta?"

Hope briefly explained the offer she'd received to host her own radio show.

"When were you going to tell me, Hope?"

"I just told you."

"That's not what I'm talking about, and you know it. If I hadn't proposed to you, would you have confided in me? Were you waiting for the movers to load their truck before—"

"Stop it, Kendall," she said, cutting him off.

"No, Hope, I will not stop. Why haven't you given them an answer? Are you holding out for more money?"

She was irked by his mocking tone. And for the first time since meeting Kendall, she saw him as a spoiled little boy who wasn't going to get his way.

"It has nothing to do with money." She refused to tell him how much she was being offered, or that one of the perks included a home in an upscale suburb.

"If it's not the money, then what is it?"

Hope stared at him, letting seconds tick by. "I have to decide whether I want to leave my home, my family and you."

A look of tenderness softened Kendall's gaze. "Whatever you decide, I'll be here for you. Even if it means relocating to Atlanta to be with you."

She was momentarily speechless. "What about your company?" Kendall had entered into a partnership with several investment and mortgage brokers two years before.

Curving an arm around her shoulders, Kendall pulled Hope close. "I have to wait another year before I can sell my share of the business." He kissed her forehead. "Meanwhile I'll accumulate a lot of frequent-flyer miles commuting between here and Atlanta to be with you."

Hope closed her eyes as a new and unexpected

warmth surged through her. She was lucky to have found someone like Kendall. Most women complained about men who were unable to commit, but she had a man who was willing to commit *and* relocate to share her life and their future.

A smile softened her mouth as she buried her face against her lover's shoulder, and within minutes she had fallen asleep.

# Two

*My baby has no name yet.*

—Kim Nam-Jo

Hope slipped out of Kendall's bed at sunrise while he lay on his back, snoring softly. It was a rare occasion when she woke up before him. Most times he was up and preparing breakfast for her whenever she slept over at his loft. However, the same wasn't true when he slept at her Harlem brownstone. They usually lingered in bed, either talking or making love. For Hope, early morning lovemaking was the best medicine for starting her day.

She made her way to the guest bathroom and filled the bathtub with water. She had decided to use this bathroom instead of the one adjoining the bedroom so she wouldn't wake Kendall. Half an hour later she had brushed her teeth, bathed, and pulled a black, sleeveless cotton knit sheath dress over a set of matching lingerie. She had just finished brushing her hair and securing it in a French twist when Kendall's image joined hers in the wall mirror.

"You're leaving now?"

Turning, she smiled at him. "Yes. I have a breakfast meeting with my editor at seven and a GYN appointment at nine-thirty." She had requested the early morning meeting to discuss the possibility of her continuing to write her column if she decided to accept the talk show position.

Kendall angled his head. "Are you feeling all right?"

"Not really," she answered truthfully. "Even though I'm on the Pill, my cramps are getting worse and my flow heavier."

"Do you want me to go to the doctor with you? My flight isn't due to leave LaGuardia until three this afternoon." He was scheduled to attend a four-day conference for African-American CPAs in Las Vegas.

Closing the distance between them, Hope kissed his stubbly cheek. "No, thank you. I want you to have a safe flight, and don't forget to have some fun."

He frowned. "You know I don't gamble."

"I wasn't talking about gambling. You can always take in some of the shows."

"I'll think about it."

She kissed him again. "Don't think too hard, darling. Gotta go or I'll be late. My driver will be here in a few minutes." She had contracted with a car service to drive her around the city because it was more convenient than taking the bus, subway, or attempting to hail a taxi to take her uptown at odd hours.

She rushed out of the bathroom and pushed her bare feet into a pair of suede-covered mules. She gathered the stack of letters, put them and several disks into a manila envelope, then slipped them into her leather tote, along with her laptop computer.

Making certain she had everything, she picked up her tote and shoulder bag, and headed for the door.

*The driver pulled up* to the curb in front of a diner a block off Hudson Street. Getting out, he circled the car, opened the rear door and extended his hand to help Hope alight.

She gave him a warm smile. "Thank you."

He nodded. "You're welcome, Miss Sutton. I'll be back to pick you up at nine."

Hope thanked him again, then headed toward the twenty-four-hour diner where she frequently met with her friend and editor, William Cullen. She spied him as soon as she walked into the restaurant. He rose to his feet in his favorite booth, waiting until she sat across from him before retaking his seat.

"Good morning, Bill."

William's bright blue eyes crinkled. "Good morning to you, too. I hope I'm not out of order when I say you're positively glowing this morning. Is something spectacular going on in your life I should know about?"

Hope stared at the tall, freckled, raw-boned, middle-aged man with a head full of flyaway graying red hair, to whom she owed her journalism success. They'd met for the first time when William had become the temporary guardian for his at-risk adolescent niece, Erin, during a family court PINS hearing. He and the girl had been referred to her as private clients for individual and family therapy sessions. Toward the end of treatment, he had asked her to write an advice column for his newspaper.

"I've been offered a position as a late-night, call-in host for an Atlanta talk radio station."

The color drained from William's face. "Let's order something to eat, then we'll talk."

Hope ordered half a cantaloupe, scrambled egg whites on wheat toast, and coffee, while William requested a mushroom omelet with a rasher of bacon and tea. Over breakfast she outlined the terms of the radio station's proposal.

"I don't want to stop writing the column."

"And you don't have to," William said quickly, "but will that become a conflict of interest for you?"

She shook her head. "I don't know. I'm scheduled to meet with the station's producer in three weeks."

William lifted a reddish eyebrow. "If they don't have a problem with you working for them and the paper, then I'd love for you to continue. What I need to ask is, will you have the time to do both?"

"I believe I will."

"And if you don't?"

"I refuse to consider not being able to do both. Instead of delivering my disks to you by messenger, I'll attach them to e-mails. I love the personal contact of writing too much to give it up right now."

"And I don't want you to."

William gave Hope a long, penetrating stare. She was one of the most intelligent and confident women he had ever met. And if she hadn't worked for him, he would have considered asking her out after she had discharged him as one of her clients.

Hope lingered long enough to have a second cup of coffee. She gave William the envelope with the letters and disks and promised she would have another batch completed before the end of the week. She checked her watch. It was minutes before nine.

"I have another appointment."

William paid the bill and escorted Hope out of the diner and onto the sidewalk teeming with New Yorkers. "Where are you headed?" he asked.

"Uptown." She slipped on a pair of sunglasses to ward off the rays of the bright Manhattan sunlight. "My driver will be here soon." Seconds later, a sleek black car cruised up to the curb.

William opened the rear door, smiling at Hope after she slid gracefully onto the leather seat. He nodded, closed the door, and stood motionless, watching the car as it moved into the flow of uptown traffic. There was no need to wish Hope luck with the radio show. She had something more precious than luck.

She was blessed.

*Hope stared up at the ceiling.* She did not think she would ever get used to the degradation she felt during an internal examination. Just lying on her back, heels in the stirrups, legs and knees spread, and someone peering into her with a light was tantamount to helplessness. The sound of the doctor removing his latex gloves signaled the end of her ordeal.

Dr. Booth stood up. Deep grooves furrowed his lined forehead. "As soon as you are dressed, I'll see you in my office."

Why, Hope thought, did the doctor's statement sound like a pronouncement of doom? Words he had said to her many times before were delivered in a monotone void of emotion. Sitting up, she ripped off the paper gown and retreated to a small dressing room.

A sixth sense told her that there was something wrong. Within seconds she recalled the letters from women who had written about being diagnosed with ovarian cancer, delivering a stillborn, miscarriages, mastectomies, and so many other women's health problems. Most times she had to remind them that medical personnel offered healing; clergy, salvation; and mental health professionals, hope.

And if there was something wrong with her, who would be there to offer her the hope she would need?

*Hope sat at* one of a quartet of bistro tables shaded from the sun by a large black-and-white umbrella and took a sip of herbal tea. Her right hand shook slightly as she lowered the china cup to a matching saucer. "I've been diagnosed with endometriosis."

Dr. Booth had described the origin, symptoms, and treatment options, while she'd sat numbed by the possibility that she might not be able to bear a child. She'd never imagined that she would *not* have children.

Hope's best friend, Lana Martin, a registered nurse turned professional herbalist, went completely still, her hazel eyes widening. "What has he recommended?"

"He's increasing the dosage of my hormone therapy. I have to take the Pill every day for the next four months to stop my period. I'm scheduled for a follow-up visit early October. At that time he'll assess whether I'll have to undergo surgery to remove the endometrial lesions. The last alternative is a hysterectomy. His other recommendation was to 'go home and have a baby.' "

Lana shook her head and smiled, shoulder-length reddish dreadlocks moving around her flawless gold-brown face with the motion. She knew Hope's doctor wanted to suppress her ovulation for an extended period to curtail endometrial tissue growing around her ovaries, colon, bladder, or fallopian tubes.

"He's right, you know. I like his advice for you to go home and have a baby. Damn, Hope, you're thirty-eight years old. What are you waiting for? A change of life baby?"

"I'd like to get married first, thank you."

"What's up with you and Kendall?"

Lana mentioning Kendall's name reminded Hope that he had proposed marriage twelve hours before. She took another sip of the fragrant rose hip tea, peering at her friend over the rim of the cup. "Last night he asked me to marry him."

"Hot diggity damn! Of course you told him yes."

Hope stared at a trio of Japanese mimosa trees shading the backyard patio and flower garden of the Harlem brownstone. Lana and her physician husband, Jonathan, had bought the abandoned property five years before. They'd renovated the building, installed an elevator, and used the first floor for Jonathan's private practice, the street level for Lana's herbal enterprise, and the second and third floor for their living quarters.

Sighing, she shook her head. "I didn't give him an answer one way or the other."

"Are you crazy? You've dated the same man for three years and you can't give him a simple yes or no?" Lana rolled her eyes. "You're no different than the people who write to you about not being able to commit."

A flicker of annoyance crossed Hope's features. "It has nothing to do with my not wanting to commit."

"Then what is it?"

"I've been offered a position with an Atlanta talk radio station. The station's program manager is coming to New York to meet with me at the end of the month."

Lana's jaw dropped. "Oh, shit! That does change a lot of things."

Hope smiled for the first time since leaving her doctor's office. "You've got that right."

"Does it mean you would have to relocate?"

"Yes."

"What are you going to do with Kendall? And if you accept the position, when would you leave?"

"If I decide to accept the offer, and if all goes well with my health, then I'll move in late fall." It was easier to answer Lana's second question than the first. She did not know what was going to happen between her and KC.

"What about Kendall?"

Hope glared at Lana. She was as tenacious as a dog with a bone. "I don't know," she answered truthfully. "I suppose we could marry and he or I can take turns commuting between here and Atlanta for the next year. He still has another year before he can opt out his share of his company's partnership."

"I suggest you marry Kendall, accept the station's offer, then move into one of those fabulous upscale communities with the rest of the bougie black power couples. In that order, of course."

"You're a fine one to talk. You and your husband are the epitome of bourgeoisification. Not only have your home and practices been profiled in *Essence* but that layout in *Architectural Digest* was the cherry on the cake. So, back it up, girlfriend, when you talk about bougie black folks."

Lana threw back her head and laughed. Sobering, she said, "I have some herbal options for your condition. I'm going to give you printouts of several recipes. They're premenstrual and postmenstrual roots and herbs. You're also going to have to change your lifestyle. That means watching what you eat and drink. Limit the amount of coffee and alcohol you drink. Lighten up on red meat. Lowering your intake of animal protein and animal fat can decrease harmful levels of foreign estrogen in your body."

"Is there anything else I can do?"

"Yes. I always tell women with endometriosis who come in to see me to avoid drinking milk, juice, or bottled water that comes in plastic containers. Look for glass bottles instead."

"Why not plastic?"

"Plastics are considered to be endo-disruptors, and it is suspected that the chemical additives in plastic containers can leach into liquids and foods. You don't have to concern yourself with tampons or sanitary napkins, which are bleached white with chlorine, because you shouldn't see your period for the next four months. But, if you do have breakthrough bleeding, then make certain you use unbleached, unscented, nondeodorant cotton pads that are available at many health food stores."

"How can I thank you, Lana?"

Reaching across the table, Lana grasped Hope's hands. "By marrying Kendall and making me godmother to your children."

* * *

*Sitting in the middle* of her bed that night, Hope cradled a cordless telephone under her chin. She sighed audibly. Why couldn't her sister be happy about KC's proposal? At thirty-eight and thirty-five respectively, Hope and Marissa were too old for sibling rivalry, but Marissa always bragged about being married before Hope. "Have you forgotten that we've been seeing each other exclusively for three years? It's time we commit to a future together."

There was a prolonged silence before Marissa spoke. "You're right. It is time you married and give Mama a few more grandchildren. Congratulations."

"Thank you, Little Sis," Hope said, using her nickname for Marissa. "Don't tell Mama or Daddy until I make it official."

"I won't. I don't mean to change the subject, but remember we're still planning the cookout for Daddy's retirement."

"Have you set the date?"

"The Saturday of the Memorial Day weekend."

"Good." She was scheduled to meet with the radio program manager two days before.

"Are you bringing KC?"

"Yes."

"Then I'll add his name to the list."

Hope spoke to her sister for another ten minutes, laughing as Marissa gave her an update on her six-year-old twin sons, who apparently had embarked on a mission to make their mother lose her celebrated temper on a regular basis.

"Last night I told Trey that as soon as school is out I'm taking the weekends off. I don't intend to shop for food or do laundry. I'm going to leave the house early Saturday morning, and not come back until Sunday evening. After a few weekends of having to forage for food, clean socks and underwear, they'll get themselves together."

"That sounds wild."

"I am wild, Big Sis. Thanks to you, I've become a pit bull in a skirt with dreams that go beyond being a wife and a mother. I've made up my mind to go back to school and get my degree."

At that moment Hope wished she could be with Marissa. Her sister had dropped out of college to become a stay-at-home wife and mother.

" 'Give all to love; obey thy heart.' "

Marissa chuckled softly. "Ralph Waldo Emerson. What I truly like is Maya Angelou's, 'All God's children need traveling shoes.' "

"You still know your poets." Hope could imagine her sister's dimpled smile.

"Know *and* love them. That's one of the reasons why I've decided to get my butt back in school."

"We'll talk about everything when I come for Daddy's cookout."

That said, Hope rang off and replaced the receiver in its cradle. Sinking down to the mattress, she stared up at the ceiling's plasterwork design. She had decided to accept Kendall's proposal, become his wife, complete the recommended four months of hormone therapy, and then hopefully become pregnant.

# Three

*Wine comes in at the mouth and love comes in*
*at the eye.*

—William Butler Yeats

*Hope stood at* the steel door, cradling a bouquet of flowers under her left arm. She tightened her grip on the decorative shopping bag containing a card and a bottle of champagne. Searching in the pocket of her slacks, she took out a key and inserted it into the lock, turning it until she heard the tumblers click. The door to the expansive loft opened silently, and she went completely still. The smell of bacon lingered in the air.

She frowned while moving quietly into the entryway. She had come to Kendall's apartment a day earlier than his scheduled return from Las Vegas to leave the flowers and champagne as pre-celebratory gifts. Her step was determined as she made her way toward the kitchen. Had Kendall returned and neglected to call her?

She heard his voice, then another voice over the

music coming from a radio in the kitchen. Curious, she took half a dozen steps until she stood several feet beyond the arched entrance to the gourmet kitchen.

Kendall stood with his back to her at the cooking island . . . with another man. The tall, slender stranger sported a tank top and a pair of spandex biker shorts that clung to his toned buttocks like a second skin. Kendall was butt naked, the stranger's arm around his trim waist.

They shifted, facing each other while sharing a smile. The stranger reached down and fondled Kendall, who groaned and rolled his naked hips against the groping hand. Hope took a step backward, unable to pull her gaze away from the erotic coupling.

Swallowing back the bile rising up in her throat, Hope turned and practically ran across the living room to the door, the rubber soles of her running shoes making tiny squeaking sounds on the wood floor.

Somehow she found the strength to close the door quietly, and she left as silently as she had come. Tears blurred her vision the instant she reached the sidewalk. Reaching into her shoulder purse, she took out a pair of sunglasses to cover her tear-filled eyes. She walked slowly, placing one foot in front of the other, along the Esplanade, heading toward the Brooklyn Bridge.

Hope glanced at an elderly couple, sitting on a bench on the Esplanade and staring into each other's eyes. *Everlasting love*, she thought. As she neared them, she handed the flowers to the woman and the bag with the champagne to her companion.

"Here's a gift to love." She did not register their shocked expressions as she quickened her pace.

She walked until she reached the bridge's pedestrian roadway, then continued onward, walking past City Hall, Chinatown, Little Italy, and Soho to the West Village. Hot, exhausted and hungry, she stopped at an outdoor café and ordered lunch. She thought it odd that she could think of eating when all she wanted to do was scream at the top of her lungs. Scream and cry until she exorcised the sharp pains in her chest.

After taking a few bites of food, she pulled the cell phone from her purse and called her car service to take her home.

*Hope arrived home* and stripped off her clothes. Leaving them on the floor in the bathroom, she filled the bathtub and retrieved a bottle of wine from the kitchen. She climbed into the tub, sat in the hot water, and put the bottle to her mouth and drank deeply.

The water had cooled by the time she emptied the bottle. The tears came so quickly that she couldn't stop them. They streamed down her chest, heaving breasts, and into the water. Using her toes, she pulled the lever to empty the tub and sat staring at the water as it swirled down the drain.

Time ceased to exist for her. She tried to get out of the bathtub and failed. A wave of dizziness hit her. The sensation was similar to the dizzying pull of the ocean tide she had experienced at the age of ten, the year she'd learned to swim. Her grandmother had warned her about going into the water because of a tropical storm off the coast of South

Carolina's Lowcountry. All of the residents on Mc-Kinnon Island had stocked up on supplies, then they'd waited to see if they had to evacuate before the storm hit the islands.

But she was not a ten-year-old curious girl spending her summer on McKinnon Island, ignoring a direct order not to go swimming, but a thirty-eight-year-old psychologist sitting in a bathtub in a Harlem apartment, too intoxicated to get up without falling.

Once she'd realized the folly of her self-destructive behavior, she laughed. She refused to think about Kendall, his lover, or her fear that Kendall may have infected her with a sexually transmitted disease.

An hour later she managed to get out of the tub in a drunken stupor and stumble to her bedroom on wobbly knees. She lay facedown across her bed in a haze as the sun shifted its position in the sky, sinking lower, below the horizon. The soft chiming of the telephone on the bedside table and the sound of callers leaving messages on the answering machine went unheard and unanswered as she slept. Then the sun rose in the sky to signal the beginning of a new day, and still she slept on.

It was more than twenty-four hours after she had walked into Kendall's apartment that Hope woke and stared up at the ceiling as if she had never seen it before. Suddenly all of it came rushing back—what she had seen, how she had reacted. She closed her eyes when the designs on the ceiling blurred, then she scrambled off the bed and raced to the bathroom to purge her stomach. She was sick, sicker than she had ever been in her life. The smell of toothpaste caused another bout of dry heaves as she brushed her teeth.

She felt a bit more in control of her reflexes after she'd showered and dressed. As she made her way slowly to her kitchen, the telephone rang, and she decided to let the answering machine pick up the call. After four rings, a familiar male voice came through the speaker.

"Hey, baby, I just got back."

"Liar!" she screamed at the machine.

"I miss and love you like crazy. Call me, sweetheart, when you get the chance."

"I don't think so," she mumbled under her breath. All she wanted to do was eat something to settle her stomach. No, what she needed was comfort food: grits, biscuits, and soft scrambled eggs. What she actually wanted was grits and fried fish like she used to eat on Sunday mornings on McKinnon Island.

It was the second time within hours she had thought about McKinnon Island, South Carolina. She had spent her childhood summers there in the small, one-story house that her maternal great-grandfather had built with his own hands. Shaded by tall pines, hickories, gums, and oaks, it was surrounded by thick underbrush and stood less than two hundred feet from the Atlantic Ocean. Her grandmother, who knew Hope loved summering on the island more than her sister and two brothers, had willed the house and property to her. It had been more than three years since she had visited the island even though she had had the house renovated and paid an elderly man to inspect it several times a year to make sure it did not fall into disrepair.

The house and the island were a part of her family's history and legacy. Her grandmother's people had been descendants of former slaves from West Africa, who had populated the Sea Islands. They were known as Gullahs. Grandmomma talked funny, but after spending several summers with her, Hope had come to understand the Gullah she spoke. Her mother understood the dialect but refused to speak it, and she forbade Hope from speaking it, too.

Hope gathered the ingredients for her breakfast. The aroma of grilling beef sausage patties mingled with the smell of freshly ground coffee beans and baking biscuits. She whisked two eggs until they were a fluffy yellow froth and poured them into a skillet minutes after the golden brown biscuits came out of the oven.

Carrying her gastronomical feast to the table in a corner of the large eat-in kitchen, Hope savored her meal without a care for the amount of calories it contained. Just once, she wanted to let go—to not care what she ate or where she needed to be.

Despite her intentions, she ate only two of the half dozen biscuits. Before she had become Dr. Hope, she would've eaten all six. Something in her head would not permit her to relapse into eating the copious amounts of food that had once pushed her well above the two-hundred-pound mark. The extra weight had compromised her health, and as she neared middle age, maintaining good health had become her number one priority.

Breakfast concluded, she cleaned up the kitchen and headed back to her bedroom. She remade her bed and climbed into it, reaching for a book on the bedside table. Kendall called twice while she read, leaving messages that she should call him. After he called a third time, she turned down the volume on the answering machine so she wouldn't hear the two-faced, lying, deceitful snake, and drifted off to sleep.

*Several hours later* Hope stirred, coming awake slowly at the feel of warm lips caressing her cheek. Her eyes widened when she realized Kendall was perched beside her on the bed.

"Hey, baby."

Hope forced herself not to react, or she would pick up the bedside table lamp and smash it against Kendall's head. He wasn't worth her being arrested or serving time for assault.

Forcing a smile, she said, "Hey, yourself. What are you doing here?" She pushed herself into a sitting position.

Kendall angled his body to face her. "I came over because you weren't answering your phones."

"I'd turned down the volume."

"Why?"

"Put my keys on the table and I'll tell you."

"What?"

"You heard me, KC. Give me my keys." Her dangerously soft voice held a silken thread of warning.

He shifted, pulling a set of keys from the pocket of his slacks and placing them on the table. His expression changed from shock to distress as he watched Hope reach into the drawer of the nightstand and withdraw the key to his duplex.

Reaching for his hand, she dropped it into his open palm. "Now we're even."

Kendall's hand closed over the metal. "What the fuck is going on here?"

His reaction amused Hope, because it was on a rare occasion that Kendall said the four-letter word. She angled her head. "Did you really think I was going to marry you when you are *fucking* a man?" He went completely still and tried to speak, but only garbled sounds came from his throat.

"I saw you with your lover yesterday," she said, deciding to press her attack. "You didn't see me because you were getting your jollies off. I left before I could see anything else."

"It's not what you think," Kendall said in his defense.

"Are you calling me a liar?"

"No, baby."

The endearment snapped what was left of her fragile self-control. "Don't 'baby' me!"

He pulled back his shoulders. "Okay, Hope. It's not what you thought."

"And don't tell me what I think!"

"Otis and I are not lovers."

"And I'm five-two, a size four blond with blue eyes."

"I swear on my dead father that I've never slept with him."

"Then what the hell was he doing at your place? You told me you wouldn't be back until today, yet I saw you yesterday with a man who had a good old time jerking you off. And it must have felt good because you were groaning before you put your tongue down his throat." Her voice quivered. "I trusted you, Kendall, and you betrayed me. I can compete with another woman for you, but not a man."

For an instant a shadow of wistfulness stole into

Kendall's expression. "I was curious, Hope. I've been curious about other men for a long time, and yesterday was the first time I acted on it."

She left the bed and sat down on the padded bench at the foot of the wrought-iron bed. She could not bear to be close to him. "Why didn't you tell me? Why did I have to find out like I did?"

Shaking his head, Kendall stared at the twisted sheets. "I didn't think you would understand."

"Understand!" The single word exploded from her. "Did you forget that Dr. Hope has an answer for everyone!" she practically shouted. "If you had told me I would've let you go. I'm not saying it wouldn't have hurt, but not as much as finding out the way I did."

Kendall met her angry gaze with one that pleaded for understanding. "You were never Dr. Hope to me. You are the woman I've fallen in love with. The woman I want to marry and have my children."

"It's too late for that, KC." Her voice had softened. "I can't marry you because I don't trust you, and I refuse to wait for you to assuage your curiosity while you engage in a same-sex relationship."

"Why . . . why did you come to my place yesterday?" he asked.

"I wanted to surprise you. I'd planned to leave a bottle of champagne and flowers, because I had decided I wanted to become Mrs. Kendall Clarke." She blinked back tears. "Now, please go. And you don't have to worry that I'll tell someone about your double life. Your secret is safe with me."

Kendall lowered his head. It was a full minute before he pushed off the bed and left Hope's bedroom. Without a word, he opened the front door and walked out of Hope's life.

# Four

*Time was. Time is. Time shall be.*

—Carl Sandburg

Hope had set up a lunch reservation with the program manager of Atlanta talk radio station WLKV at Londel's Supper Club. Over a pre-lunch cocktail, Derrick Landry outlined the talk show's call-in format to her.

She touched a corner of her cloth napkin to her mouth. "When is your projected broadcast date?"

Derrick dropped his gaze. "October eighth."

Hope studied the features of the very attractive black man in his early sixties. His lightweight wool suit had been tailored to fit his tall, slim body to perfection. She hadn't missed the admiring female glances directed at him when the maitre d' had shown him to her table.

"I may not be available to start. To be honest, I'm not certain whether I'll be able to accept the offer. I may have to undergo a surgical procedure around that time."

"When will you know for certain?"

"I have a follow-up visit with my doctor October first."

"If you do have the surgery, how soon will it be before you will be able to resume your normal activities?"

She shrugged. "I don't know. Maybe three to four weeks."

"I'll have to relay this news to my boss, then I'll get back to you with his decision."

Hope pulled a business card from her purse and handed it to Derrick. "You can contact me by phone or e-mail."

Nodding, Derrick slipped the card into the breast pocket of his jacket. "What do you recommend for dessert?"

She smiled at him. It was apparent he wasn't going to brood about her reluctance to commit to his station's proposal.

"Warm bread pudding with a caramel sauce."

"It sounds wonderful. What are you having?"

"Nothing, thank you. I'm going to pass on dessert."

Derrick angled his head. "But you hardly touched your food."

"I don't have much of an appetite."

And she didn't—not since the day Kendall had come to her. Hope had told herself to get over Kendall's deception, but she couldn't. He was a man she had fallen in love with, planned to marry. Several times a week she woke up sobbing into her pillow. There were times when she stayed in bed most of the day, unable to motivate herself to eat or change her clothes. Forcing herself to read and answer letters had become a monumental task.

She missed Kendall. Missed his companionship, missed sharing a bed and her body with him. He'd filled up the empty spaces in her life.

A waiter took Derrick's dessert selection, and twenty minutes later they stood at a corner on Frederick Douglass Boulevard, hailing a taxi to take him back to his Midtown hotel. Hope shook his hand, then watched as he got into the taxi. She waited until the taxi pulled out into the flow of traffic before she turned and headed back to her apartment.

Like an aging, celebrated actress getting Botox injections, Harlem was undergoing a face-lift. Every week more and more pale faces blended with the black and brown ones eating in restaurants, attending church services, enrolling in schools, and riding the subway and buses downtown to towering office buildings. One young white couple with two children and a biracial couple with a child on the way had purchased the last two remaining abandoned brownstones on her block. The changes on One-Two-Five Street were phenomenal. Major store chains had set up shop to offer goods and services to the residents of the historically black neighborhood.

A black-owned bookstore had recently opened its doors, and Hope had made it a habit to frequent it at least once a week. Every time she perused the self-help section, she thought about writing her own book based on the letters published in her "Straight Talk" column. She usually dismissed the idea because she did not have the time to devote to writing a book.

Now that she wasn't seeing Kendall she had time—lots of it. She had time, and she owned property on McKinnon Island. Her pace quickened, her step lighter as she turned down the block leading to her brownstone apartment building.

She wasn't impulsive by nature, but within seconds she knew what she had to do to heal her mind while she waited for her body to heal. She would spend this summer on McKinnon Island.

Marissa Sutton-Baker met Hope as she parked her rental car behind a row of others lining the driveway at their parents' Teaneck, New Jersey, home. She stuck her head through the open driver's side window. "Where's Kendall?"

Hope removed the key from the ignition. "He's not coming."

Straightening and stepping back, Marissa folded her hands on her hips. She watched Hope get out of the midsize Toyota. "Why not?"

"I'm not seeing him anymore."

"But . . . but aren't you engaged?"

Shaking her head, Hope curved her arm through her sister's and walked around the house to the backyard patio, where their father sat with their mother and several aunts. "I broke off the engagement. Close your mouth, Marissa," she said in a quiet voice.

"Get the fuck outta here!"

"Watch your language, Rissa," Patrick Sutton warned, lines of frustration creasing his forehead. He couldn't understand why his daughter couldn't speak without using profanity.

Marissa frowned at her father. "Remember, I'm grown, Daddy."

"Then act grown and responsible, baby daughter.

After all, there are children here. They hear enough foul language in the street without hearing more from family."

Hope squeezed Marissa's hand as her sister rolled her eyes at their father. Of the four Sutton offspring, Marissa had been the rebel and most difficult to control. She had spent more than half her childhood banished to her room, where she'd passed the time reading poetry and writing in her many journals.

"Let me say hello to Daddy, then I'll meet you in my old room."

Hope kissed all the women at the table, then went over to her father. Leaning over, she kissed his clean-shaven cheek. His light brown eyes sparkled like citrines. She had inherited her mother's coloring and body type and her father's clear brown eyes.

"Congratulations, Daddy. You made it." Her father had retired as postmaster at the Wyckoff, New Jersey, post office.

Smiling, Patrick Sutton curved an arm around her waist. "Thanks, Hope." His smile faded. "You still losing weight?"

"A little." It was a lie. Over the past two-and-a-half-weeks she had lost twelve pounds. She now weighed one hundred fifty-eight pounds. When she graduated high school she'd weighed more than that.

"Don't get too thin," he warned softly. It was a known fact that Patrick liked women with a lot of flesh on their bones. "Where's your boyfriend?"

"I'll never be thin, and Kendall couldn't make it." Reaching into her shoulder bag, she took out an envelope. "Here's a little something to help keep you in shape."

Patrick took the envelope and opened it, his eyes widening in surprise. "Well, I'll be."

"What did you get?" asked one of his sisters-in-law.

"A gift certificate for golf clubs." He stared at Hope. "How did you know I wanted a set?"

"Mama."

Patrick stared across the table at the woman whom he had married forty-two years ago, and smiled the dimpled smile that had enchanted her the first time they'd met. Hope straightened. Her many nieces and nephews were having fun splashing in the pool the elder Suttons had had installed the summer before. Their parents lay on webbed chaises under the protective covering of large umbrellas, dozing or talking quietly to one another.

"I'm going inside for a few minutes."

Flora Sutton frowned at her eldest daughter. "Why don't you get something to eat first? I made your favorite—fried ribs."

"I'll eat later, Mama." And she would. She would fill up on her mother's wonderful Gullah dishes before driving south to McKinnon Island.

"You're wasting away to nothing."

Hope smiled as she made her way toward the house. There was no pleasing her family. First she was too heavy, now she was too thin. She waited for her eyes to adjust to the dimmed coolness of the house, then climbed the staircase to the second story. She found Marissa in her childhood bedroom, sitting on a cushioned window seat.

Marissa patted the cushion beside her. "Sit down, Big Sis."

Hope complied, staring at the pattern on the

area rug. "I broke up with Kendall because I found out that he's bisexual." She told Marissa what she had witnessed and the subsequent meeting with Kendall when he'd come to her apartment.

Her sister launched into a string of explosive expletives that shocked Hope, who thought she had heard it all. "I knew it," Marissa said angrily. "I knew there was something wrong with him last year when the two of you came here for the Fourth of July cookout. He couldn't take his gaze off Trey when he came out of the house wearing his swim trunks. His eyes lasered in on my man's johnson like he was a piece of ass."

"Why didn't you say something?"

Marissa sucked her teeth. "Do you think you would've believed me? You probably would've accused me of being jealous." Her glare dared Hope to refute the accusation.

"You're wrong, Marissa." The softness of Hope's words belied her rising annoyance.

"We've always disagreed about men."

"That's because we have a different perception of who we want as lovers or life partners."

"Trey may not have a college degree or wear designer labels to work, but he's still better than that freak you've been sleeping with."

Marissa's words revived the pain Hope had tried to exorcise. She loved Marissa, but her sister's tongue was a weapon.

"Trey not having a college education never bothered me, Marissa. His insecurities and not wanting you to get your degree does."

Marissa's eyes filled with tears. "I know that, and I don't care, because I'm going back in the fall. I need to feel as if I've accomplished something other than being a stay-at-home wife and mother. I'm not Mama." Shifting slightly, she curved her arms around Hope's neck. "I'm sorry. I shouldn't have said what I did about you sleeping with a freak."

Hope hugged her sister back. "Kendall's not a freak. He's just confused."

"I don't believe you. How can you be so calm and understanding?"

"I've treated many clients who are conflicted about their sexuality. As to being calm—I have to be, or I would put a serious hurting on him."

Marissa pulled back, eyes wide in surprise. "You were thinking about hurting him?"

"Big time."

"You should've called me. I would've had Trey page a few of his dawgs from 'round the way who've spent more time in jail than out. They would've given Kendall an instant sex change without benefit of anesthesia or a scalpel."

Throwing back her head, Hope laughed until tears rolled down her cheeks. She could always count on Marissa to make her laugh.

"Have you had yourself tested?"

The question sobered Hope immediately. She met Marissa's direct stare. "Yes. It came back negative." Even though Kendall said he hadn't slept with his lover, she knew she would not relax until she'd taken the test.

Marissa smiled her attractive, dimpled smile. "Good for you. I don't know what I'd do if anything happened to you. I love you, Hope."

"And I love you, too, Little Sis." She glanced over her sister's shoulder. "I'm going away for the summer."

"Where to?"

"McKinnon Island."

"Why?"

Hope let out an audible sigh. "I need to get away and relax, unwind. I've been toying with the idea of writing a book based on the letters I've received for 'Straight Talk.' I know I'll never write it if I stay here. There are too many distractions. The island will give me the solitude I need."

"What about your column?"

"I'll continue with the column. I've submitted enough responses to run until the end of September."

"When are you leaving?"

"Tonight."

"Is that why you're driving a rental?"

Hope nodded. "Yes. I'll drive until I get tired, then I'll stop and check into a motel. I've packed my laptop and a printer, so we can always communicate by cell phone or e-mail."

"Are you certain you're not running away from yourself?"

"No. What I'm probably doing is trying to find myself. I'm thirty-eight, unmarried, and childless. I need to discover who I am and what I want. I know you, Junior and Bobby never liked spending the summers on McKinnon, but I've always loved it."

Marissa shivered. "It was too spooky for me. And whenever I complained, Grandmomma said it was the spirits of dead slaves trying to find their way back to West Africa."

"*Ghosses* and *ha'nts* best be on da look out fo' me, 'cause I be home soon."

The two women hugged again, then rose to join the other family members.

**Part Two**

## REBECCA LEIGHTON-OWENS

*Our love has been dying for years.*
—*Anna Swir*

# Five

*This is hard to say simply, because the words have grown so old together.*

—David Wagoner

*Rebecca Leighton-Owens* sat at the table in the breakfast nook of a spacious kitchen in a Charleston suburb sipping her second cup of coffee. The remains of one cigarette smoldered in a ceramic ashtray, while an unlit one lay close at hand. She allowed herself two cups of coffee and two cigarettes each day. It was a ritual she had established last year, and although her husband and children did not approve of her smoking, it was something she refused to give up. Cigarettes had become her only vice and overt act of rebellion.

"Mama?"

Rebecca closed her eyes. "What do you want?"

"Look at me, Mama. Please."

Rebecca opened her eyes and came to her feet. It wasn't her daughter's tears that bothered her, because it seemed as if the teenage girl cried more than she smiled, but the angry abrasion on her chin.

"What happened to you?" Her protective maternal instincts had surfaced.

"Kyle found my diary," Ashlee wailed in a trembling voice.

"I'm not talking about your diary. What happened to your chin?"

"I fell down the stairs." She backed up at the same time her mother extended a hand. "Please don't touch me, Mama. You stink of cigarettes."

Rebecca's hand fell limply to her side. Her child had injured herself, yet she did not want her to touch her. She stared at her hand as if it were an offending object that did not belong to her. What, she asked herself, and not for the first time, was she doing to herself and her family?

"I'll wash my hands."

Ashlee nodded, watching her mother as she disappeared into the bathroom off the kitchen. Walking to the table, she picked up the unlit cigarette and dropped it into the cup of coffee.

Rebecca returned to the kitchen with a bottle of peroxide, cotton swabs, and a tube of antibiotic salve. Easing Ashlee down to a chair, she tended the abrasion. The eyes staring up at her were filled with the trusting innocence of a young child instead of those of an adolescent.

Leaning forward, she kissed her forehead. "I'll talk to Kyle about bothering your things."

Ashlee rolled her eyes. "You said that before."

Rebecca nodded. "I know I did. But this time I mean it." She planned to talk to Kyle, Ashlee, *and* her husband about something that was certain to change everyone. "You'd better get dressed, or you're going to be late for the school bus."

"Don't forget I'm spending the weekend with Sonia."

Rebecca smiled for the first time that morning. "Have fun."

Her daughter planned to spend the weekend with her best friend, Kyle had left Charleston for a weekend class trip to Washington, D.C., and earlier that morning her husband had informed her that he wanted her to help him host a dinner party for a new client and his wife that night.

*Rebecca slipped into bed* and turned off the lamp on her nightstand. She had fulfilled her role as hostess, and now all she wanted to do was sleep. Closing her eyes, she feigned sleep as Lee walked into the bedroom. She held her breath as he got into bed beside her. He moved closer and gathered the fabric of her nightgown, pulling it up over her hips.

"No, Lee."

His fingers stilled. "What's the matter?"

"Nothing's the matter. I just don't want you to touch me."

Lee withdrew his hand. "You didn't want me to touch you last night, or the night before. What's going on, Becky?"

She stared at the shadows on the doors of the wall-to-wall walk-in closet. He was too close. He was smothering her, like everything else in her life. "I want a separation."

Lee fell back to the mound of pillows and stared up at the ceiling.

"I've been faithful to you these past two years."

"I know that, Lee." Her voice was soft, calm.

"You've met someone." His question came out like a statement.

"No. I haven't met someone." Her tone was flat.

"If not a who, then *what?*"

The words Rebecca had kept locked inside of her screamed for escape. The frustration, anger, disappointment, and despair merged. Pushing up into a sitting position, she turned the switch on the lamp nearest her.

She stared down at her husband. She had thought herself blessed when she had caught the eye of Charleston's most eligible bachelor. Lee Baxter Owens, a descendant of one of South Carolina's leading black families, had it all: good looks, breeding and wealth. But none of it mattered to Rebecca, because she was trapped.

"I need a break."

"What kind of a break, Becky?"

She gritted her teeth. Lee knew how much she hated for him to call her that, yet he insisted on shortening her name. "A vacation."

He released her hand and pulled her closer until her head rested on his shoulder. "The kids will be out of school in a couple of weeks. We'll all go away together for a week or two."

Shaking her head, Rebecca pulled out of his embrace. "No, Lee. Not with you. And not with Ashlee and Kyle."

His dark eyes widened before they narrowed, and Lee stared at her as if she weren't his wife but a stranger. "What the hell are you talking about?"

"Don't, Lee." Her voice was soft, pleading.

"Don't 'Lee' me, Becky."

She bit down on her lower lip to stop it from trembling. She had permitted her husband to program her life right down to her day-to-day existence.

It had begun the day she had become Mrs. Lee Owens. She'd never had to make a decision because he had been the one to do that. Unknowingly, she had surrendered her will, life, and her future to a man she had come to love more than herself.

"I want to take a vacation—alone." Rebecca was hard-pressed not to smile. She had said it!

"Alone," Lee repeated, as if testing the word.

"Yes, alone."

He peered closely at her. "Is there something you're not telling me? Are you sick? Did you find out something from your last exam you don't want me to know?"

She shook her head. "I'm not sick. I'm just tired, tired of the same day in, day out routine." The words and emotions she had buried for years came rushing out. "I feel unappreciated. I've become your hostess and your maid. And I'm nothing more than a cook, chauffeur, nurse and laundress to Ashlee and Kyle. I can't remember the last time any of you said thank you, or I love you."

Lee trailed his fingertips over her sculpted cheek. "I do love you, Becky."

Her golden-brown eyes shimmered with moisture. "You love what I give you, Lee. I take care of our home, nurture our children, and when you want a warm body I'm available for you. You love me because whenever you entertain you don't have to hold your breath, because I know what to wear and say. You parade me before your clients like a trophy you've won in a competition. I am not a trophy, nor do I like being eye candy. The only time you tell me you love me is when I spread my legs for you. And at that moment I could be any woman."

Easing back, he folded his arms under his head and closed his eyes. "You're wrong, Rebecca. It's nothing like that."

"Then how is it, Lee? I have a degree in history and teaching credentials, yet I haven't taught in fourteen years. Why? Because you want me home."

"The children need you at home."

Leaning on an elbow, she leaned closer to him. "Wrong! *You* want me home."

He opened his eyes, glaring at her. "That's not true!"

Rebecca held his gaze. There would have been a time when she would have retreated, but it was too late for that now. She had opened Pandora's box, and repressed anger and pain had escaped out and into the universe. Lee had lost his sway over her. His matinee idol looks and his pedigree meant nothing, because if she did not fight to empower herself, then she would cease to survive.

She decided to press her attack. "If that's the case, then I'm going to apply for a teaching position at one of the high schools."

Lee closed his eyes for several seconds. He could not believe what he was hearing and wondered to whom Rebecca had been talking. It couldn't be any of the wives in their social circle, because those women did not work, nor did they want to work outside their homes. Hosting fund-raisers took up most of their free time.

One thing he did know: He was losing his wife. *That* he refused to accept. And he had almost lost her before, when she'd discovered that he had been sleeping with a business client. He'd sworn an oath that it would never happen again—and it hadn't. No woman would ever lure him into her bed again.

"Why don't you join some of the clubs you used to belong to?"

"And do what, Lee?"

"Whatever it is you women do and talk about."

"We talk about everything and nothing. I don't need to sit around all day with a group of bored, sexually frustrated women who'd rather sleep with pool boys or the young men who come to landscape their property than their husbands. These are the same women who turn their noses up at women who choose to have babies out of wedlock, yet they have the morals of an alley cat in heat. No, thank you."

Lee smiled at Rebecca. "We'll talk about it tomorrow, Becky."

She shook her head. "No, we won't. And stop calling me Becky."

"But . . . your father calls you that."

"He's my Daddy, and you're not!"

Lee did not know the woman in bed with him. Something or someone had set her off, and he intended to identify who or what it was. "What do you want me to do, Rebecca? If you're asking my permission to let you go off somewhere by yourself, then my answer is no."

"I don't need your permission, Lee. I'm merely informing you that I intend to take the summer off. As soon as the kids are out of school, I'm going away. I've given you the past sixteen years of my life, and now all I'm asking for is two months for myself."

"What about Kyle and Ashlee?"

"What about them?" she said, answering his question with one of her own. "You're an intelligent man, Lee. If you're savvy enough to run a bank, then you should know what to do to take care of your children. However, if you have a problem balancing your career and fatherhood, then I'll call my parents and ask them to come down to look after their grandchildren in my absence."

Turning away from him, Rebecca switched off her lamp, then lay with her back to her husband and closed her eyes.

# Six

*If only I knew the truth, I swear I would act on it.*
                                                    —Paul Goodman

Rebecca woke up to find the space next to her empty.

It was Saturday morning, and Lee had gotten up early to play golf. Her children were away, and she had the house to herself, at least until late afternoon when Lee returned from the country club.

Turning over on her belly, she buried her face in the pillow, smothering the laughter bubbling up in her throat. She'd done it! She had freed herself from the invisible shackles that made her a prisoner. Now, all she had to do was decide where she was going to spend the summer. She thought about the pile of brochures she had hidden away under a stack of papers in a desk drawer.

She took a leisurely shower, singing loudly at the top of her lungs. After going through the ritual of moisturizing her body, she pulled a pair of cotton shorts and a tank top over her underwear. Returning to the bedroom, she slipped her bare feet into a pair of leather sandals she should have discarded last summer, then went into the kitchen to brew a pot of coffee.

After her second cup of coffee and cigarette, Rebecca went into her parlor to call her mother to inform her about her plans for the summer. A stack of brochures and pamphlets advertising Sea Islands vacation properties littered the surface of an antique mahogany desk. She had just ended the call when the doorbell rang.

Nothing in her expression revealed her surprise at seeing her mother-in-law standing on her doorstep. "Good afternoon, Mother Owens."

She barely tolerated Lee's mother. Rebecca knew Georgina had never forgiven Lee for marrying her; not only did she not have the requisite pedigree to marry an Owens but also she was not a Southerner.

"May I come in?" Georgina Owens's smile seemed forced.

Rebecca opened the door wider. "Of course." She waited until the older woman stepped into the spacious entryway, then closed the door to keep out the sultry late spring heat and humidity. The two women moved into a room off the expansive living room Rebecca had set up as her parlor. It was here that she always received and entertained her mother-in-law. The other rooms in the five-bedroom, six-bathroom house were off limits to Georgina except when everyone got together for formal family gatherings.

Georgina sat on a tapestry-covered floral straight-back chair, crossing her legs at the ankles, while Rebecca took a matching chair opposite her.

"Mother Owens, may I get you something cool to drink?"

"I did not come to socialize, Rebecca." Georgina made no attempt to disguise her annoyance as she lifted an arched eyebrow. "I need to know why you've decided to abandon your husband and children like some drug-addicted welfare tramp who is only concerned with her own selfish needs."

Rebecca stared at the tall, thin woman dressed in ice blue silk. The slim skirt and matching blouse had not come off a department store rack. Georgina Owens had used the services of the same seamstress for more than twenty-five years. A wide-brimmed straw hat with a white grosgrain ribbon shaded her unlined nut-brown face from the hot sun.

"You come to my home unannounced, then you have the audacity to insult me to my face."

Georgina sat up straighter. "It is not my intent to insult you."

"Then why are you here?"

"I'm here because my son called me this afternoon with some very disturbing news."

"Your son or *my* husband?"

Georgina Owens placed a manicured hand over her breasts. "Are you on your menses, Rebecca?"

Heat stung Rebecca's cheeks as she registered Georgina's query. "Excuse me?"

"You heard me."

Rebecca stood up. "You have just worn out your welcome."

Georgina also rose to her feet. "If you do anything to disgrace my family, I'll—"

"Disgrace," Rebecca spat out, cutting her off. "Lee managed to do that all by himself when he screwed his business client, got her pregnant, then paid for her abortion."

She felt a perverse sense of satisfaction when Georgina's mouth closed with an audible snap. "I'm going away for the summer not only to save myself but also to save my marriage. And you don't have to worry about *my* children, because my mother and father have agreed to come down and take care of them while I'm away."

The fight seemed to go out of Georgina with this disclosure. "I'd planned to take them to Williamsburg, Virginia, for a few days before we spend a month at the lake house."

"You should've checked with me before you made those plans."

"But I've never had to check with you before. Kyle and Ashlee have always stayed with Mitchell and I for the month of July."

"That was the past. Ashlee and Kyle are my children, therefore I say who they will stay with and where they will go. You've had *your* grandchildren every summer since Ashlee was six years old, but now it's time for my mother and father to have *their* grandchildren. They will be coming down next week to stay *here*. I will draw up the necessary documents giving them joint guardianship with Lee in my absence. Whatever you and Mitchell have planned for my children will have to be approved by my parents."

"What about Lee? He is their father."

"Lee will go along with whatever I say." There was a threatening edge to the softly spoken statement.

"I thought you had worked through your propensity for revenge during your marriage counseling sessions. Lee still harbors enough guilt about his indiscretion without you bringing up the past."

Rebecca shook her head slowly. "I've forgiven Lee. He's the one who hasn't forgiven himself."

"That's because he knows you'll use his *mistake* to get your way."

"Good afternoon, Georgina." It was the first time she'd called her mother-in-law by her given name. "I hope you'll forgive me if I don't see you to the door."

Rebecca walked out of the parlor, leaving Georgina staring at her back. She still had to determine where she planned to summer. She had narrowed her search to three Lowcountry Sea Islands: Edisto, Hilton Head, and McKinnon. The latter was the more remote and lesser known, which meant it would be less populated.

McKinnon Island. She hoped it would be as mysterious and laid-back as the printed material in the brochure depicted it to be. Located south of Hilton Head Island, and southeast of Daufuskie Island, McKinnon Island had yet to garner the attention of developers who had forced out many of the longtime descendants of African slaves and ex-slaves to put up hotels, golf courses, and private residential communities.

She walked down a wide hallway to the rear of the house and into the climate-controlled patio, where she sank down to a chintz-covered chaise. Kicking off her sandals, she closed her eyes and rehearsed what she wanted to tell her children about the plans she had made for their summer.

\* \* \*

*Lee returned within* minutes of his mother's departure. Rebecca stared at him as he stood at the entrance to the patio. He had come back earlier than she had anticipated.

He walked in and sat down on the side of the chaise. Leaning over, he pressed a kiss to her forehead. "Good afternoon."

Rebecca gave him a narrowed look. "Your mother came to see me—unannounced." She related her conversation with Georgina without dropping her gaze. It was apparent that Lee was as shocked as she had been at Georgina's reference to her acting like a drug-addicted welfare tramp.

A muscle in his lean jaw twitched. "I'll talk to her. I'd called her to let her know that you were going away for the summer. I never imagined she would come here and say those hateful things to you."

"There's no need to say anything to her, because it's not going to change her opinion of me."

Cradling her face between his hands, Lee stared deeply into Rebecca's eyes. "Wrong, darling. My mother is still angry because I did not marry the girl she wanted me to, but you are the woman I fell in love with and married. I will not put up with her insulting you."

"Let it go, Lee."

He shook his head. "No, Rebecca, I won't."

She placed her fingertips over his mouth. "I'm begging you to let it go."

Closing his eyes, Lee nodded. "Okay, baby."

Rebecca traced the outline of his sensual mouth with her fingertips, then kissed him. It wasn't the burning, passionate kisses they'd exchanged in the past, but one that was soft and healing.

Gathering her into his arms, Lee shifted and positioned her to sit between his outstretched legs. He rested his hands over her flat middle. "When are you going to tell the kids?"

"When they get back tomorrow afternoon."

"Do you want me with you when you tell them?"

"No. I want them to know that this is my decision, not yours."

"Have you decided where you want to go?"

Tilting her chin, Rebecca smiled over her shoulder at Lee. "McKinnon Island."

His eyebrows shot up in surprise. "McKinnon. I've heard it's little more than a swamp."

"So was Hilton Head, Kiawah, and the others before greedy, unscrupulous developers took over and displaced our people."

Lee drew his lips in thoughtfully. He knew Rebecca was right about the developers descending on the unsuspecting longtime inhabitants of the Sea Islands to buy up property and force them off lands that had been cultivated by their ancestors.

"Have you made any reservations?"

"Not yet. I'll do that on Monday."

Reclining in his protective embrace, she told him her parents had agreed to come to Charleston to look after Ashlee and Kyle. They talked about Ashlee starting high school in the fall and Kyle wanting to try out for his school's football team. They talked about their children, parents, and Lee's estranged sister. They talked about everything except what would happen at the end of the summer when she returned from McKinnon Island.

"What do you say we go out for dinner tonight?" he whispered close to her ear.

"Where do you want to go?"

"Someplace real nice where I can show Charlestonians that I'm married to the most beautiful woman in the whole damn city."

Rebecca giggled like a little girl. "When are you ever going to stop talking trash, banker man?"

"Never."

*Rebecca shifted her gaze* from her son to her daughter as they flanked her on the love seat. Neither of them had inherited her physical characteristics. It was as if she had had nothing to do with their conception except carrying them beneath her heart for nine months. Both of them claimed Lee's coloring, features, and his height and lankiness. The only obvious trait that indicated she had been a contributor to their gene pool was her curly hair. Her children had returned from their weekend outings, and she had asked them to meet with her in the parlor before they retreated to their bedrooms to prepare for the last three days of the school year.

"What's up, Mama?" Ashlee asked.

Rebecca could always count on her daughter's outspokenness. Ashlee was so different than Rebecca had been at fourteen. "I'm going away this summer," Rebecca replied. She knew there was no other way but to be direct with her children.

Kyle stared, unblinking. "What do you mean, going away?"

"Your grandmother and grandfather are coming from Massachusetts to stay with you for the summer."

Ashlee stared at her with wide eyes. "Why?"

"I'm going away by myself, and they've agreed to look after you until I return."

Her daughter's eyes welled up with tears. "Are you and Daddy getting a divorce?"

Rebecca dropped an arm over Ashlee's and Kyle's shoulders, pulling them close to her body. She and Lee had tried not to involve their son and daughter in their marital affairs, but they hadn't been totally successful once their children had discovered their father had become involved with another woman.

"No, baby." She dropped a kiss on their heads.

"Then why, Mama?" Ashlee's voice was soft and trembling.

"I'm tired, my darlings."

"Why don't you go to bed and sleep?" Kyle asked.

Rebecca smiled. "It's not that easy."

"Why not?" questioned Ashlee.

"I get up every day and do the same thing over and over. I prepare breakfast, make lunch for you and Kyle, then I make beds, dust, vacuum, put up several loads of wash, shop for groceries, and cook dinner. After chauffeuring the both of you to softball and football practice and sleepovers, I'm too tired to even think straight."

"What if Daddy got you a maid," Kyle quipped, grinning from ear to ear.

"Would the maid be expected to act like a referee when you invade your sister's privacy?" She gave her son a level look. "You've been told about going into Ashlee's room and searching through her things." Ashlee stuck her tongue out at her brother.

"And you're not exempt from adding to the chaos, young lady," Rebecca continued, cutting her eyes at Ashlee. "I'd like to have a dollar every time you come home crying and slamming doors because you've seen Bobby Jackson with another girl. It's normal for you to have a crush on a boy, but it's unrealistic to think an eighteen-year-old would be interested in someone fourteen."

Ashlee gritted her teeth. "He's an idiot."

Rebecca smiled. "He may be an idiot, but he's still too old for you."

Kyle patted his mother's arm to get her attention. "Are you going away to die, Mom?"

"Why would you say that, Kyle?"

"Andrew's mother was sick and tired, so his daddy sent her away, and she never came back."

"Andrew's mother had cancer. Even if she hadn't gone away, she still would've died."

"So, you're not going to die?"

"No, Kyle. At least I hope not for a long, long time."

"I like Gram and Gramps," Ashlee said. "Especially when they take us fishing."

Rebecca was surprised. "But don't you fish when you go to the lake house?" The Owenses had built a vacation home close to Lake Marion.

"Nope," Kyle quipped. "Grandma Owens won't let us bring fish in the house because she says it stinks up everything. So, we have to throw them back. But Gramps lets us keep the fish, and Gram cooks it."

"Gram and Gramps, along with your father, will be responsible for you while I'm away."

"Can we come and visit you?"

Rebecca pondered her daughter's question. She hadn't thought they would miss her enough to want to come and see her. Last year they'd spent their entire summer vacation at Lake Marion with Lee's parents, and when she'd come up to visit with them, they had hardly given her a glance or spoken to her.

"I don't see why not. I'll rent a place with enough room so we won't be all over one another."

Ashlee hugged her mother. "Cool."

Hard-pressed not to let out an audible sigh, Rebecca smiled. It had gone better than she'd thought it would. Both Lee and their children were resigned to her leaving them for the summer.

Twin emotions of elation and fear attacked her. In another two months she would celebrate her fortieth birthday, and she planned to go to a strange place to discover what Rebecca Leighton-Owens wanted.

**Part Three**

# THEODORE HOWELL

*somewhere i have never traveled, gladly beyond
any experience, your eyes have their silence.*
—*e. e. cummings*

# Seven

*I know everything, don't argue with me!*
                    —Marina Tsvetaeva

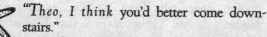 "Theo, I think you'd better come downstairs."

Helen Bryant's soft voice broke the silence of the large, glass-walled room.

Theodore Howell ran a large hand over his close-cropped hair and rolled his head from side to side, attempting to ease the tight muscles in his neck and shoulders. He glanced at the clock. It was ten-forty. He had been writing nonstop for the past two hours.

"Didn't I tell you I did not want to be disturbed?"

"Suit yourself. I'll just tell the police officers to take your brothers down to the station house for processing."

Theo jumped up, his chair tipping over and falling to the floor with a loud clatter. He stared at his housekeeper. "What did you say?"

Folding her arms under her breasts, Helen snorted under her breath. "Christian and Brandon are in some kind of trouble." She stepped out of the doorway just in time to avoid being run over as Theo ran down the staircase, taking two steps at a time.

"*Damn them!*" The two words were squeezed from between teeth clenched so tightly that his jaw ached.

He had become legal guardian to his two half brothers and sister after their mother and father died in a commuter plane crash. The tragedy had turned theirs and Theo's daily existence upside down. He had been on his own since he'd turned twenty-one, and now, at forty, he did not want to be responsible for anyone but himself. However, he wasn't given a choice, once calls from a social worker and his mother's lawyer informed him that he had to take care of three grieving adolescents he hardly knew.

Standing in the middle of his living room were two tall, muscular, uniformed black LAPD officers and his teenage siblings. Brandon's chin rested on his chest, while Christian held his head at a cocky angle.

Theo blew out his breath. He was in luck. He knew one of the two officers. "What happened, Russell?"

"We were called in to break up a party that had gotten out of control. I found this one having sex." Theo could see his large hand tighten on Christian's neck. "I doubt if she's more than thirteen." He glared at Brandon. "And mister life of the party was having a good old time taking stokes off a blunt in between shots of tequila."

"I was for taking them in, but my partner said

you would take care of them," the other officer snarled.

Theo's hands curled into tight fists. "He's right. I will take care of them." He walked over to his brothers, who had taken a sudden interest in their shoes. He grabbed each by their T-shirts, pulling them up close to his chest. They stank.

"Thank you, Officers. I can assure you that there will not be a repeat of what occurred tonight as long as they live under *my* roof."

After the officers drove away, Theo hauled the two boys across the living room and into the family room. He shoved them down into a leather love seat.

Light from table lamps illuminated the fear radiating from sixteen-year-old Brandon's eyes, but not so with Christian. At seventeen, Christian stood an even six foot and had begun adding muscle and bulk to his lanky frame from a daily weight-lifting regimen.

Even though they'd had different fathers, and there was an age difference of twenty-three and twenty-two years, respectively, the physical resemblance between the three was remarkable. People often took Theo for their father instead of their older brother. They shared the same lean face, large dark-brown eyes, and high, flat cheekbones. Even their coloring was the same—a warm cinnamon-brown.

Sitting down on a chair opposite them, Theo gave each a long, penetrating stare. "This is the first and the last time the police will show up at my door because of your stupidity." He turned his angry gaze on Christian. "Have you gone and lost your damn mind? You don't need to be having sex, especially with an underage girl."

Christian cocked his head as he gave Theo a half-smile. "You're just jealous, because no one wants to fuck you because—" Whatever else he was going to say died on his lips when he felt the sting of Theo's open hand on his left cheek. Before he could catch his breath, he caught another hard slap on the other cheek. He was too stunned and in too much pain to react. Blood spurted from his nose, flowed into his mouth, and onto his T-shirt.

Brandon jumped up.

"Where the hell are you going?"

Theo's shout halted him in his tracks. "I have to go to the bathroom."

"Stay!" The single word was enough to make him sit down again.

Christian's T-shirt ripped as Theo held him in a punishing, viselike grip. "If you ever use that language in this house again, someone will have to call nine-eleven to keep me from taking you out." He shook him several times before releasing him. "Go clean yourself up, then get into bed. Don't you dare ask me to go anywhere for the rest of the summer."

Christian wiped his arm across his nose. "You can't hit me."

"I didn't hit you," Theo countered. "I slapped you, little brother. Perhaps you would like me to hit you?"

Christian sniffled, holding the hem of his shirt to his nose. "You're not my father."

"You've got that right, because if I'd been your father you'd have more respect for yourself. Now, get out of my sight!"

Christian turned and walked out of the room.

Towering over Brandon, Theo stared down at

his bowed head. "What happened to your common sense?"

Brandon tried blinking back tears but was unsuccessful. "I'm sorry, Theo."

"Sorry doesn't cut it, Brandon. Binge drinking and drugs will put you in an early grave. What if someone had laced that joint with crack or angel dust?"

"I'm sorry," he said over and over as mucous streamed from his nose.

Theo threw up a hand. "Clean yourself up. And the same goes for you as Christian. Don't ask me to go anywhere. Not even to the corner. You'll come home from school and stay in. Are you sober enough to understand what I'm saying?"

"Yes. May I go now?"

"Yeah, go."

Brandon ran, holding his hand over his mouth as he headed for the nearest bathroom.

"What happened to Chris?"

Theo turned to look at Helen. "What do you mean what happened to him?"

"He's bleeding."

"I slapped him. Is there anything else you'd like to know?"

Helen stared at her employer, measuring her words carefully. Since she had come to work for Theodore Howell, he had never exchanged a cross word with her. But all of that had changed once his siblings had come to live with him. He did not seem to understand that the children were grieving the loss of their mother and father.

"May I tend to his injuries?"

"There are no injuries, Helen. He has a bloody nose."

"It looks like more than a bloody nose."

"If he had been locked up tonight he'd have more than a bloody nose. And he's lucky the officer who brought him home is a friend. Either I bloody his nose for mouthing off at me, or some rogue cop will beat him senseless because he's a young black male."

Helen's faced turned a deep pink with the mention of "young black male." "But—"

"But nothing, *Miss Bryant*," Theo said, cutting her off. "I pay you to cook and to keep my house clean, not to give me advice on how to deal with my brothers and sister."

"And I can quit, too."

He stared at the petite woman, whom he had hired as a live-in housekeeper a week after he had moved from northern to southern California. Never married and childless, sixty-year-old Helen had gathered Brandon, Christian and Noelle to her bosom like a mother hen protecting her brood. She spoiled and pampered them shamelessly, thereby undermining his role as their guardian and authority figure.

"Then quit!"

She shook her head. "No, Theo. I'm not going to quit and leave those motherless children alone with a monster like you."

"Oh, I'm a monster? I rearrange my life to take in three angry, defiant, and rebellious teenagers, and you call me a monster. I think not."

The sparkle went out of her blue eyes. "I know you're doing the best you can, but they're still hurting."

"They're hurting because they don't want to accept the fact that their parents aren't coming back."

Although he shared the same mother with Christian, Brandon and Noelle, his relationship with Mary Howell-Anderson had not been that of a mother and her son. Mary had gotten pregnant at fifteen and moved to Los Angeles to live with an older cousin until she'd delivered her baby. Mary had never revealed the identity of Theo's father. She'd returned to San Francisco for a week, long enough to leave her three-week-old son with her own mother. It had been his grandmother, Esther Howell, whom Theo had called Mama. And it wasn't until Mary had married Hollywood still photographer James Anderson and given birth to her second child that she'd returned to San Francisco to introduce her infant son to his older brother. Theo had been twenty-one years old when he'd been introduced to his mother, her husband, and Christian for the first time.

Helen managed to look contrite. "I know I was out of line for calling you a monster."

"Yes, you were."

She ignored his retort. "And I know it has been hard on you, but if you don't mind, I'd like to help you care for them."

"You've done enough."

He wanted to tell Helen that Mary had done her children a disservice by indulging their every whim. It was as if she'd sought to give them what she hadn't given her firstborn. What Mary did not know was that his grandmother had given him all of the love he would ever need. Esther had protected and nurtured him until he had been able to take care of himself. And once he had sold his first script to a major movie studio, he'd assumed total responsibility for supporting his grandmother. She had died in his arms, and there was never a day when he did not think of her.

"I want you to remember that I'm here if you need me for more than cooking and cleaning."

"I know that, Helen."

She gave him a warm smile. "Good night, Theo."

"Good night, Helen."

He waited for her to leave before he sank down into the love seat and buried his face in his hands. He hadn't meant to slap Christian.

"I'm not cut out for this fatherhood crap," he whispered. He had lost count of the number of women he had slept with over the years, but he was certain of one thing. He had never fathered a child. There was never a time since he had become sexually active that he had *not* used a condom.

Theo had grown up wondering about the man who had gotten his mother pregnant. Had he known Mary was pregnant? Had he offered to help her, or had he walked away, leaving her to face the shame of becoming a teenage mother alone? Had he been so horrible that Mary had sought to exorcise him from her life when she'd relinquished all claim to her first-born to her mother?

Bracing his elbows on his knees, he lowered his hands and stared at the floor. Seeing Christian and Brandon with the two cops had shattered his concentration, and he knew he would not be able to go back to working on his script. It was taking him longer than usual to develop the characters for his latest project, and he still had to complete six one-hour television scripts before the end of September.

There was no way he was going to develop the

pilot and the additional five scripts for the cable network to debut next spring. Not with one family crisis after another. Tomorrow he would call his agent to inform him that he would have to find another scriptwriter.

# Eight

*The night has a thousand eyes, and the day but one.*
*—Francis William Bourdillon*

**Theo hadn't realized** he had spent the night on the love seat until the rays of the rising sun inched their way across the room, settling on his cheek. He had done something he had not done in years—drink while he was writing.

The possibility that his brothers could have been arrested was a wake-up call that he had to get his priorities in order. Becoming legal guardian to his siblings wasn't something that had been dumped on him. During a rare meeting with Mary, she had informed him that she and James were drawing up wills, and she'd asked if he would take care of her children if anything ever happened to her. He hadn't hesitated when he'd given his consent. After all, Mary was only sixteen years older than he was, and chances were she would live to see all of her children reach their majority.

But fate was tricky and fickle. Mary was fifty-six

when she died, leaving a mountain of debts and sole custody of her children to a son she had denied within weeks of his birth.

Peering at a clock on the fireplace mantel, Theo noted the time. It wasn't quite six o'clock. Groaning at the effects of last night's drinking, he made his way toward the staircase to the second level. He met Helen as she came down the stairs carrying a wicker basket filled with dirty bath towels. She cut her eyes at him, then moved closer to the banister when she caught a whiff of the stale alcohol on his breath.

"Good morning, Theo," she said cheerfully. "It looks as if it's going to be a beautiful morning."

"Yeah, yeah."

She flashed a Cheshire cat grin. "What's the matter, *Boss?* Did you drink something last night that didn't agree with you?"

Theo mumbled a curse under his breath as he concentrated on putting one foot in front of the other until he made it to the top of the curving staircase without falling. He walked past the bedrooms belonging to the three children, and climbed another half dozen steps until he stood outside the door to his own bedroom. The alcove off the sitting room had become his office and his sanctuary. The glass walls brought the outside in, and the natural beauty of the panoramic landscape had become his muse.

Stripping off his T-shirt, shorts and underwear, he walked into the freestanding shower stall and turned on the cold water. He welcomed the biting sting of the water as it beat down on his head. He adjusted the water temperature and washed his hair and body.

Twenty minutes later, Theo sat at his desk, dial-

ing the number of his agent, Jeff Helfrick. The call
was answered on the third ring.

"Whoever the hell is calling me at this hour better be talking a multimillion-dollar deal, or your ass
is mine."

"Jeff, Theo."

"Theo?" Jeff's voice lost its gravelly tone.
"What's up?"

"I'm not going to be able to do the pilot for you."

"What!"

He quickly related what had happened the night
before. "Look, man, it's too stressful for me to try
and play daddy to kids who are still bleeding emo-
tionally."

"I thought you had them in counseling."

"I did. They went for a few sessions, then they
opted out. And forcing them to go isn't the answer."

"Look, Theo, I don't mean to sound insensitive,
but you know you're the best writer for this project.
Didn't you tell me that you've been waiting all your
life to write a television drama featuring black actors
who weren't portraying entertainers, cops, inmates or
pimps?"

Jeff was right, but that did not make Theo's decision any easier. He had written more than a dozen
movie scripts, two of which had received Oscar
nominations. The nominations had made him a
more sought-after writer, but his dream since graduating film school was to write a television drama for
a predominantly black cast. And now that he was
being offered the opportunity, he had to turn it
down because he had promised a dead woman he
would take care of her children.

"I can't write the scripts while trying to reconcile

with my family." Suddenly it hit him. This was the first time he had thought of Noelle, Brandon and Christian as his family. "My little sister cries and sulks more than she talks, while Christian is hell-bent on turning nerdy Brandon into a thug. They have less than a week of school left, and I'm thinking of taking them away for an extended vacation."

"Where?"

"I haven't decided where."

"Look, Theo, maybe I can help you so we both can get what we want."

"What's that?"

"I built a little place off the South Carolina coast for myself whenever I need to disappear from my ex-wives. It's on McKinnon Island. It's small and laid-back. The tourists have yet to discover it, or it would be overrun like some of the other islands in the region. The house has four bedrooms and four full baths. It's only a few hundred feet from the ocean, is centrally heated and cooled, and equipped with modern appliances. The kids can hang out, go fishing and crabbing, while you can write your ass off."

Theo smiled. "You make it sound very tempting."

"I'll hold off telling the network that you won't be able to do the project until next week. If you change your mind, then call me. I'll arrange for a private jet to fly you and your family into Savannah. I'll also arrange for a vehicle for you to use during your stay on the island."

"I won't promise you anything, but I will think about it."

Theo ended the call. Before he made any decision, he would discuss it with his family.

\* \* \*

*Three days later* Theo sat at the dinner table with Noelle, Brandon and Christian. They ate without talking. It had been that way since Christian and Brandon's Saturday night fiasco.

Placing his fork next to his salad plate, Theo cleared his throat. "I'd like for all of us to go away for the summer."

"Where?" Noelle asked.

Theo gave his sister a gentle smile. She was the most vulnerable of the three. Her parents were killed the day before her thirteenth birthday. Tall and willowy, she reminded him of a startled doe, with her large eyes and delicate features. She wore her relaxed shoulder-length hair in a profusion of tiny braids.

"McKinnon Island, South Carolina."

Brandon glanced up and stared at Theo. "What would we do there?"

"The house where we would stay is close to the ocean, so that means swimming, boating and fishing."

"Will there be kids our age, or old farts sittin' around talking about their grandkids?" Theo glared at Christian, who dropped his gaze. "Sorry. We can't swim."

Theo stared at each of them. "None of you know how to swim?" They shook their heads. He smiled. "Would you like to learn?"

"Yes," chorused three voices.

"Then that settles it. We'll leave for McKinnon Island Sunday. And tomorrow we'll go to the mall after school and shop."

Noelle sat up straighter. "What are we shopping for?"

"Bathing suits, sandals, tank tops, three disc players, several dozen CDs . . ." His words trailed off as his sister and brothers exchanged high fives.

"Is Miss Helen coming?" Brandon asked.

A powerful sense of relief swept over Theo. He had gotten them to agree to summer on McKinnon Island with him.

"Yes, Brandon, Miss Helen is coming. She lives with us, and because she does, we have to think of her as family."

*Family.* He was getting used to saying the word. His grandmother had been his only family for many years, but now he had his brothers and sister.

As a realist, Theo knew it wasn't going to be easy, but at least spending the next two months on an island off the Carolina coast was a beginning—for all of them.

# ⭐Part Four

## McKINNON ISLAND

*I saw the tracks of angels in the earth.*
—*Petrarch*

# *Nine*

The sea its millions of waves is rocking, divine.
                                    —Gabriela Mistral

*Hope smiled.* She had come home.

The sight of the saltwater marshes wrapping around the west and south sides of McKinnon Island made her pulse race. She'd left Charlotte before dawn, driven to Savannah, then had taken a road, now referred to as a causeway, to the landing, where a ferryboat made more than a dozen trips a day to Daufuskie, Hilton Head, and McKinnon Islands.

Slowing the rental car, she became a tourist and sightseer, noting changes in her surroundings. Road signs pointed the way to a new development, Palmetto Haven, advertised as a future gated community. Her heart sank in her chest. Developers had discovered McKinnon. And she knew they would be like the others, offering Gullahs money they truly did not need to leave their ancestral land.

Her grandparents and their grandparents before

them had supported themselves with things that came from the land and water. They grew their own crops, and raised chicken and cattle in their yards. Everyone learned to fish, crab, shrimp, and pick oysters. Nobody had much, but they always had enough.

She drove along a recently paved road for a quarter of a mile, then turned off to the one that led to her property. Tall pines and ancient live oaks bearded with Spanish moss formed a natural canopy, shutting out the intense rays of the sun. Movement rustled bushes, and Hope shuddered slightly. It would take time for her to get used to the island's wildlife: snakes, rabbits, coons, foxes, and probably a few surviving bobcats.

The thick underbrush gave way to a clearing, where the first of a quartet of houses stood facing the water. The last time she'd visited McKinnon, two of the three other houses had still been vacant after their elderly residents had passed away several years before. She wondered if anyone lived in them now. Delicate curtains hung from the windows at two of the once-vacant, one-story clapboard houses, while vertical blinds hanging from the third answered her query as to whether the homes along Beach Road were occupied.

Hope maneuvered into the sand-littered driveway to the newly painted white clapboard house at the end of the half-mile road. The caretaker had carefully tended the property. A new asphalt roof had replaced the corrugated tin, and the addition of dark green shutters matched wicker porch furniture swaddled in plastic. She cut off the car's engine, got out and made her way up to the porch. Her key turned easily in the lock, and as the door opened on well-oiled hinges, a blast of heat met her, much like the one that would send her back several feet whenever she would open the door to her grandmother's wood-burning stove. Working quickly, she opened all of the windows to let the stifling heat escape and a salt-water breeze in.

It took her forty-five minutes to unload her car of luggage, her computer and printer, and put them in their respective rooms. The food she had pur-chased in a Savannah gourmet shop was stored in the refrigerator. She planned to take a bath, go to bed early, and sleep late. Driving more than eight hun-dred miles over a period of twenty-eight hours had left her totally exhausted.

*The sun was high* in the sky, the tide had receded and a gentle ocean breeze wafted through the screened-in windows by the time Hope came awake. A smell, peculiar only to McKinnon Island, brought back memories of the mornings when she'd woken up in the large iron bed she'd shared with Marissa. She hadn't needed an alarm clock to tell her to get up, because the smell of frying bacon, percolating coffee, and baking biscuits was all she needed to pro-pel her out of bed, wash, and dress quickly so that she could eat breakfast with Grandpapa before he left to go fishing. Folks on McKinnon said that Simon Robinson was one of the island's better fisher-men. There was never a time when he failed to return with a boatload of crabs, shrimp, lobster, or oysters. Most of his catch was sold to restaurants in either Savannah or Charleston. What he did not sell he brought home to his family.

It wasn't the urge to eat that prompted Hope to get out of bed this morning but curiosity. She wanted to reunite with the people who clung to the old ways and made her proud of her Gullah heritage.

After completing her morning ablution and letting her sister know she had arrived safely, Hope began the task of mixing tinctures of the six herbs Lana had recommended as a premenstrual formula. A shelf in the small kitchen held a plethora of dark apothecary bottles filled with seeds, herbs, barks, roots, and flowers that probably could be found on the island.

Fortified with a cup of the herbal tea, dressed in her favored white man-tailored shirt with the sleeves rolled up to the elbows, a pair of cropped navy blue pants and running shoes, she left the house and walked along Beach Road and into town to reacquaint herself with her mother's ancestral home.

As she removed her sunglasses, Hope's smile matched that of a man standing behind the counter at McKinnon's mini-market. "Ya famemba me?" she asked, lapsing easily into the Gullah dialect.

Charles Hill's smile widened. "Who be dat?" he teased. "How could I ever forget the prettiest girl to ever step foot on McKinnon." He came from behind the counter, arms extended. Hope moved into his embrace and hugged him.

She kissed Charles's cheek. He was still handsome. His dark gray eyes were incongruent in his tobacco-brown face. It was rumored among the Gullahs that his grandmother had been kept by a white man whose ancestors had owned the island's largest rice-producing plantation.

"It's good seeing you again, Charles."

He held her at arm's length. "How long has it been?"

Shaking her head, Hope said, "I can't remember. The last time I visited three years ago, your father told me you'd moved to Tennessee to coach a high school football team."

She and Charles had dated briefly during their seventeenth summer. Whenever he hadn't been working in his family-owned store, they had spent their time together swimming or sitting on the beach reading their favorite novels. He had not had the money to take her to Hilton Head or Savannah, because he'd been saving every penny for college. When Hope had offered to pay for the ferry ride and dinner, he'd broken off with her. It was her first introduction to what she would come to recognize as machismo.

Charles nodded. "I did. I'm back this summer to help out in the store. Mama called me a couple of months back to say that Poppa's sugar is up again. She complains that he's been working too hard, so here I am. What's up with you, Dr. Hope? Why have you come back?"

It was apparent her old friend was familiar with her column. The last time she had come to McKinnon, her column had not yet celebrated its first anniversary. "Please don't call me that," she chided. "I'm thinking of writing a book, so I decided McKinnon is the best place to find a little peace and quiet."

"It's so quiet that if you're not careful you'll fall asleep standing up."

Hope laughed and Charles joined her. They talked, reminiscing about the residents who had passed and moved away, and those who had remained. Charles proudly showed her photographs of his wife and two young daughters, who had elected not to vacation on the island this summer.

Charles left to wait on a customer, and Hope wandered around the general store. It was stocked with as many hardware items and over-the-counter drugs as foodstuff. A door at the far end of the store led to a space that doubled as the post office. Incoming and outgoing mail was processed in Savannah and transported to and from McKinnon Island by ferry.

Waving to Charles, she left the store and made her way along the two-block business district. She peered into the plate glass window of The Fish Net. It was noon, and the restaurant was filled to capacity. Vehicles with license plates from Florida, Georgia, North and South Carolina crowded the parking lot. The Jessup brothers' reputation for fried catfish, barbecued shrimp, and their secret-recipe basted roast pig was legendary throughout the Lowcountry.

She lingered in front of the small movie theater. The marquee advertised a film Hope had seen more than three months ago. At the far end of the street was a three-story brick structure where bales of cotton had once been stored before being shipped north. After the Civil War had ended the plantation economy, the warehouse had been left empty. In the mid-1990s a North Carolina theater troupe had converted the warehouse into a playhouse for their summer stock productions. This year's playbill featured an updated version of Leonard Bernstein's *West Side Story*. The last production she'd attended at the playhouse had been an upbeat rollicking Motown Revue.

Hope continued her tour, noting the price of

gasoline from the single pump service station. It was twenty cents lower than the comparable octane in New York. Half an hour later she found herself inside McKinnon's largest black cemetery. She found the headstones marking her grandparents' graves, as well as those of many other long-deceased family members who had lived all of their lives on the island.

She stopped again, this time near the Brule River, where her grandfather and other fisherman had hauled nets filled with fish and traps with crabs into their boats. The dilapidated remains of a wooden marina leaned at a precarious angle. It was there fishermen had sold their surplus seafood to visitors who had returned empty-handed from the daily fishing excursions.

Retracing her steps, Hope stopped at The Fish Net for a boxed take-out lunch. The woman who took her order did not recognize her, but Sally Ann Jessup had gone to school with Hope's mother, Flora. She paid for her purchase, thanked Sally Ann, and returned home. The heat and humidity were too high to continue on foot.

*Hope spent the afternoon* and early evening on the porch, rocking and listening to the portable radio on a nearby table. The sound of the waves washing up on the beach was calming and hypnotic. It was the first time in years she had spent more than four hours doing absolutely nothing. The slam of a car door captured her attention, and she shifted on the rocker and stared at a woman who had just gotten out of a late-model luxury sedan. Slender and petite, she was fashionably dressed in a pair of celadon green slacks with a matching sleeveless blouse. She smiled at Hope, who waved and returned her smile.

Hope watched the woman take several pieces of luggage from the trunk of her car. Although their houses were separated by ninety feet, Hope was able to discern the brilliance of precious stones on her left hand.

*She's married. But where is her husband?*

Shrugging off her unwarranted curiosity, Hope pushed to her feet and went into the house. She walked into the bedroom, where her grandmother and grandfather had slept together for more than forty years. She opened the drawer in a double dresser and took out a swimsuit. The sun had sunk lower in the sky, the surf was calm, and conditions were perfect for a swim in the ocean.

# Ten

*He brewed his tea in a blue china pot, poured it into*
*a chipped white cup with forget-me-nots on the*
*handles, and dropped in a dollop of honey and cream.*
*"I am," he sighed deeply, "contented as a clam."*
— Ethel Pochocki

Rebecca closed the door to the small three-bedroom house, unable to control her trembling hands. She was frightened; no, she was scared. It was the first time in her life that she had found herself completely alone. As a child she had vacationed with her parents, then with Lee when they were dating, and later as a wife and mother.

After opening all the windows, she removed her shoes and sat down on a worn armchair, staring at her surroundings. The house was little more than a cottage, which could fit in her Charleston house twice, with room to spare.

She had left Kyle and Ashlee with her parents, fighting back tears when she'd lectured them about obeying their grandparents. Lee hadn't seen her off. His absence had spoken volumes. He knew he could not stop her from going away, yet he hadn't totally supported her decision to summer by herself.

She missed her children, her husband, and the spaciousness of her home. Placing a hand over her mouth, she wept silently.

*The sun had shifted* overhead by the time Rebecca moved off the chair. She had had her crying jag, and now she was ready to face what would become an uncertain two months. She wasn't going back to Charleston, and she'd made up her mind it was time to settle into her vacation house.

Walking across the living room, she made her way into the kitchen and flipped a wall switch. The ceiling light did not come on. She opened the refrigerator. The bulb in the outdated appliance did not light. Her mouth tightened in frustration as she circled the refrigerator to check if it had been plugged in. It was, but there was no humming sound.

The real estate agent who had handled the rental of the house had told her that everything was in working order. She left the kitchen and checked the lights in the other rooms. The electric was on in the three bedrooms and living room, but not the kitchen and bathroom.

Glancing at her watch, Rebecca noted the time. It was after seven, and in another ninety minutes it would be dark. She had to find someone to check out the electricity in the bathroom and kitchen.

She left the house, her bare feet making little *slip-slap* sounds on the porch's floorboards. She inhaled a lungful of salt-filled air, held her breath, then let it out slowly. A hint of a smile softened her mouth. The summer rental had come short of her expectations, but she could not complain about the setting. A house, albeit small, on the beach was ideal.

Walking to the end of the porch, she spied her neighbor. Warm golden light spilled from the windows of the house, which was glowing bright in the evening shadows.

Rebecca leaned over the peeling railing. "Good evening."

Hope glanced up when she heard the greeting. There was no drawl in the clear, feminine voice. Rising from the rocker, she walked over to the opposite end of her porch. Smiling, she said, "Hi. I saw you moving in earlier."

"I'm Rebecca Owens. I hope you can help me."

"With what?"

"I need someone to check the electricity in my kitchen and bathroom. It's not working."

"Are you certain you don't need to replace the bulbs?"

Rebecca shook her head. "I don't think it's the bulbs. The refrigerator is plugged in and it's still not working. Do you know of anyone who can come out to help me?"

Hope thought of the elderly man who took care of her house. She nodded. "Yes, I do know someone. I'll call him and see if he'll come over."

Rebecca smiled. "Thank you, Miss . . ."

Hope returned her smile. "Hope Sutton."

There was a moment of silence before Rebecca said, "The Hope Sutton who writes the 'Straight Talk' column?"

Hope had learned early on that it was impossible to remain anonymous, because her photograph always appeared in her column. "Yes."

A soft gasp escaped Rebecca as she stared at the advice columnist to whom she had written two letters that she'd never mailed. She'd wanted to pour out her heart to Dr. Hope and unburden herself, but a week later, she'd shredded both letters.

"I'll be right back."

Rebecca nodded. "Thank you." Her neighbor's porch had furniture, while hers was completely bare. If she wanted to sit outside, she would have to use a kitchen chair.

After she'd recovered from the sparseness of the house where she would spend her summer, she saw its quaint charm. When she had spoken to the realtor who'd represented the owner of the property, she'd been told that she would have to bring her own bed linens, cookware, and utensils. The house had been cleaned and aired, the plumbing and electrical checked and found to be in working order, and the grass and brushes around the house cut back. The bedrooms were small, kitchen appliances were more than thirty years old, and the wallpaper throughout the house bore traces of water stains, but the roof was purported to be sound.

She made her way off the porch and across the sandy lawn. Twin lamps flanking Hope's front door and an overhead fan stirring the ocean breeze invited her to sit and stay awhile. Rebecca wasn't certain what she'd expected Dr. Hope Sutton to look like in person, but it wasn't the tall woman who had offered her a warm smile.

Hope reappeared, and Rebecca stared up at the advice columnist. Her hair was pulled up in a ponytail, while a dark brown bare face shimmered under the glow of the porch lamps.

"You're much prettier than your photograph."

Hope blushed, nodding. It wasn't often that she received a compliment from a woman. "Mr. Turner says he will be over around nine."

"Nine o'clock. I can't wait that long. Is there anyone else you can call?"

Hope was taken aback by the waspish tone. "No, there isn't."

Her mouth tightening in frustration, Rebecca said, "I suppose I don't have much of a choice."

"No, you don't." Hope was hard-pressed to keep the sarcasm out of her voice.

"Thank you for making the call for me."

"Don't mention it."

Hope stood on her porch and watched Rebecca as she walked back to her house and disappeared inside. "Ungrateful pseudo-snob."

Hope sat down on the rocker and picked up the book she'd been reading. There was something about Rebecca Owens that annoyed her. She had asked her for help, yet she'd acted as if she'd been wronged because someone had not rushed to do her bidding. What her new neighbor had to learn was that no one moved quickly on McKinnon Island. That is the way it always was and would always be.

*Rebecca unpacked* as she waited for Mr. Turner to arrive. As she changed into a sleeveless dress, she made a mental note to buy a supply of candles just in case of an emergency. She'd found an old radio on a countertop in the kitchen, and she plugged it into an outlet in the room she had selected as her bedroom. Fiddling with a dial, she found a station that featured light contemporary songs, which were a welcome relief from the rap and hip-hop music her son and daughter blared so loudly that pictures vibrated on the walls.

Mr. Turner came at nine-thirty, and within minutes he replaced several blown fuses. He refused to take any money from her and mumbled something in a dialect Rebecca could not understand. Waiting until he was halfway out the door, she pushed the bill into the pocket of his shirt and quickly closed and locked the door behind him.

She extinguished all of the lights except those in her bedroom and the bathroom. At ten-thirty she crawled into bed after a lukewarm bubble bath, and fell asleep minutes after her head touched the pillow.

*It was late evening* the next day when Rebecca saw Hope again. She was sitting on the porch, reading. "Good evening, Hope."

Hope's head came up. "Good evening, Rebecca."

"May I come over?"

Hope put aside the book. "Yes."

She was on her feet by the time Rebecca came up the porch steps, seeing things about her neighbor she had not noticed the day before. She was not only petite but also very thin. The gold streaks in her short, curly hair matched her eyes. Rebecca smiled, and dimples winked in her cheeks.

"I'd like to apologize. I know I sounded ungrateful yesterday, but I've been a little out of sorts lately."

Hope ignored Rebecca's apology and asked, "Did Mr. Turner fix your lights?"

Rebecca blushed. "All he had to do was replace some blown fuses."

"Thankfully that was all he had to do."

"You're right. But I'd like to thank you for your help. Perhaps we could have dinner together one of these evenings."

Hope knew Rebecca was offering the olive branch, and she decided to accept it. She nodded. "Okay. Would you like some sweet tea?"

Rebecca smiled again. "Yes, thank you." She had noticed that Hope referred to iced tea as sweet tea. Even though Hope did not sound like a Southerner, Rebecca knew instinctively that she had Southern roots.

Hope pointed to a cushion-covered wicker chaise. "Please sit down. I'll be right back."

Rebecca sat down, closed her eyes and let out an audible sigh, the sound blending with the chirping of crickets and the rattle of palmetto trees in the cooling nighttime breeze. *This is nice.*

The soft click of the screen door opening made Rebecca open her eyes and come to her feet. Hope had returned, carrying a tray with two tall glasses and a pitcher filled with ice and a red liquid.

Hope placed the tray on the table with the radio. "I hope you like rose hip. I've added natural sweetener instead of sugar." Lana had recommended she use a sweet herb called stevia. She filled the glasses with tea, handing one to Rebecca.

Rebecca took a sip, her eyes widening. "I'm not much of a tea drinker, but this is delicious." She took another swallow. "Would you mind giving me the recipe?"

Hope smiled. "Not at all. Lately, I've become quite the tea connoisseur. I plan to have many afternoon teas during my stay."

"How long do you plan to stay?"

"I'll be here through the summer. How about yourself?"

Rebecca stared at the diamond engagement ring and matching band on her left hand. "I have to be home before my children go back to school."

A comfortable silence followed as the two women sipped tea and stared out at the blackness of the ocean. Hope did not know how, but she felt Rebecca's tension. After she placed her glass on the coaster on the table, Rebecca twisted her wedding rings around the third finger of her left hand as if she couldn't decide whether to take them off or leave them on.

Hope hadn't come to McKinnon to play therapist to others. She needed to get her own head together. Once she settled her inner turmoil, she planned to outline a book based on the letters she had received over the years. Writing the book would become her therapy and take her mind off her medical condition. She did not think about the offer to host the talk radio show. Derrick Landry had promised to get back to her, but so far she hadn't heard anything from him on whether his station was willing to move back the projected broadcast date.

"Would I be imposing if I asked to share afternoon tea with you?"

"Of course not. In fact, I'd love company."

A smile softened the lines of tension around Rebecca's mouth. She ran a hand through her short, curly hair. "If you'll make the tea, then I'll bring the little cakes and accoutrements."

"That sounds wonderful."

Rebecca stood up and extended her right hand. "Thank you for the tea and your company."

Rising, Hope shook her hand. "You're quite welcome. I'll see you tomorrow—say around four?"

"Four it is. Goodnight, Hope."

"Goodnight, Rebecca."

Hope waited until the petite woman with the haunted golden eyes walked away, then she sat down again. Rebecca Owens was in pain. It was obvious she had come to McKinnon Island alone, and the therapist in Hope wondered why. She thought of endless possibilities before reminding herself that whatever the reason was it was none of her business.

It began raining at sunrise, and by late afternoon the steady downpour slashed against the roof and windows. The radio newscaster reported a tropical storm would drop more than two inches of rain along the Carolina coast before losing its intensity.

Hope got up early and took the ferryboat to Savannah to shop for enough food to stock her refrigerator and pantry. It had taken only two days on McKinnon to revive her appetite.

At the supermarket she gathered organic steaks and hamburger patties, bottled juices, and dairy products. She paid for her purchases, loaded the trunk of her rental car, then drove across the causeway to wait for the ferryboat.

As she maneuvered her car onto the ferryboat, she noticed that a black Lexus SUV bore South Carolina plates. Normally she would've left her car to stand at the rail to watch vehicles and passengers board and disembark at each island, but not in today's stormy weather.

The rear doors to the Lexus opened, and two young black men wearing baseball caps, T-shirts, shorts, and deck shoes stood at the railing and pointed as Hilton Head Island came into view.

"*Thankfully the rain stopped.*" Rebecca placed a large wicker basket on a chair in Hope's kitchen. "I kept listening to the radio, waiting to be told that we would have to evacuate."

Hope removed a small dish of sliced lemons from the refrigerator. "We would have to have a lot more wind and rain before that happens." She spied the picnic basket. "What on earth did you bring?"

A mysterious smile curved Rebecca's mouth. "Oh, just a little something."

Rebecca's little something turned out to be ruby tea biscuits filled with red jam. She'd also brought an exquisite porcelain tea set emblazoned with tiny violet flowers. Hope watched as she placed the pot and matching cups and saucers on the white linen tablecloth. Reaching into the basket, she pulled out two sterling place settings and matching serving pieces.

Hope was impressed. When she'd asked Rebecca to join her for afternoon tea, she hadn't thought it would be comparable to high tea at Buckingham Palace. "Everything is so elegant."

Flashing her dimpled smile, Rebecca curtsied. "I'd like to think of us as McKinnon's Sophie Ladies."

"Sophie Ladies?"

Rebecca sobered. "This summer you and I will become the island's Sophisticated Ladies. But only during high tea, madam."

Hope laughed. "I like you, Rebecca. You've got lots of class."

Hazel eyes shimmered with excitement. "Why, thank you, Hope." The famous Dr. Hope Sutton thought she had class, while her mother-in-law viewed her as a gauche interloper from the North whose family pedigree boasted factory and mill workers, day laborers, and civil servants. Rebecca was the first Leighton to graduate from college.

She had gone to Hilton Head earlier that morning to shop and had stopped in a gift shop to look for items she could send back to Charleston for her parents and children. She'd spied the tea set and hadn't been able to resist buying it. After she'd told the shopkeeper she planned to have afternoon tea with a friend while summering on McKinnon, the woman had suggested she add the sterling silver place settings.

She glanced around the kitchen. "This place is lovely. It's a lot more modern than where I'm staying."

"That's because I had it done over."

Rebecca's eyes widened. "You're not renting?"

"No. I inherited this house and the surrounding property from my grandparents." There was half an acre behind the house that led into the woods, where her grandparents had kept their livestock and tended a vegetable garden.

"Please tell me about your family."

Over several cups of lemon verbena tea and jam-filled tea biscuits served on a warm plate, Hope wove a mesmerizing tale of the summers she had spent on McKinnon as a child. Rebecca listened, enthralled. She envied Hope and the time she'd spent with her brothers and sister. She had become an only child at nine after her younger sister had died in a hit-and-run accident.

"I remember the first time I helped my grandmother cook chitlins."

Rebecca grimaced. "I'd eat chitterlings if I could get past the smell."

Hope arched an eyebrow. "Oh no, you didn't call them chit-ter-lings, girlfriend."

"Isn't that what they are?"

"Not!" Hope stated emphatically. "Down here they're *chit-lins*." She peered closely at Rebecca. "Do you have *any* Southern roots?"

A rush of color darkened Rebecca's cheeks. "I don't think so."

"Where are you from?"

"Lowell, Massachusetts."

"How many generations?"

"At least six."

Hope shook her head. "That's a shame, Yankee girl. If you intend to spend the summer on McKinnon, then get ready for an infusion of Gullah culture and language."

Throwing back her head, Rebecca laughed until tears rolled down her cheeks. It had been a long time since she had really laughed without constraints. Picking up a napkin, she dabbed her eyes. Before she'd married Lee, before she had become a mother, she'd laughed all the time. When had her life become so serious?

"When I got off the ferryboat yesterday, I asked a man how to get to Beach Road, but I couldn't understand a word he said," she confessed.

"He probably said, 'Down yondah' and pointed in the direction of the ocean."

"That's the only word I understood."

Hope gave Rebecca a basic course on the Gullah language. She told of the annual gatherings in Beaufort, on Hilton Head, and on Georgia's Sapelo Island that celebrated a fading language and way of life. They talked until the pot of tea cooled and nightfall blanketed McKinnon.

Hope offered her neighbor a quick tour of the small, three-bedroom house. "My grandmother and great-grandmother pieced all of the quilts."

Rebecca fingered a faded, multicolored quilt covering an iron bed in the smaller of the bedrooms. It was stitched together using various colors and fabrics. "It's beautiful." Her attention was directed to a trio of small round baskets on a table under a window. She peered inside. They were filled with dried flowers and herbs.

"Those baskets and all of the others in the house were woven here on the island."

Rebecca gave Hope a direct stare. "Who wove them?"

"I don't remember who in particular, but I'm certain some of the older women still make sweetgrass baskets."

"Can you introduce me to them?" Rebecca did not feel comfortable enough to seek them out on her own because she did not understand their Gullah dialect.

"Do you want to buy some?"

"No. I want to learn how to weave them."

Hope stared at her new friend. Rebecca had come to McKinnon Island wearing raw silk and expensive jewelry, had purchased sterling silver pieces and a Sevres tea set for their afternoon tea, yet she wanted to learn to weave baskets like her African ancestors.

"Give me a few days to find out who would be willing to give you lessons, then I'll let you know.

Anything else you'd like to learn to do while you're here?"

"How to quilt by hand."

"I'll ask about both."

Rebecca smiled again. "Thanks, girlfriend."

Hope returned her smile. "You're quite welcome, girlfriend."

After Rebecca left, Hope retreated to the bedroom, where she had set up her temporary office. She plugged her laptop into a telephone outlet and checked her e-mail. There were three new messages.

Hope read Derrick Landry's from WLKV:

*Hope, The show's producer has decided to push back the broadcast launch for "Straight Talk" to accommodate your full medical recovery. Please advise as to a tentative start date. Cordially, Derrick.*

The second one was from Lana, wishing her well.

The third was from Kendall:

*Hi, Baby. I hope you are well. Miss you. Love, KC.*

Hope shook her head. *Sorry, KC, I don't do threesomes.*

With a click of the mouse, she deleted his message.

She answered Lana's and Derrick's e-mails, then inserted a new disk and began outlining the topics she wanted to cover in her book. It was after two when she finally turned off the computer and readied herself for bed.

# Eleven

*Sea, wave, low places and the high air.*
                                    —Hilda Doolittle

Theodore Howell mounted the half dozen steps to the wraparound porch and unlocked the front door. Jeff, a native New Yorker who now made his home in Los Angeles, had built a vacation home on a South Carolina Sea Island reminiscent of a Louisiana Lowcountry plantation-style house. The smell of freshly hewn wood was redolent in the air. The interior smelled new.

He smiled. Foul-mouthed and at times irascible, his agent had made good on his promise to assist him in completing the pilot. Jeff had arranged for a private jet to fly him and his family to Savannah, Georgia. It had been raining when the jet had touched down, and less than an hour later they had been on their way to the landing to wait for the ferryboat to take them to McKinnon Island. Luggage for five had taken up most of the cargo space in the SUV, and that had meant he and Helen would have to return to Savannah to shop for enough food to last at least two weeks. He flipped a wall switch near the door, and warm, gold light from sconces mounted on walls and columns separating the living and dining rooms brightened the gloomy interiors.

Turning, Theo met the curious gazes of his brothers and sister. "Chris, I want you and Brandon to unload the truck and put everyone's bags in their room. Then get out of those wet clothes." They had preferred standing out in the rain during the ferryboat ride to McKinnon. He smiled at Noelle. "If you want, you can come with me and Miss Helen."

Noelle stared at Theo, her expression impassive. "Where are you going?"

"Back to Savannah to shop for groceries."

She pushed back the hood to her bright yellow slicker and rearranged her braided hair.

"No, thanks."

He gave her a narrowed look. His sister had been unusually quiet during the coast-to-coast flight. She hadn't eaten any of the food served by the flight attendants, and she had spent the time either sleeping or listening to her disc player.

"Suit yourself. I expect you to have all of your clothes put away before we come back." He directed his attention to his brothers, who were checking out the stereo equipment behind the doors of a massive armoire. "Chris, you're in charge. And I should not have to remind you that I don't want strange kids in the house when I'm not here."

Christian gave Theo an incredulous look. "You're buggin'."

"I may be buggin' but the rule still stands, Mr. Personality." Christian's grin was sheepish. There was something about the seventeen-year-old's personality that was infectious. He made friends easily, and girls were drawn to him like a moth to a light. He had a deep voice and a smile sensual enough to make older women forget his youth.

"Which room is ours again?" Brandon asked. He was to share a room with his brother in one of the two first-floor bedrooms, while Theo would take the other.

"You and Chris get the one in the back."

Jeff had explained the layout of the house to Theo. Two bedrooms with adjoining full baths, sitting and dressing rooms took up the entire second floor. Two guest bedrooms were on the first floor. The one in the rear of the house was larger than the one in a wing off the kitchen, which faced southeast and afforded a view of the ocean and unlimited daylight.

Theo took a quick tour of the spacious house while the boys unloaded the bags from the SUV. The house and what he had seen of the island were ideal for his work. He knew Helen would be more than pleased with the large, state-of-the-art kitchen. Each bedroom had a fireplace, and the French and Colonial furnishings were in keeping with the house's eighteenth-century design.

The seating arrangement in the family room, with angled sofa, chairs, and a love seat, was more appealing than if the furniture had been positioned parallel to the walls. French doors and mullioned windows let in light despite the cloudy, rainy weather.

Theo walked out to the porch and found Helen waiting for him. "How do you like it?"

Helen stared out at the mist above a copse of oak trees shrouded with soggy Spanish moss. The rain was tapering off. "It's not me, Theo, but those kids."

"You don't think they'll like it here?"

Shifting, she stared at her employer. Theodore did not have a clue. She might not have had any children, but she was aunt to enough nieces and nephews to know something about children. "It's too remote. Will there be other kids their age to interact with? How long will it be before they become bored?"

"I don't know and I can't think about that now."

He wanted to tell Helen that the money he would earn for writing the pilot and scripts would generate enough income so that he would not have to accept another project for the next five years. And he needed to devote the next five years to his siblings. In five years Christian and Brandon would have graduated college and Noelle would be entering college. Brandon, a student in an accelerated academic track who had advanced a grade, was now a high school senior along with Christian.

Cradling an arm under Helen's elbow, Theo escorted her to the Lexus. Waiting until she was seated and belted in, he rounded the vehicle and took his seat behind the wheel. Glancing at the porch before turning on the ignition, he saw his brothers and sister standing together. They were watching him.

Suddenly it hit him! He was all they had. They were watching him leave, wondering if he would come back or vanish within seconds, like their parents. He turned the key but did not shift into gear.

Seconds later, he opened the door and walked back to the porch. He was met with three quizzical stares.

"Come on."

Uncertainty filled Christian's gaze. He and Brandon had changed their clothes. "I thought you said we had to unpack."

Theo smiled. "You have the rest of the summer to unpack. We'll eat out, then we'll shop for food."

"Hot damn," Christian whispered, while Brandon led Noelle to the Lexus.

Theo curved an arm around Christian's neck, holding him in a tight embrace. "You are going to have to watch your mouth when the ladies are present, brother."

"What ladies?"

"Miss Helen and Noelle."

"Noelle's a girl."

Theo tightened his grip. "She's a lady, Chris, and I want you to respect her. You're her role model when it comes to selecting a boy she'd like to date. And if she's used to hearing profanity, then she won't be repulsed by it."

"Are you really that lame, Theo? I've read stories about you dating four honeys at the same time. And I used to say to myself, 'Man, he's got it goin' on.' But after living with you, I don't know what to think."

"They were just stories."

"Are you saying you don't get *none?*" Christian asked in a low voice.

Theo dropped his arm and angled his head. "If you're asking if I sleep with women, then the answer is yes, but never two, three or four at one time. I've always had a problem keeping names straight, so I decided it's easier to sleep with one woman at a time. And always with a condom. Remember, going out with a woman doesn't mean you have to sleep with her." A slight smile curved his mouth. "But, I must confess that I haven't had any female companionship since you guys came to live with me."

Christian managed to look embarrassed. It was the first time he and Theo had discussed sex. "What are you going to do? Wait for Noelle to move out before you get a girlfriend? By that time you'll be so old you'll forget how to do it."

Theo laughed, and so did Christian. "It's like riding a bike. You never forget. But, on a more serious note, I will not bring a woman into the house as long as any of you live with me."

"That's old school, man. I know kids whose mothers bring men home after their fathers move out."

"I'm very conservative about certain things because I was raised by my grandmother, not *our* mother."

Christian's brows drew downward in a frown. "What was up with that?"

It was apparent Mary hadn't told his siblings about her life before she met and married James Anderson. "I'll tell you about it one of these days."

Theo knew the day of reckoning could not be avoided forever. Brandon, Noelle and Christian had known that they had a much older brother, but what Mary had neglected to tell them was that she had waited more than two decades to acknowledge and reconcile with her firstborn. On his thirtieth birthday, Theo had called Mary, and they had had a mother-son talk for the first time in their lives. He'd thought turning thirty had precipitated the telephone call, but it wasn't until after he had hung up that he'd realized it had been because he missed his grandmother, whom he had buried two months before. It was as if he'd had to connect with some-body—anybody with whom he shared blood.

"When?"

"Before we leave here. Now, let's go. I want to get back before the last ferryboat pulls out."

In the six months he had lived with Theo, Christian had learned enough about his older brother to know when to concede—except the night when L.A.'s finest escorted him and Brandon home. After the first slap from Theo, he realized it was dangerous to open his mouth before he engaged his brain. A couple puffs of weed had left him tem-porarily insane. Once his head cleared the following morning, he swore he'd never physically challenge Theo again, because if he slapped that hard, he did not want to find out how hard he could punch.

*Theo stared at Noelle* across the table, flanked in the booth by Helen and Brandon. They had arrived only minutes before a large crowd had gathered out-side the door to Johnny Harris, the city's oldest restaurant.

"Have you decided what you want?"

She did not glance up from the menu in front of her. "I'm not hungry."

"But you haven't eaten anything all day, sweet-heart," Helen crooned.

Noelle pushed out her lower lip. "I *said* I am not hungry." She had spoken through her teeth.

"Noelle!" Theo raised his voice, and diners from

a nearby table turned in their direction. He closed his eyes and covered his mouth with his right hand. His sister continued to push buttons he never knew he had. He opened his eyes and lowered his hand. "Please apologize to Miss Helen."

Noelle glared at him. "What did I say?"

"It's not what you said, but how you said it."

"Apologize, Ellie," Christian said, using his pet name for his sister. He could feel the tension coming from Theo.

Tears flooded Noelle's eyes, and she bit down hard on her lower lip. "I'm sorry, Miss Helen," she said after a long silence.

The pink color on Helen's cheeks began to fade. "Apology accepted."

Noelle perused the menu again, then said, "I'll have the broiled lobster, if it's not too expensive." There was no price next to the selection.

"Don't worry about the price," Theo said. "Just order whatever it is you want."

Brandon closed his menu. "If that's the case, then I'll have the lobster, too."

"Hey. I'll take one also," Christian chimed in.

Theo sighed. James and Mary Anderson had indulged their children beyond their financial limitations. Mary rarely cooked, preferring instead to dine in expensive restaurants. She thought nothing of pulling her children out of school to accompany their father on location, where she utilized the services of tutors hired by movie studios for their child actors. At first it was a novelty for the young Andersons to visit major cities and foreign countries, but as they'd grown older and formed friendships with their schoolmates, they'd begun to balk at leaving home. Mary had continued to accompany her husband, and when she had she'd left her three children in the care of a full-time housekeeper.

Theo studied the menu. "We'll order four lobsters, mussels in a butter sauce, crusty fried oyster, and soft-shell crabs."

Noelle wrinkled her nose. "I don't like oysters."

"She never ate them," Brandon volunteered.

Theo looked at Brandon under lowered lids. "If she says she doesn't like oysters, then she doesn't have to eat them."

Noelle smiled for the first time in days. "Thanks, Theo."

"How about the fried frog legs?" Helen asked. The response was a chorus of yucks from the others at the table.

A waiter came to take their order.

The food lived up to the restaurant's fabled reputation as all conversation ended and everyone concentrated on eating everything on their plates.

"What's the damage?" Brandon asked after the waiter placed the check on the table. Everyone had eaten so much that they found it hard to move out of the booth.

Theo picked up the itemized bill, barely glancing at the total. "Are you paying, Brandon?"

He flashed his shy smile. "Could be."

Noelle rolled her eyes at him. "Where did you get money?"

"I saved it from my allowances," he said proudly.

Theo nodded in approval. "That's what I like. A man who knows how to manage his money."

"Suck up," Noelle and Christian spoke in unison.

"There will be no name-calling," Theo warned softly.

Noelle pushed out her lower lip. "You say that because Brandon's your favorite."

All eyes were trained on Theo as he leaned back against the dark red Naugahyde booth. He gave each one a long, measured stare before he fixed his gaze on Noelle. "What have I done to make you think I love Brandon more than I love you or Christian?"

With wide eyes, she asked, "You . . . you love me—us?"

"If you'd asked me that question six months ago, or even a month ago, I would've said no."

"And now?"

Theo smiled. "Now, pumpkin, I realize I love you and your brothers enough to sacrifice whatever it takes to make certain you're safe and happy."

Christian cleared his throat. "What would you sacrifice?"

He told them about the television project for the cable network and the September thirtieth deadline he had to complete the six scripts. He also revealed that he had been willing to pass on the project until his agent had offered the use of his house on McKinnon Island.

Christian looked at his brother and sister, then decided to become the spokesperson for the group. "In other words, you need us to stay out of your face until you complete the scripts?"

Theo shook his head. There was something about Christian that reminded him of himself when he was his age. Outspoken, confident. He could also assume a take-charge posture when called upon.

"All I'm asking for is your cooperation. You

know I usually get up early to write, so I would appreciate not being disturbed unless it is a life-and-death situation. Miss Helen is more than capable of answering your questions and solving problems. The afternoons and evenings will be our time together. I promised to teach you all to swim, and I intend to keep that promise.

"If you want to go somewhere, then let me know the day before. Christian, you have your driver's license, and I've already cleared it with Mr. Helfrick that you may drive his SUV, but only on McKinnon Island. If you need to leave the island, then either Miss Helen or I will accompany you. Every Sunday night I will give each of you a weekly allowance. If you spend it before the next Sunday, then you'll have to wait." He paused. "Are there any questions?"

Christian bit back a grin. "It sounds good to me."

Theo glanced at Brandon. "How about you?"

"It's cool, Theo."

"Noelle?"

She shrugged her shoulder. "I suppose it's okay."

Theo paid the bill and left a generous tip. As he waited for everyone to get into the SUV, he thought about Noelle's response. Why, he thought, was it so hard for him to get through to her? She had accused him of favoring Brandon when it was she he had bent over backward for. He had heard people say it was easier to raise a boy than a girl, and for the first time in his life he believed it.

# Twelve

*You will have the road gate open, the front door ajar.*
                                    —Patrick Kavanagh

Hope sat on her porch, drinking her second cup of tea.

Yesterday's storm had passed over the island, leaving the sky a startling blue. Bright NO SWIMMING orange pennants flapped wildly from metal stakes placed along the beach. Children who had visited or grown up on McKinnon learned quickly not to ignore the colorful flags. The pennants, usually posted before or after a storm, indicated rough surf and dangerous undertow, which could sweep the strongest swimmer under within seconds.

Her gaze narrowed when she spied a lone figure walking the beach. Someone was up early. She continued to sip the flavorful herbal drink as she watched the figure come closer and closer. Then, Hope went completely still when she saw the person turn and walk toward the water.

*Don't you see the orange flags?*

Within seconds the figure was on the beach, then gone, swept away by the tide. Dropping her cup, Hope bounded off the porch, racing toward the water. Her bare feet sunk into the wet sand as she sprinted and dove into the ocean. Her heart pounded painfully in her chest as she searched under the water. She came up for air, filling her lungs with oxygen, then dove under again. Then she saw her. Braided hair fanned out around her brown face like octopus tentacles.

Reaching out, Hope caught the braids and began pulling as she fought the force pulling her and the girl downward. She wrapped the braids around her fist, and kicked her legs until she broke the surface. Then she began swimming back to the beach. Her eyes burned and her throat was raw from swallowing salt water.

She collapsed on the beach, her chest heaving as she struggled to catch her breath. Head lowered, she crawled on hands and knees to the slender figure lying facedown in the foaming surf. Hope turned her over, her eyes widening when she stared down at the face of a young girl who stared up at her with a flat, hard expression. The hatred blazing from her eyes chilled Hope even more.

"Who told you to pull me out?"

Hope's fear was supplanted with rage so intense that she wanted to slap the girl for risking not one, but two, lives. "What did you say?" The question had come out in a raspy whisper. The girl closed her eyes and turned her head. The fragile rein on Hope's temper snapped, and she reached out and pulled the girl up, shaking her until her head rolled limply on her shoulders.

"If you want to kill yourself, then you should've done it further down the beach where I couldn't see you!" The girl opened her eyes, glared at Hope, then broke down and cried.

Seeing the girl cry was Hope's undoing. The girl was a little more than a child. Her wet T-shirt clung to a slender body with just a hint of budding young breasts. Wrapping her arms around her shoulders, Hope held her, rocking her like a mother would a fretful infant. "It's okay," she crooned softly. "You're going to be all right, sweetheart."

Noelle heard the soothing feminine voice, and suddenly she felt safe. "Mama," she sobbed before another wave of tears flowed unchecked.

Hope went completely still. The girl thought she was her mother. She decided to play along. "Yes, baby? I'm here for you."

"Why did you have to die, Mama? Why couldn't you and Daddy wait to come back another day?"

Easing back, Hope stared at the girl's grief-stricken expression. She could tell from the look in the girl's eyes that she was beginning to realize she wasn't her mother.

"Let me go!"

"Not yet."

Her delicate chin quivered. "Please."

"Not until you tell me your name."

Panic rioted within Noelle. She needed to get away. "I can't."

Hope smiled. "Why not?" She had affected her therapist voice.

"Because you'll tell my brother."

"Tell him what?"

"That I tried to kill myself."

Hope's hands moved up, and she cradled the girl's face. Sand clung to her forehead and cheeks. "Did you really want to kill yourself?"

Noelle's lashes fluttered wildly. "I don't know." She shrugged a narrow shoulder under her wet T-shirt. "I don't know how to swim."

"Do you know what the orange flags on the beach mean?"

"No."

"They are put there to warn people not to go into the water."

Noelle sniffed loudly. "I didn't know."

"I want you to come back to my house with me, where you can clean yourself up."

"Will you tell my brother what I tried to do?"

"I can't answer that question because I don't know who you are."

Biting down on her lower lip, Noelle closed her eyes. "My name is Noelle Anderson."

Hope dropped her hands and smiled. "What a beautiful name."

Noelle opened her eyes. "I was born a week before Christmas." There was a hint of pride in her voice.

"How old are you, Noelle?"

"Thirteen."

*Thirteen, suicidal, and an orphan,* Hope mused. It was definitely a dangerous combination.

"Does your brother know where you are?"

Noelle shook her head. "No. But I told Miss Helen I was going for a walk."

Hope did not ask who Miss Helen was. "They're probably going to be looking for you if you don't get back soon. Come into the house with me and wash your face. Then I'll take you home."

Reaching out, Noelle clutched Hope's wrist. "Promise me you won't tell my brother that I tried to hurt myself."

*Hurt.* The girl had tried to kill herself, and she'd thought of it as an attempt to hurt herself. And why did Noelle think Hope would know her brother? The name Anderson was not one she was familiar with.

"I won't tell him if you promise not to go into the water by yourself again."

An expression of indecision crossed Noelle's young face before she finally said, "I promise."

*Hope waited* while Noelle washed her face and rinsed her braided hair. She handed her a towel to absorb most of the water. Hope didn't have any clothes that would fit Noelle, so the girl would have to go back home wearing her wet shorts, sneakers, and T-shirt.

They walked along Beach Road in silence, and it wasn't until they made their way toward a winding unpaved road that Noelle asked, "What's your name?"

"Hope."

Noelle gave Hope a sidelong glance. The woman who had pulled her out of the water was beautiful. Her strange-colored eyes glowed like bits of gold in her dark brown face.

"Who named you that?"

Hope smiled. "My mother. She had had two boys, so when she discovered she was going to have another baby, she hoped I would be a girl."

"I guess it's a nice name."

"I'd like to think it's a wonderful name."

Noelle pointed to her left. "I'm staying there." The house was built on a slight incline less than a hundred feet off the road.

Hope sighed. It was one of the newer houses on McKinnon. First there was one, two, then the self-contained, gated communities. In less than twenty years the landscape and the faces of the inhabitants would probably change completely. How long would it be before a developer arrived, checkbook in hand, to offer her an astronomical amount for her to sell her heritage?

"Do you want me to go in with you?"

Noelle shook her head. "I'll be all right." She pulled her lower lip between her teeth, blinking back tears. "Thank you, Miss Hope."

"You know where I live, Noelle, so if you need someone to talk to, then just drop by. My door will always be open for you."

A smile trembled over Noelle's mouth. "That's okay. I won't bother you."

Hope returned her smile. "It's not about bothering me. I was thirteen once."

The teenager nodded, then turned and made her way slowly toward the two-story house overlooking the beach. Hope watched until she disappeared from view before she turned to retrace her steps.

*Noelle made her way* around to the back of the house, opening a rear door that led into a mudroom. She removed her wet shoes and brushed grains of sand off the soles of her feet, then walked into the kitchen.

She came to a complete halt when she saw Theo leaning against the cooking island, sipping coffee.

There was no way she could make it up to her bedroom without him seeing her wet clothes.

"Theo?"

He turned, his gaze widening when he took in her wet hair and T-shirt. He set down the mug in slow motion. "What happened to you?"

"I went into the water." She had decided to tell the truth.

Theo closed the distance between them. "Didn't you see the orange warning flags?"

"I didn't know what they meant."

Curving his arms around Noelle's shoulders, he pulled her to his chest. "I don't know what I would do if something happened to you."

Noelle had expected Theo to yell at her, not console her, and that shocked and confused her. The floodgates opened, and as she sobbed against his shoulder, she confessed how she had tried to kill herself by drowning and about the woman who had jumped into the ocean and pulled her to safety.

Lowering his head, he kissed her damp hair. "It's all right, pumpkin."

"You're not mad at me?"

Theo closed his eyes and mumbled a silent prayer of thanks. All that mattered was that Noelle was safe. He opened his eyes. "No, baby girl, I'm not angry with you."

She pulled back and stared up at him. "That's what Daddy used to call me."

"Baby girl?" She nodded. "Would you prefer I not call you that?"

Her smooth brow furrowed. "It's okay if you do." She appeared so much younger than thirteen.

Theo's gaze met and fused with his sister's. "I

can't replace your father, but I promise to take care of you, be there for you in good times and not so good times. I don't have any experience with children, teenagers in particular, so I need you to be patient with me."

The corners of her mouth lifted. "You do yell a lot, Theo."

He frowned. "Do you have to remind me of that?" Theo cradled her face in his hands. "If you need to talk about anything, I want you to come to me first."

"I promise you I won't try it again."

He knew he had to watch Noelle carefully, because if she'd attempted suicide once, then there was always the possibility she might try it again. "I'm going to hold you to that promise, otherwise you're going back into counseling."

A shadow of alarm touched her face. She hated the therapist and did not want to go back to her. "I mean it, Theo."

"If you're to become responsible for your behavior, then you're going to have to face the consequences."

"I'm grounded?"

Theo nodded. "For the next three days you will help Miss Helen around the house. And that includes doing laundry, cooking and cleaning. You will not be permitted to leave the house or hang out on the beach."

"Mama never grounded us."

He wanted to tell Noelle that parents not establishing boundaries for their children contributed to all types of antisocial behaviors. "I am not your Mama, Noelle." There was a hard edge in his voice.

"I understand." The two words were soft, barely audible.

"Good. I want you to change your clothes, then check in with Miss Helen." He cradled the back of her wet head in his hand, leaned down, and kissed her forehead. "We'll talk again later."

Theo watched Noelle as she walked out of the kitchen. He hadn't realized he had been holding his breath until he felt the tightness in his chest. The enormity of his sister's suicide attempt finally hit him, and he moved on shaking knees to a tall stool at the cooking island. Christian and Brandon had lost their mother and father, and he shuddered to think how they would react to losing their sister, too.

Resting his elbows on the granite countertop, he buried his face in his hands and did something he had not done in a very long time—he prayed. He prayed for guidance, strength, and especially for understanding. He needed all three in his attempt to become a surrogate father to his siblings.

*Hope sat at the table* on the porch and rearranged the three-by-five index cards for the third time that morning. She stared at the topics she had written with a black marker: Relationships, Marriage, Divorce, Adolescent Years, Health, Death and Dying, Spirituality, Money Matters, Lifestyles, Parenting, and Career vs. Job. There were eleven cards—an uneven number. She needed to either add one or delete one. She shook her head. All of the topics were essential, so that meant she would have to come up with one more.

Leaning back against the cushioned rocker, she closed her eyes. She had a monumental task in front of her—going through hundreds of disks to extract the letters she wanted to reprint for her book. Each disk, labeled by month and year, contained every published "Straight Talk" column. Now, if she could come up with one more topic, she would begin to review the archives.

Hope heard someone clear his throat, and she opened her eyes and sat up straighter. Standing on the first step to the porch was a tall, slender black man whose face was vaguely familiar. She had seen him before but could not remember where.

Pushing off the rocker, she stared at him as a knowing smile softened her mouth. He looked as if he had stepped off the pages of a Ralph Lauren ad, with his navy blue golf shirt, white pleated front walking shorts, and navy canvas Docksiders. She could not remember the last time she had come face-to-face with a "preppy brother." She wanted to see the eyes concealed behind the lenses of his sunglasses. Perhaps then she would recognize him.

"Good morning."

Theo's impassive expression did not change. He did not want to believe, could not believe the woman Noelle had told him about was Dr. Hope Sutton. The celebrated psychologist-advice columnist had saved his sister's life. He had seen her guest appearances on several televised talk shows, but he had to admit she was much prettier in person. Even with her hair pulled off her bare face and dressed in an oversized T-shirt with a pair of cropped pants, she was delightfully feminine.

He inclined his head. "Good morning, Dr. Sutton."

He knew who she was. "Hope Sutton."

Theo smiled for the first time. "Hope, Dr. Sutton. It doesn't matter what you call yourself, because I would like to thank you for saving my sister's life earlier this morning."

"You're Noelle's brother." The question had come out like a statement.

"One of her brothers." Removing his sunglasses, he extended his right hand. "Theo Howell."

Hope's jaw dropped slightly as she stared at the proffered hand. She did not want to believe that Noelle's guardian was the brilliant, high-profile, womanizing scriptwriter Theodore Howell.

She crossed her arms under her breasts, bringing his gaze to linger on her chest. "May I make a suggestion, Mr. Howell?"

Theo dropped his hand. "What?"

"Take good care of your sister. She's too young to be in so much pain."

"I had her in therapy," he countered, not caring if he sounded defensive.

Hope lifted an eyebrow. *"Had?"*

"She wouldn't stay."

"She's only thirteen, and at that age she should not be allowed to make her own decisions on her emotional well-being. She's the child and you're the adult. I suggest you act like one."

Theo struggled to control his temper. "You're really a piece of work, aren't you?"

"What are you talking about?" It was Hope's turn to be defensive.

"I viewed the *Sixty Minutes* segment on you, and I wanted to come through the television when you tried to defend your hard-as-nails stance when the topic of bashing black men came up. Why can't you cut us some slack? All of us aren't irresponsible, trifling, or a turncoat when one decides he wants to marry a white woman."

Her golden eyes darkened in fury. How dare he! He had no right to talk about her when his own sordid reputation was touted in every sleazy supermarket tabloid several times a year.

"You've thanked me for helping your sister. Now I'm going to ask that you leave my property, Mr. Howell."

Turning on her heel, she opened the screen door and walked into the house, leaving him staring at her back.

Theo stood motionless, staring at the space where Hope Sutton had been. He was losing it. He had come to a woman's house and insulted her. Helen had called him a monster, and this time he had to agree with her.

Because he owed Hope for saving his sister, he would give her time to cool off before approaching her again. His grandmother had accused him of being too prideful, and she'd been right. There were occasions when pride had to be laid aside in order to move forward, and this was one of those times. Theo put his sunglasses on the bridge of his nose and walked down to the beach.

*Hope stood at the window,* peering through the sheer curtains. Theo stood on the beach, arms folded over his chest, staring out at the pounding surf. He'd said he was *one* of Noelle's brothers. Did that mean he was guardian to more than one child? Noelle needed counseling, and it was apparent her guardian also needed counseling.

She turned away from the window, not seeing him as he turned and walked back the way he had come.

# Thirteen

*I believe that you are here to become more of yourself
and live your best life.*

—Oprah Winfrey

Hope slowed her car over the muddy,
rutted road to avoid hitting a slow-moving
dog that stopped, looked at her, and then
continued crossing the road at the same unhurried
pace. She smiled. Even the pets on McKinnon were
laid-back.

She'd decided to complete her tour of the island
and follow through on her promise to Rebecca to find
someone who could teach her to weave sweetgrass baskets. If anyone knew the artisans living on the island,
then it would be Charlotte Field. While many of Mc-
Kinnon's first families had left the island, the Fields had
stayed, keeping the Gullah language and culture alive.

Hope maneuvered into an unpaved driveway
and parked behind an ancient pickup truck. She
opened the door and shaded her eyes as she spied
the raw-boned figure of an elderly woman rise from
a rocker on a screened-in porch.

"Afternoon, Miss Charlotte."

Charlotte Field moved slowly to the porch door, squinting. Her snow white hair was braided in two thin plaits that hung over her narrow shoulders, while a pair of glasses had slipped down to the end of her short, broad nose. Her white hair was a startling contrast to a face that appeared blue-black in color.

"Who be dat?"

"Flora Robinson's girl," Hope replied, smiling broadly.

"Who?"

"Queenie Robinson's grandbaby girl."

Charlotte grinned, displaying a set of short, straight teeth darkened from a lifelong habit of chewing tobacco and dipping snuff. Opening the door, she extended her arms. "Hey, baby. Come give Mizz Charlotte some *shuga.*"

Hope mounted the stairs to the porch and hugged the elderly woman, registering the fragility of her slight frame under a flower-sprigged cotton dress. She kissed her withered cheek. "You look beautiful, Miss Charlotte."

"No, child, you look beautiful." She pointed at a rocker next to the one she had just vacated. "Come set and rest yourself. You want a cool drink?" A Mason jar filled with lemon slices in a yellowish liquid sat on a nearby table.

"No, thank you, Miss Charlotte."

Hope smiled, nodding as Charlotte launched into a lengthy discourse, using short, quick Gullah phrases, bringing her up to date on everything and everyone on the island. She stopped intermittently to drink from the Mason jar. Her husband of sixty-four years still

went out on his fishing boat six days a week with
their eldest son. Her granddaughter had graduated
from beauty school and had set up a salon in a little
shed out back.

"Dat girl can really do some hair." She peered
closely at Hope's thick hair swept up in a ponytail.
"You gwine let Precious fix you up?"

"I'll let you know. If I have someplace special to
go to, then I'll have her do it." She was not ready to
commit to Precious doing her hair until she saw her
work.

Waiting for another pause, Hope asked Charlotte
about some of the women who still made baskets
from sweetgrass. The older woman gave her a skeptical look until she explained that a friend who came
from "yondah" wanted to learn the technique. She
pointed upward, indicating "up north."

Charlotte gave her the names of several women
who still wove baskets and sold them to tourists
who booked boat excursions of the Georgia and
South Carolina Sea Islands.

"The best one be Janie Saunders. Her weave a
basket so tight it don't lose a drop of water."

Hope thanked Charlotte for her help and
promised to come back and "set" awhile. Charlotte
would not let her leave without a jar of her legendary peach preserves. Hope thanked her again,
kissing her cheek. The preserves would be a perfect
topping for hot biscuits or scones. As she drove to
the north end of the island, she recalled that her
Grandmomma had refused to have anything to do
with the Saunders because she'd said they tried too
hard to be uppity. Too many of them were direct
descendants of the owners of the largest cotton plan-

tation on McKinnon, and they had sent their children to colored schools in Hilton Head rather than the one-room schoolhouse on the island.

Once educated, most of the Saunderses had left McKinnon, but Janie had returned, after graduating from college, with her husband, who looked white, although he claimed to be a Negro. The federal government had given the state of South Carolina money to expand and renovate the school, and Janie and her husband had joined the faculty of three to offer a quality education to the children on McKinnon. They'd also purchased the property where Janie's relatives had been the oppressor and oppressed, and they had begun restoring it to its original grandeur.

Hope found Janie Saunders-Smith at home, cradling a grandchild on her lap. Although in her early fifties, Janie looked much younger. She listened intently as Hope explained what Rebecca wanted. Her expression was impassive, then she smiled and agreed to help, claiming it would give her something to do to pass the summer other than spoiling her grandchildren.

Hope drove home, feeling as if she had put in a full day's work. She had rescued a teenage girl, met with one of the island's oldest surviving residents, and had set up a meeting with a Gullah artisan for her summer neighbor.

She parked her car at the rear of her house on Beach Road, noticing that Rebecca's wasn't in its usual space. Smiling, she wondered if Rebecca had gone to Hilton Head again to shop for expensive pieces.

As she got out of the car, she noticed a field of

flowers growing in wild abandon. The caretaker had cut the grass and weeded the area where her grandmother had planted her vegetable garden. Grandmomma had told her that at one time the land behind the house had looked like a jungle. "Back in dem days" Hope's great-grandfather had cleared the land and expanded his house to include a third bedroom. The house was modest by island standards, not having indoor plumbing until the late 1920s.

She lingered, picking enough flowers for a colorful bouquet before going into the house. As soon as she unlocked the door, she saw it. Someone had slipped a small envelope under the door.

Picking it up, she walked into the kitchen and left the jar of preserves and flowers on the countertop. Sitting down at the table, she opened the envelope, her eyes widening in surprise. The note card was from Theodore Howell.

> *Sorry!*
>
> *Theo*

She stared at the two-word, two-line note. He had used one word to apologize, but for what? Being rude, arrogant or opinionated?

A smile crinkled the skin around her eyes. "Apology accepted," she whispered. The fact that he had made the attempt to apologize meant he did claim a modicum of humility.

Pushing off the chair, she put the flowers in a vase, then made her way to the bathroom. After a shower and a light lunch, she intended to relax on the porch until her afternoon tea with Rebecca.

\* \* \*

*Theo leaned against* the porch column to Hope Sutton's house for the second time that day, watching her as she dozed. She looked different than she had earlier that morning. Her unbound hair curved under her jaw as she rested her head at an angle on the cushioned rocking chair. A white cotton halter and matching slim skirt ending below her knees had replaced her T-shirt and slacks. He felt like a voyeur as he watched the gentle rise and fall of her breasts.

His gaze roved lazily over the curves of her calves and down to a pair of slender ankles and feet. Hope looked different, natural, so unlike the professionally coiffed and made-up woman he'd seen on television. Now he needed Dr. Hope Sutton's assistance. Folding his body down to the top step, he sat, stretched out his legs, and waited for her to wake up.

*Hope woke up* and stared at a pair of broad shoulders. "I accept, Mr. Howell."

Hope's low, husky voice brought Theo to his feet. He turned and found her standing several feet behind him. He hadn't heard her get up.

A slight frown appeared between his large, penetrating eyes as he stared directly at her. "Excuse me."

Hope smiled at Theo for the first time. "I said I accept your apology." He returned her smile, the gesture so endearing that it caused Hope to catch her breath. Seeing the scriptwriter up close verified why women were drawn to him. He was handsome and shockingly virile.

Theo angled his head, his sensual smile still in place, and offered his right hand. "Perhaps we should start over. Good afternoon, Miss Sutton, Theo Howell."

Hope placed her hand in his larger one, a slight shiver of awareness racing up her arm when his fingers tightened over hers. "My pleasure, Mr. Howell."

"Theo," he insisted.

She inclined her head. "Hope." He released her hand, and she pointed to the rocker. "Please sit down. May I offer you something to drink?"

"No, thank you."

He waited for Hope to take the chaise before he sat on the rocker. The haunting scent of her perfume had penetrated the seat and back cushion. The chaise was angled so he could see her without turning his head.

Resting his elbows on the arms of the chair, he rocked back and forth in a smooth, measured rhythm and stared out at the beach. "This is nice."

Hope nodded but did not respond. Crossing her legs at the ankles, she waited for Theo to reveal why he had come to see her for the second time in one day.

"I'd like to talk to you about Noelle."

"What about her?"

Theo ran his right hand over his short-cropped hair before he massaged the tight muscles in the back of his neck. Even though he had extracted a promise from Noelle that she would not attempt to hurt herself again, he still did not feel comfortable.

"I'm worried about her."

"And you should, Theo. After all, she did try to kill herself."

He gave Hope a direct look. "She blames herself for her parents' deaths."

"Was she directly responsible for their deaths?"

Theo shook his head. "No. They died in a plane

crash. She feels guilty because she'd asked them to change their travel plans to return to L.A. to celebrate her thirteenth birthday."

"Your sister is dealing with grief, loss and guilt. She's also thirteen, female and somewhat fearful of you."

His eyes widened. "No she's not."

"Yes she is, Theo," Hope countered. "She wanted me to promise her I wouldn't tell her brother that she tried hurting herself."

"But she did tell me."

"She probably told you because she was more afraid of your reaction if you had found out on your own."

He closed his eyes and shook his head from side to side. "Six months ago I became guardian to two brothers and a sister whom I had seen exactly four times before we were reunited at their parents' funeral."

"You had the same father?"

Theo opened his eyes. "No. Mother," he said after a long pause. "My mother was a month past her sixteenth birthday when she had me, and I was three weeks old when she left me with her mother. I met her for the first time when I turned twenty-one."

"Did you resent her deserting you?"

Shifting slightly, he smiled. "No. I wouldn't be who I am if Mary had raised me."

"Do you see her as a bad mother?"

The corners of his mouth lifted. "I'd rather say she wasn't a good mother. My brothers and sister have serious boundary issues."

"And what are your issues, Theo?"

His jaw tightened. "You think I have issues, Hope?"

"Of course. Everyone has issues. And you are in denial if you think you don't. The fact that you've come to see me indicates that you do."

"I've come to see you about Noelle."

Hope refused to relent. "You've come to me because you have parenting issues. You're in a dual role as older brother/surrogate father. You must see your siblings as individuals with different personalities, wants and needs."

"I think I'm better with my brothers than my sister. I'm used to interacting with women, not young girls."

Hope laughed. "There's not much difference between the two. One you sleep with, the other you don't."

His black arching eyebrows lifted as he gave her an incredulous look. Then he leaned back on the rocker and smiled. "I never thought about it like that."

"I did not come to McKinnon for the summer to counsel patients, but I did tell Noelle that my door would always be open to her if she wanted to see me."

"She didn't tell me that."

Hope heard the censure in Theo's voice. "I would not have talked to her without first getting your parental consent."

"What would you talk about?"

She shrugged a bare shoulder. "Probably things a mother would share with her daughter—talk about clothes, books, music, cute boys, and hot movie stars." She wrinkled her nose. "Inane things."

"That sounds like fun, all except for the cute boys."

"You can't expect us to talk about cute girls, can you?"

Throwing back his head, Theo laughed. "No, but I can."

What he wanted to tell Hope was that he thought she was more than cute. She was pretty and very sexy. And he found himself drawn to her. And not because he had been celibate for six months but because her looks matched her intelligence. A combination he had not found in all of the women he had ever dated.

His smile faded. "What brings you to McKinnon Island?"

Hope wanted to say a medical dilemma and the shocking revelation that the man she'd planned to marry was bisexual. "I used to spend my summers here as a child," she said instead.

"You have family on the island?"

She shook her head. "I used to. I inherited this house after my grandparents passed away. My mother and her brother didn't want it, and neither did any of my siblings, so it was willed to me. How about yourself? Why have you come to McKinnon?"

"My friend is loaning me his place for the summer so I can complete a few scripts."

"How much is a few?"

"Six."

Hope stared at Theo, complete surprise on her face. "Six movie scripts?"

He shook his head. "No. Television."

Her smile was dazzling. "Good for you. When do you have to submit them?"

"The last one must be completed by the end of September."

"You only have four months." It was already the first week in June.

"That's plenty of time." And it was. Once he completed the pilot, Theo knew he could realistically complete one script every two weeks. "If you're not doing anything Sunday afternoon, I'd like to invite you over to the house for dinner . . ." His words trailed off. "And, of course, to meet the rest of my family," he added, as if an afterthought.

She thought about turning down the invitation, then thought about Noelle. She wanted to see her again. Smiling, she said, "I'd like very much to meet them."

"I'll pick you up at two."

Hope felt the intensity of Theo's stare. It was as if he were photographing her with his eyes. To say he was handsome was an understatement, and it was obvious women were drawn to him for more than his ability to write award-winning scripts.

It wasn't vanity that told her that Theodore Howell was interested in her for more than her help with his sister. But right now she did not want him or any man to become interested in her. Not while the image of Kendall with another man still lingered along the fringes of her mind, resurfacing in her dreams.

"There's no need to pick me up." She did not want the dinner to be misconstrued as a date.

Theo's nostrils flared slightly. "I'd rather bring you than have you come on your own. My brothers and sister have never seen me with a woman since they've come to live with me. I believe it would be more comfortable for them if they see us together when I make the introductions."

"Are you saying they're going to reject me out-right?"

"I don't know how they'll react," he said honestly. "After all, they do have problems with boundaries."

What he did not say was that he did not know his siblings well enough to predict their reactions to anything. He was almost certain Noelle would wel-come Hope, but he had his doubts about Christian.

Hope nodded, her curiosity aroused. "I'll be ready at two."

Theo stood up and smiled. The gesture was as intimate as a kiss. "Thank you, Hope."

"You're welcome, Theo."

She did not move off the chaise for another hour—long after Theo had disappeared beyond the beach. The sound of an approaching car signaled Rebecca's return. Hope glanced at her watch. It was almost three o'clock. Waiting until after she'd heard the solid slam of the door to Rebecca's Mercedes-Benz sedan, she got up and went into the house. It was time to prepare for their afternoon tea.

# Fourteen

*Sometimes we are stuck in a maze of our making and could use a helping hand.*

—Sark

Rebecca walked into the cottage, grimacing against the wave of heat rushing at her. She had left all the windows open. Not even the cooling breeze coming off the water could counter the buildup of heat. She had become too accustomed to central air-conditioning.

Making her way to the tiny kitchen, she opened the refrigerator and placed a decorative airtight container filled with vanilla meringue kisses on a shelf. She kicked off her sandals, retrieved her cell phone from her purse, and pressed the speed-dial number to her home.

"Hello."

Rebecca recognized her mother's voice immediately. Felicia Leighton's New England inflection sounded strange, because after living in South Carolina for more than half her life, Rebecca had become so used to the drawling cadence of Southerners.

"Hello, Mom. What's going on?"

"Not much since your last call, and that was just about twenty-four hours ago."

She ignored her mother's retort. "Where are Ashlee and Kyle?"

"Georgina took them out with her. She said something about having them volunteer at a summer camp for the next month—"

"What summer camp!" Rebecca exclaimed, interrupting Felicia.

"I don't know the name of it. She said something about them becoming CITs."

"Counselors-in-training."

"Yes, dear, that's it."

The tight ball forming in her stomach forced Rebecca to sit down. "The sneaky, manipulative witch! She waited for me to go away . . ." Her words trailed off.

"What's the matter, Rebecca?"

"Georgina only orchestrated this subterfuge so you and Dad won't be able to spend time with your grandchildren. Does Lee know about this?"

"Of course he does."

She glanced at her watch, wanting to talk to her husband before he left work. "Look, Mom, I'll talk to you later."

"Rebecca, please take care of yourself."

"I will." She pressed the End button, then dialed Lee's private line. His secretary answered, then connected her to Lee.

"Hi, baby."

"Don't you dare freakin' 'baby' me, Lee Owens. What the hell does your mother think she's doing?"

"What's the matter, Becky?"

"She's sabotaging my plans for my children."

"Your children? Am I not their father?"

"I don't know. There are times when you don't act like their father. You knew my parents were going to take care of Kyle and Ashlee for the summer, yet you let your mother woo them away with a volunteer summer job."

"They said they wanted to do it."

"When did this all come about? It certainly wasn't yesterday, when I spoke to them."

There was a pause, then Lee said, "I'm not going to get into it with you now, Rebecca. But let me remind you that it was you who decided to leave your children because you *need* to find yourself. So, whatever it is they want to do during your absence should not concern you as long as I approve it."

She bit down on her lower lip to cut off the words threatening to explode from her mouth. Words she knew she would regret later. Lee was as manipulative as his mother.

"You're right, Lee. I'm not the first Owens woman to leave Charleston and not come back, and I'm certain I won't be the last." Her forefinger hit the End button, terminating the call.

Lee's younger sister Phyllis had left Charleston to attend college in California. She'd sent her parents a letter in the middle of her second year, telling them she'd dropped out because she was pregnant and was living with a former classmate of whom, she was certain, they would never have approved. Phyllis had not indicated a forwarding address, so her family had never known if she'd married, or the sex of the baby. That had been sixteen years ago. Phyllis was past the manipulation, and Rebecca was quickly getting to that point. And if she returned to Charleston it would be to get her children, then leave—for good.

*Hope sat across* the linen-covered table on the porch, staring at Rebecca's trembling hands. "Are you all right?" Rebecca was attempting to pour the pitcher of ice tea into tall glasses but couldn't.

Rebecca placed the pitcher on the table, shaking her head. "No."

Reaching across the table, Hope captured her hands. They were moist and trembling. "What's the matter, Sophie Lady?"

Rebecca smiled, blinking back tears. She related her telephone conversation with her mother and the subsequent one with her husband. "Lee knew I wanted my parents to take care of Ashlee and Kyle, yet he let his mother usurp my parents' plans." She pulled her hands out of Hope's loose grip.

"You left your husband and your children. You can't control what's going on in Charleston as long as you remain here."

"Are you saying I should go back home?" Rebecca's tone became chilly.

Leaning back against her chair, Hope shook her head. "I'm not saying anything. It's obvious the telephone conversations with your mother and husband have upset you. And the only reason you're telling me about them is because you need a friend right now."

"I need Dr. Hope right about now."

Hope shook her head. "If you want Dr. Hope, then you're out of luck. I did not come to McKinnon to do therapy. But if you want a friend, then I'm here for you." Pushing back her chair, she stood up.

"What do you say about McKinnon's Sophisticated Ladies skipping tea and going out to dinner?"

Rebecca smiled. "Yes."

*Hope and Rebecca* arrived at The Fish Net in the middle of the dinner rush. Waitresses, shouldering trays with mouthwatering dishes, moved quickly, ladening log-hewed tables with steaming plates of greens, broken crab and okra stew, oysters, barbecued spareribs, pork chops with gravy, and chitlins. Thick slices of buttered corn bread and fluffy biscuits accompanied each entrée.

"This place is really hopping," Rebecca whispered.

Hope nodded, smiling. "It hops from the time it opens before dawn for breakfast until closing time."

"Who would get up at dawn to eat breakfast?"

"Fishermen."

Sighing, Rebecca glanced around the crowded room and wrinkled her nose as if she had caught a whiff of something malodorous. When Hope had suggested going into town to eat, she never would have expected to dine at a place that was literally a hole in the wall. The log cabin housing The Fish Net did not look large enough for twenty people to stand together without touching. It was incredible that they had managed to set up at least twenty tables with just enough space for the waitresses to navigate between each.

"Mercy! It's a shack."

Hope noted Rebecca's expression and declaration and decided to reserve comment, because what she wanted to say would not come out very diplomatically. She would tell Rebecca that she was a snob, an outsider and—if she had to go there—a Northerner. Although she herself had been born and raised in New Jersey, she was proud of her Southern roots and her Gullah heritage.

How long, she wondered, would it be before her neighbor abandoned her designer wardrobe for the ubiquitous shorts and T-shirt? This evening she wore a stunning Donna Karan pale pink silk sheath dress, matching Jimmy Choo stilettos, and a trendy Kate Spade handbag. Everything about Rebecca Owens screamed money, from her Rolex watch to her top-of-the-line Mercedes-Benz sedan.

"Someone is waving at you, Hope." Rebecca gestured to her left.

Shifting, she saw Noelle sitting with Theo at a table against the wall. He smiled, pushing back his chair as he rose to his feet. She watched him as he wove his way through the tables. He had changed from his shorts and T-shirt into a pair of white jeans, matching cotton short-sleeve shirt, and a pair of tan leather sandals.

Hope hadn't realized she had been holding her breath. There was something about the white against his red-brown skin, the way he moved, walked, smiled that had her watching him closely. He was strong, masculine, and beautiful.

"Hello again."

She also liked the deep sound of his voice. Hope gave him a dazzling smile. "Hello yourself."

Theo could not take his gaze off Hope. He'd returned to her house a second time that day because he'd been unable to stop thinking about her. Reluctantly pulling his gaze away, he smiled at the petite woman dressed to the nines. She reminded him of some West Coast women who put on haute couture just to walk their dogs.

He inclined his head to Rebecca. "Good evening."

Hope grimaced. She had forgotten her manners. "Theo, Rebecca Owens. Rebecca, Theodore Howell."

Rebecca flashed a brilliant, dimpled smile and extended her right hand. "My pleasure, Mr. Howell."

He shook her hand. "Theo." He released Rebecca's hand, his penetrating gaze returning to Hope. "Would you ladies mind sharing a table with me and my sister instead of waiting?"

Wiggling her toes in the stiletto sandals, Rebecca said, "I'd love to." Her calves were beginning to burn. It had been a while since she'd worn four inches of heels. She glanced at her neighbor. "Hope?"

"Yes. Thank you, Theo."

He moved aside, and the two women made their way to the table, where Noelle sat staring at them. She had been the one who'd noticed Hope first, her sullen expression vanishing like a flash of lightning crisscrossing a summer sky. She had spent the morning and afternoon in her room, inconsolable. It had taken some urging, but he'd gotten her to agree to go out to dinner with him. Christian and Brandon were content to spend their time on the beach listening to music.

Theo waited for Hope to sit down beside Noelle, leaving him to share the bench seat with Rebecca.

Hope moved closer to Noelle, their shoulders touching. "Hi."

Noelle flashed a shy smile. "Hi."

"Noelle, this is my friend, Rebecca Owens. She's staying in the house next to mine for the summer."

Rebecca smiled at Noelle, who had dropped her gaze. "Hi, Noelle. I have a daughter who is about your age."

Noelle appeared suddenly alert. "How old is she?"

"Fourteen."

"I won't be fourteen until December. Is your daughter here?"

"Noelle," Theo admonished softly.

"That's okay," Rebecca countered. "Ashlee and my son, Kyle, are working at a country day camp as counselors-in-training for a month."

Theo stared at Hope and lifted his eyebrows. It was the most animated he had ever seen his sister. He ignored Rebecca and Noelle's conversation, smiling. "You look very nice in that color," he said to Hope. She had paired a pink sleeveless linen blouse with a calf-length, leaf green wrap skirt with large pink flowers. Her shoes were black patent leather mules.

"Thank you." Hope wanted to tell Theo that he looked fabulous in white, but said instead, "Have you ever eaten here?"

He picked up a menu. "No, so you're going to have to help me out. What's good?"

She scanned the selections. Nothing had changed since her last visit. "Everything. However, I'm partial to the barbecued shrimp, country-fried cabbage with ham, and the okra gumbo."

Rebecca studied the menu next to Theo's right hand. "They have chitterlings."

"Chitlins," Theo and Hope chorused before bursting into laughter.

Rebecca managed to look insulted. "I'm going to fix you both when I order them."

"Good," Hope and Theo chorused again.

They decided to order half a dozen entrées so each could sample different selections. The busboy placed pitchers of icy sweet tea, frothy beer, and half carafes of white and red wine on the table, along with baskets of corn bread and hot, fluffy biscuits as a waitress took their orders.

Someone had fed the colorful jukebox in an alcove between the kitchen and the main dining area, and the blues of Professor Longhair and Bobby "Blue" Bland blared from the speakers. The jukebox selections had not been updated in more than a decade.

Hope, Rebecca, and Theo fell into an easy camaraderie as they discussed the movies Theo had scripted and the more popular topics covered in her "Straight Talk" column. Theo made certain to include Noelle in the conversation. All talk came to an abrupt end as serving bowls of chitlins, Sea Island okra gumbo filled with pieces of ham hock, fried shrimp, cucumber and tomato salad, barbecued turkey wings, and seafood rice were set on the table, along with a complimentary portion of The Fish Net's celebrated roast pig. Rebecca spooned a small portion from the steaming bowl of chitlins onto her plate. Picking up her fork, she bit into the hog intestines and swallowed, her eyes widening.

Hope lifted an eyebrow. "Do you like them?"

Sucking her teeth and reaching for the bowl, Rebecca filled her plate. "Please, girlfriend, 'like' wouldn't begin to describe it. It's delicious."

Theo and Hope exchanged a smile before they

began filling their own plates. Theo took surreptitious glances at his sister under lowered lids, pleased that she had taken the initiative to take portions from each bowl, then he turned his attention to serving himself. It took Hope, Theo, Rebecca, and Noelle two hours to eat everything put out before them. When the waitress arrived with the check, all three reached for their purses and wallet.

"I've got it," Theo said.

Rebecca, her face flushed from several glasses of wine, shook her head. "No, I've got it. Please, let this be my treat."

Hope gave her a direct look. "I'll leave the tip."

Theo grimaced. "I'm not used to women paying for my meals."

"Don't stress yourself, Theo," Hope said softly. "When McKinnon's Sophie Ladies meet for dinner the next time, we'll be certain to invite you and you'll be given the opportunity to pick up the tab."

His eyebrows shot up. "Sophie Ladies?"

"Sophisticated Ladies," Rebecca and Hope said in unison.

He held up his two pinkies. "Well, la-de-da!"

Everyone laughed as Rebecca and Hope settled the bill. Ten minutes later, they stood in the parking lot.

Hope hugged Noelle, smiled at Theo, then followed Rebecca to where she had parked her Mercedes-Benz. She slipped into the passenger seat and blew out her breath.

"I can't believe I ate so much."

Rebecca turned the key in the ignition. "You! I must have ingested five thousand calories."

Hope gave her a sidelong glance. "What would

you know about counting calories? There's hardly anything to you."

"I wasn't always this thin," Rebecca admitted. "I lost thirty pounds after I found out that my husband was having an affair a couple of years ago." She backed the sedan out of the lot, heading for Beach Road. "I never knew Lee was cheating. He came home every night, and we still made love two to three times a week. Sometimes, when the kids stayed over at my in-laws, it was more often."

"Did he tell you why he felt the need to have an affair?"

A wry smile touched Rebecca's mouth as she shook her head. "All he said was that it wasn't my fault. The woman happened to have been his business client. One day he took her out to lunch, and after several drinks they wound up at a motel outside of Charleston. It became a weekly ritual until she discovered she was pregnant."

"That's when your husband told you."

Rebecca gasped. "How did you know?"

"You forget I get thousands of letters from women who are confronted with unfaithful husbands and boyfriends. Usually when the other woman tells her married paramour that's she pregnant, she's hoping that he'll leave his wife for her. If he doesn't, and if she's the ambitious type, then she'll opt for an abortion." Hope peered at Rebecca. "Did she get an abortion?"

"Yes, she did."

"It's a classic scenario. Did you go to marital counseling?"

Rebecca nodded as she maneuvered into the driveway of her summer rental. Not bothering to turn off the engine, she unhooked her seat belt and stared at Hope. "My mother-in-law accused me of being spiteful to Lee because I decided to vacation alone this summer."

"Are you, Rebecca?"

"What?"

"Being spiteful."

Rebecca chewed her lower lip. "I can't honestly answer that question. I know there's something that will not permit me to forgive Lee. That may be because I'm also angry with myself because I don't like who I am, who I've become."

"And that is?"

"Superficial and opinionated. I find fault in everything and everyone. I've become the very person I like least: my mother-in-law."

Hope stared at Rebecca's strained profile. "Could it be you're competing with your mother-in-law for your husband's affection?"

Her head jerked around. "I'm Lee's wife."

"And your mother-in-law is his mother—the first woman in his life, the one whose influence helped mold him into what he's become. You should identify what it is that made you fall in love with this man, marry him, bear his children, and continue to stay with him. Whatever it is has to be greater than his infidelity."

Sighing, Rebecca nodded. "You're right. I bet you'd never find yourself in my situation."

Hope gave her a long, penetrating look, then said, "You're wrong. I was in your situation. A man I loved very much and hoped to marry deceived me with someone else. No one is exempt from a cheating partner. Not even Dr. Hope." She unbuckled her seat belt and unlocked the passenger side door. "I'm waiting for a call from Janie Saunders-Smith, who has agreed to give you weaving lessons. As soon as she calls, I'll take you to meet her." Hope opened the door. "Thanks for dinner."

She got out of the air-cooled car and walked the short distance to her own house. It wasn't until she had opened the door and latched the screen behind her that she felt a wave of sadness move her to tears. Rebecca talking about her philandering husband had dredged up the scene with Kendall and the other man.

At least Rebecca had experienced what it felt like to be a wife and mother, unlike her, who doubted whether she would ever marry or have a baby. The thought that Kendall preferred a man to her elicited a momentary panic that gnawed at her confidence. For the first time in years, she questioned her femininity.

She might have had some answers for Rebecca, but none for herself. Perhaps, as it would for her neighbor, the summer on McKinnon Island would yield what she was looking for.

# Fifteen

*The soil you see is not ordinary soil—it is the dust of
the blood, the flesh and bones our ancestors.*
   —Shes-his Reno Crow (late nineteenth century)

"It's a plantation," Rebecca gasped, staring at the house coming into view. The grand structure, framed by ancient cypress trees, wing pavilions, a Greek Revival façade and a Regency-style entrance topped by an octagonal cupola gave the structure a wedding cake appearance.

Hope took a quick glance at Rebecca's gaping mouth. "It *was* a plantation. In fact, it was the largest cotton-producing plantation on McKinnon. I'll stop there, because Janie will tell you her family's history."

Janie Saunders-Smith was waiting for them as they alighted the car. Smiling, she said, "Welcome back, Hope." She nodded to Rebecca. "Please come in out of the heat."

"I'm sorry, but I can't stay, Janie. But I'll come back later to pick up Rebecca." Hope made the introductions as the two women shook hands.

Janie's smile widened. "That's all right. Either Thomas or I will drive her back."

"Thanks, Janie."

Hope was grateful for the offer because she wanted to get back to her writing. She had gotten up early and gone for a walk along the beach before returning to the house to outline the information she wanted in each section, stopping only when Rebecca had rung rang the bell to let her know she was ready to meet Janie.

Rebecca followed Janie into the spacious entryway and felt as if she had stepped back in time. Squares of black and white marble flooring set the stage for twin curving staircases leading to the second floor. A towering grandfather clock softly chimed the hour. It was one o'clock.

"Your home is beautiful, Mrs. Smith."

Janie wagged a finger. "None of that 'Mrs. Smith' business around here. I'm Janie, and I hope you will permit me to call you Rebecca."

Rebecca flashed a dimpled smile. "But of course."

"You're in luck, Rebecca, because not only will you get a crash course in weaving baskets, but also a history lesson. My brother-in-law arrived yesterday. Ezra has been contracted by the University of Arkansas Press to write a book chronicling South Carolina Gullahs and Georgia Geechees and their African heritage. McKinnon is his last stop on what has become a two-year, twelve-island field trip."

"This is incredible. I have a degree in American history, yet I know nothing about the people of the Sea Islands."

"What is it you'd like to know?" asked a deep voice behind them.

Rebecca turned to find a tall, solidly built, middle-aged man with graying, straight blond hair, dressed in a pair of khaki shorts, matching shirt, work boots and thick cotton socks. Despite the light-colored hair, his skin was as dark as hers. He smiled, and minute lines fanned out around his dark eyes.

"Everything about the Gullahs."

Ezra Smith's smile faded, and he angled his head. "New England?"

It was Rebecca's turn to smile. "Massachusetts."

Janie watched the friendly interchange. "Rebecca, this is my brother-in-law Ezra Smith, professor emeritus of history at the University of Arkansas, Fayetteville. Ezra, Rebecca Owens."

Ezra closed the distance between them. "My pleasure, Ms. Owens."

"If you insist on calling me Ms. Owens, then I must address you as Professor Smith."

Crossing his arms over his broad chest, Ezra shook his head. "Please don't."

Rebecca decided she liked Janie and Ezra. Both were friendly and down-to-earth. She was startled that she and Janie looked enough alike to be related. Ezra's sister-in-law was petite, honey-gold complexioned, with light brown curly hair and dark gray eyes.

"Do you also teach, Rebecca?" Janie asked.

"I used to, but that was a long time ago."

"What are you doing now?" Ezra asked.

"Vacationing." It was the first thing that came to mind.

Janie smiled tentatively. "Please, let's retire to the sun parlor, where we can talk about what it is you want to do while vacationing on McKinnon."

"Madam." Ezra extended his arm to Rebecca,

who placed her hand in the crook of his arm. He leaned down from his impressive height. "You must tell me about Massachusetts. I was there once, but only for a day when I was a commencement speaker at a Boston high school."

She smiled up at him. "I was raised north of Boston. I'm from Lowell."

"Ahh-hh! Lowell represents the rise of New England's cotton and textile mills, and its fall, culminating with a major strike in 1912."

Rebecca was impressed. Ezra Smith knew his history. "I'm certain you know that the workers went out on strike because they felt they were being exploited. The introduction of child labor laws doomed the mills in the North."

Ezra patted the tiny hand in the crook of his arm. "Wasn't Jack Kerouac born in Lowell?"

"Like right, man," Rebecca crooned, intimating those from Kerouac's Beat generation.

Janie smiled over her shoulder. "It looks as if you two are going to get along quite well."

*Her hostess's statement* was prophetic, because Rebecca lost track of time as she spent the afternoon with the Smiths. Thomas, a younger, slimmer version of Ezra, fired up an outdoor grill, cooking steaks, corn, and skewered vegetables to perfection.

After waiting more than an hour for their food to settle, Janie took Rebecca on a tour of the historic late-eighteenth-century house. Differing sizes and shapes of sweetgrass baskets sat on tables and shelves in the large, brick-walled kitchen. Rebecca followed Janie up the curving staircase.

"I'm a direct descendant of the family who once

owned this house, this land, and the people who planted and picked the Sea Island cotton that made them wealthy." At the top of the stairs, Janie turned and stared directly at Rebecca. "Now, *I* own it. I worked year-round for twenty years to save enough money to restore the house and grounds, and as soon as Thomas and I finish restoring the outbuildings, we're going to offer tours to school groups from the mainland. Much has been written on the Sea Islands of South Carolina and Georgia, particularly concerning pre-Civil War plantation life and Sea Island cotton. However, there is little in the literature about our people."

Rebecca trailed her fingertips over the smooth surface of an ornately carved mahogany side table in one of the bedrooms. "Won't that change with Ezra's research?"

Janie smiled. "We're hoping it will."

"Is your husband also Gullah?"

"Heavens no. Thomas and Ezra are from Osceola, Tennessee. It's right on the Mississippi, and if they crossed the river, they'd be in Arkansas. Their daddy was a white circuit judge who couldn't keep his hands off their black mama. They lived apart, because in those days she couldn't live openly with him as his common-law wife because of his position. The miscegenation laws changed, and eventually they married, but only when the judge lay dying. Ezra and Thomas were his only heirs, so when their mother died, they inherited everything."

"Better late than never," Rebecca whispered.

Janie nodded, smiling. "You can say that again. We used Thomas's share of his inheritance to purchase the house."

"What about the furnishings?"

"A lot of pieces had been bought by a consortium of Charleston antique dealers, and it took me almost a year to negotiate an amount that wouldn't bankrupt me to buy them back."

Rebecca walked into the master bedroom, awed by the carvings on a massive four-poster bed. "Other than language, how are the Gullahs different from African-Americans in other parts of the country?"

Janie sat on a maroon brocade settee at the foot of the bed, patting the seat beside her. "Please, sit down, Rebecca." Waiting until her guest sat, she continued. "The words *Gullah* and *Geechee* are interchangeable. The Gullahs are from the South Carolina Sea Islands, Geechees from the Georgia Sea Islands. What makes them unique is that they are more African in their language, folklore, agriculture, and family structure than African-Americans from other regions.

"The Sea Island culture is the matrix of the African-American family, because Sea Island *extended* families have retained many features which reflect the African heritage, as well as the adjustments made to the slavery experience."

"Are you saying they have customs which are reminiscent of the various countries in Africa from which they came?"

"Yes. Like their ancestors, the blacks of the Sea Islands look at abnormalities of birth as prognosticators of the future. Probably the most widespread belief is a baby born in a caul will be gifted with the ability to see 'ghosses' and 'ha'nts.'"

"Caul?"

Janie smiled. "It's a membrane. A lot of people call it a veil. The belief that a baby born in a caul is a sign of luck or wisdom, because of their ability to see everything or discern the spirit." Rebecca gave Janie a look that spoke volumes. She did not believe her. "You don't believe me, do you?"

Rebecca lowered her head. "Not really."

"I was born in a caul." Janie watched the other woman's head snap up. "And I know why you're here. You don't want to learn to weave baskets. You've come to McKinnon Island to find out who you are. There is also an older woman with whom you are at odds." Janie lifted an eyebrow. "Perhaps your mother-in-law? You try too hard to fit in, to become what she would like you to be."

Rebecca's heart lurched. She felt hot, then cold. Her hands were shaking, and she couldn't stop them. Had Hope told Janie about her? Or was she that transparent? She closed her eyes for several seconds, then opened them.

"How did you know?" Her voice was barely a whisper.

Janie smiled. "I told you, I was born in a caul." She stood up. "Come. I'll show you the rest of the house before we go back downstairs. Ezra will tell you how Gullahs name their children, folk beliefs concerning childbirth and the significance of midwives, Christmas Eve Watch on Johns Island, the role of women in family life as mothers and wives, sisters, and grandmothers. And, of course basketry and quilting." She peered closely at her. "Are you all right?"

Rebecca folded her arms under her breasts to conceal her trembling fingers. She could not believe Janie knew her better than she knew herself. "Now, you know I'm not going to answer that."

"Don't faint on me, Rebecca."

Her eyes widened. "You just read me, and you don't think I should be freaking out?"

"No." The single word was emphatic. "All you have to do is follow your instincts, and you will live a long and happy life."

"What instincts?"

"They brought you to McKinnon Island, didn't they?"

A smile found its way through Rebecca's expression of uncertainty. "Hey, you're right about that. I'm ready for my history lesson."

"Lessons," Janie corrected. "It will take Ezra more than a few hours to cover more than four hundred years of Sea Island history."

"Do you think he would be opposed to my accompanying him on his field trips? I could act as his assistant."

Janie shrugged a shoulder. "I don't know. Why don't you ask him?"

Excitement fired the gold in Rebecca's eyes. Her confidence returned as her defenses began to subside. "I will."

# *Sixteen*

*The long waves glide in through the afternoon while we watch from the island.*

—W. S. Merwin

Hope filled a large plastic rectangular container with two-dozen sliced short-cakes, topped them with dollops of whipped cream, then strawberries with their juice. She placed the matching shortcake halves on top, covered the container, and placed it on a shelf in the refrigerator.

Glancing at her watch, she noted she had half an hour to spare. It was enough time to take another shower and change her clothes.

She was looking forward to sharing dinner with Theo and his family. Her initial impression of him had changed dramatically after their dinner at The Fish Net. She'd found him relaxed, and at times he'd exhibited a wicked sense of humor. His interaction with Noelle was attentive and gentle, and there was no doubting his deep affection for his sister.

*I like him.* Hope smiled as she undressed and

covered her hair with a plastic cap. She was still smiling as she stepped into the shower stall and closed the door.

*Theo pulled into the driveway* and shifted into Park behind a midsize car with New York plates. Opening the door to the SUV, he stepped out, leaving the engine running to keep the vehicle cool. The eighty-five-degree early-morning temperature had climbed steadily, reaching ninety-four by two o'clock. Sand grated under his rubber soles as he mounted the porch to the gleaming white house shaded by palm and palmetto trees.

Hope's house was much smaller than the one where he was spending the summer, yet it had a charming quality missing in Jeff's vacation home. Peering through the screen on the door, he pulled the cord attached to the clapper of a cowbell. He smiled. The bell was quaint and functional.

"Come in, the door's unlatched." Hope's voice came from somewhere inside.

Theo pushed open the screen door and stepped into a small space leading into a living room. White sheers swayed in the ocean breeze coming through the screen-covered windows. An overstuffed sofa in chartreuse complemented two facing wing chairs with matching footstools that were covered in a sunny yellow-and-green floral chintz print. Beyond the living room was a dining room with a long rectangular table seating eight. The table and chairs were made of mahogany.

"Good afternoon, Theo."

The sound of Hope's voice caught Theo's attention, and he turned slowly. "Good afternoon."

Hope wore a sand-beige linen tank dress that flared out around her calves. A pair of mules in the same fabric matched the dress. Instead of her usual ponytail hairdo, she had pulled her hair off her face and secured it in a chignon on the nape of her neck.

"I'll be with you in a minute. I have to get the dessert from the refrigerator."

Theo followed her. "You didn't have to bring anything."

"I was raised never to come to someone's house empty-handed. Maybe it is not the norm in California, but it's a Southern thing," she added.

He frowned, his eyes level under drawn brows. "What makes you think I don't have Southern roots?"

"Do you?"

He took two long strides, bringing them only inches apart. His dark eyes moved slowly over her face. "What do you think?"

Hope found it hard to draw a normal breath with him so close. She felt the whisper of his breath over her forehead, the heat from his body, and the sensual scent of his cologne. He looked good, smelled wonderful, and there was no doubt he was *all* male. He was dressed in white again—this time white linen shorts and shirt. The darker color of his upper body was clearly visible through the finely woven fabric of the shirt. He had replaced his sandals with a pair of white deck shoes. There was a subtle virility about Theo that radiated from him like a powerful beam of light coming from a lighthouse.

"I don't know, Theo. You tell me."

He nodded, a slight smile playing at the corners of his mouth. "I do."

She lifted an eyebrow. "Where?"

"Beaufort and Edisto Island, South Carolina."

Her smile was dazzling. "Don't tell me you have some Gullah blood flowing through your veins."

"Some." His smile was mysterious.

"How did a Gullah end up in La-La Land?"

Winking at her, he said, "I'll tell you later."

Hope opened the refrigerator door and took out the container with the strawberry shortcakes. Theo took it from her.

"What's in here?"

"Homemade strawberry shortcake, compliments of my grandmother's recipe."

"Hot damn! You made my favorite." Curving an arm around Hope's waist, he lowered his head and kissed her forehead.

There was nothing sexual in his kiss or embrace, but that did not stop her body from reacting. Her breathing quickened.

"We'd better get going, because it's too hot to leave it out for very long."

Theo dropped his arm, unable to believe he had been so impulsive as to hug and kiss Hope. After he'd done it, he realized he wanted to do more.

Theo waited for Hope to lock the front door, then he escorted her to the Lexus, helping her up onto the passenger seat before he placed the plastic container in the cargo area. He maneuvered up the hill and drove around to the side of his house, parking under the carport.

Theo cut off the engine, then turned his head slowly to meet Hope's light brown eyes. There was something about her eyes that reminded him of a cat's-eye marble. "Are you ready to meet the Andersons?"

Her lush mouth softened as she smiled. "Of course."

She did not have to wait long, because a younger version of Theo opened the passenger side door for her, his large, dark eyes filled with curiosity. Seconds later, another young man appeared, looking enough like Theo to have been his clone.

"I'm Brandon," said the first one, extending his right hand to help her down.

Her shoes touched sand-littered concrete. "Thank you, Brandon. I'm Hope Sutton."

"Theo told us you were coming for dinner. He also warned us if we were not on our best behavior he would jack us up." His voice was low, as if he were telling her a secret.

Hope's jaw dropped slightly. "Jack you up how?"

"Don't know, don't want to find out," Brandon's brother said.

Theo rounded the Lexus, cradling the container with the shortcake to his chest. "Let's go inside where we can be introduced properly."

Hope rolled her eyes at Theo. Didn't he know threats and intimidation never worked with children, especially teenagers? Flanked by Brandon and his brother, she followed Theo into a rear door that led to an air-cooled modern kitchen. A petite woman with stylishly cut silver hair and sparkling blue eyes looked up from her task of shredding lettuce and flashed a friendly smile.

"Welcome."

Hope returned her smile. "Thank you."

Theo handed Noelle the container. "Please put this in the refrigerator."

"What is it?"

"Strawberry shortcake."

Noelle stared at Hope. "Did you make it, Miss Hope?"

"Yes, I did."

"Cool."

Theo dropped an arm over his brothers' shoulders. "Hope, I'd like for you to meet my brothers. Christian and Brandon, Miss Hope Sutton."

She inclined her head. "It's nice meeting you."

"Everybody calls me Chris."

Hope noticed that Theo had tightened his grip on Christian. "Then Chris it is." She smiled at Brandon. "How about you? Do you wish to be called something else?"

Shyly, he dropped his head. "No. Brandon's okay."

Theo removed his arms and walked over to Helen. "Helen Bryant, housekeeper, peacemaker, and all-around saint. Helen, my friend, Hope Sutton."

Helen wiped her hands on a towel, extending the right one. "My pleasure, Hope."

Hope shook her proffered hand, noticing that the intense summer sun had not been kind to the woman's fair skin. The tip of her nose was a bright pink.

"Same here, Miss Helen."

The housekeeper's face flushed. "The Miss Helen is for the kids," she whispered.

"Can I help you with anything?"

Helen waved a hand. "No. You're a guest. The next time you come you won't be a guest. Then you can help me—that is, only if you want to," she added, meeting Theo's incredulous glare.

Shaking his head, he cupped Hope's elbow.

"Come sit and relax. As soon as the meat and fish are done, we'll eat."

She followed him out of the kitchen to the rear of the house. An expansive outdoor patio with Adirondack chairs shaded by large white umbrellas faced the ocean. Four rotisserie chickens turning slowly on a commercial cart grill made her mouth water. The only thing she'd had all morning was a cup of tea.

Theo pulled out a chair at a large round table with seating for six. She sat down. A pale-blue-flower-sprigged tablecloth, with a hole cut in the middle to accommodate the pole for the overhead umbrella, matched the stack of white plates with a narrow blue trim. Beside it, a wicker basket was filled with cloth napkins and silverware.

He hunkered down beside the chair, smiling. "How hungry are you?"

Hope met his gaze. "Very."

"Good. I was hoping you brought your appetite, because Helen was up before dawn cooking. She believes she's feeding a small army."

"Cooking for three teenagers *is* a small army."

"Amen to that," he whispered. "Is there anything you don't eat?"

"I'm off red meat for the summer."

Theo angled his head, his eyes narrowing. "Are you all right?"

Her expression stilled and grew serious. "Yes." The look on Theo's face said he did not believe her. "If I eat red meat, then it must be organic."

His smile was dazzling. "You're in luck. Helen only buys organic meats, fruits, and vegetables. She says foods with additives and preservatives play havoc with her hormone levels."

Hope wanted to tell Theo that she and his house-keeper had something in common. Averting her gaze, she stared at the beach. "The view of the ocean from this point on the island is spectacular." Less than a quarter of a mile away was the proposed site for Palmetto Haven, a private gated community for the wealthy.

Theo straightened. Hope had changed the subject. If she was sick, then he wondered how sick? Had she come to McKinnon to reconnect with her roots before . . . ? His thoughts trailed off. He did not want to think of her dying.

"I'll be right back with something for you to nibble on."

Theo retreated to the house, and a minute later Brandon arrived with a platter of deviled eggs and stuffed grape leaves in one hand and a bowl of shrimp and avocado seviche in the other. Noelle followed with a bowl of crispy tortilla chips and bite-size parmesan-dusted meatballs.

"I helped Theo make the meatballs," she announced proudly. Noelle speared a meatball with a toothpick, put it on a small plate, and handed it to Hope.

She took a bite, her eyes widening in surprise. "It's delicious." It had a Mediterranean flavor. After the second bite, the meatball was gone.

"Theo said the recipe comes from Greece."

"I take it your brother cooks very well."

Noelle sat down next to Hope. "He cooks better than Miss Helen," she whispered. "Please don't tell her I said that."

Hope became her coconspirator when she said, "I won't."

"What are you two whispering about?"

Theo had come up on them without making a sound. "I was just telling Noelle how much I like the meatballs." Hope hadn't lied, but it wasn't totally the truth either.

"She did most of the work. All I did was measure the ingredients." He placed two pitchers filled with icy concoctions on the table.

"Which one is for the kids?" Noelle asked.

Theo pulled her braids. "They're both for the kids. The grown-folk drinks are inside."

Brandon and Christian came out of the house, carrying a large pot and a pan of marinated meat. The pot went on one of grill's two range-top burners, the pan of meat on a side table. Helen finally put in her appearance, carrying a large wooden bowl filled with salad. The activity increased until the table literally groaned with food.

Christian assumed the responsibility of manning the grill, while Brandon acted as waiter, bringing platters of cooked and steamed dishes to the table. Hope sampled a butter toasted frankfurter roll filled with lobster salad and topped with fresh chopped chives, steamed clams in a savory leek butter, and shoestring fries dusted with kosher salt. She ate sparingly, saving room for the grilled chicken, filet mignon medallions, and the salad made with an assortment of field greens and marinated vegetables.

Their cooking and serving duties completed, Brandon and Christian sat down and began eating. The pitchers of punch disappeared quickly, and

Theo got up, returned to the house, and came back with two more.

He pointed to a pitcher filled with a pale yellow liquid. "Grown folks."

The three Andersons exchanged knowing glances, then nodded. All knew how their older brother felt about underage drinking.

Christian reached for an empty platter. "I'm going to clean up now."

Theo frowned at him. "What's your hurry? We still haven't had dessert."

He gave his guardian a direct stare. "We can eat dessert later. It's time we left for the movies, or we're going to be late."

Theo returned the stare. "Then go."

"We . . . we don't have to clear the table?" Noelle asked, her voice rising slightly in surprise.

Theo affected a stern expression. "If you're going to the movies, then go. Otherwise stay and clean up. No speeding," he called out to Christian as he shot up from the table. Then the three teenagers were gone, racing in the direction of the carport.

Helen chuckled softly. "I've never seen them move that fast."

Shaking his head slowly, Theo said, "I don't know why they're in such a hurry to go see a movie they've seen before."

Hope knew the answer. Going off without an adult chaperone was a show of independence, a sign that they could be trusted. She took another sip of her vodka lemonade, staring at Theo over the rim of her glass. What she saw in his gaze should have shocked her, but it didn't, because she felt the same.

His gaze dropped to her bared shoulders, then to

her breasts. Her hand stilled, as if paralyzed. She couldn't move, breathe. He radiated a sensuality that drew her like a magnet. Reluctantly she pulled her gaze away. Only then was she able to breathe normally.

"I'll help clean up."

"No, you won't," Helen argued. "You're a guest."

Turning her head slowly, Hope looked at Theo, who took furtive sips of his drink. "Do you plan on inviting me back?"

He seemed startled by her query. "Of course."

Placing her napkin on the table, she began to push back her chair. "Then that settles it. I'm not a guest."

Theo moved quickly, pulling back her chair. His left arm curved around her waist. "It's not good to get on Helen's bad side," he whispered close to her ear.

Hope shivered despite the heat. "Let me handle this, please." He dropped his arm, and she felt his loss immediately. She liked him touching her. "Helen, I'd like to talk to you about something."

The bright blue eyes were suddenly alert. "What about?"

Leaning down, she whispered, "Female stuff."

"Of course, dear. We'll talk in the kitchen." She stood up and motioned to Theo. "You stay and relax. Hope and I will clean up everything."

He sat back down, shaking his head. At forty years of age, he still did not understand women. In the six years he had come to know Helen Bryant, she had never permitted anyone to help her clean her kitchen, yet she hadn't known Hope more than three hours and without warning she had reversed her hard stance.

He was tempted to bring some of the dishes into

the house but quickly changed his mind. He would do as Helen suggested—sit and relax. He moved away from the table and lay on a chaise under the protective cover of an umbrella. He was not only full but also sleepy. He doubted whether he had had more than three hours of uninterrupted sleep, because his dreams were disturbed by the images of the woman who had spent the past three hours at his table.

There was no doubt his brothers were as intrigued by her as he was. Christian had whispered to him that Hope was *hot*, while Brandon surreptitiously had given him the thumbs-up sign.

McKinnon Island was good for Noelle, Christian and Brandon. It was even good for Helen. She cooked less and did not have as much laundry. Most times the teenagers lived in swimsuits, while grilling outdoors. The only thing she complained about was their tracking sand into the house.

Theo opened his eyes and smiled. Yes, McKinnon Island was very good for him because of Hope. It was the first time in a very long time that he wanted to see a woman not because he wanted her to share his bed. She made him laugh, and she challenged him. Letting out an audible sigh, he closed his eyes and within minutes succumbed to a gentle peace that had eluded him most of his life.

*Theo woke up,* startled. He thought he'd heard voices. Raising his left arm, he stared at his watch. It was almost seven. The afternoon had sped past. Swinging his legs over the chaise, he sat up. Hope and Helen were nowhere to be seen. He pushed off the chaise and went into the kitchen. Everything had been put away.

A shiver snaked its way up his spine. The house was too cool. He stopped to adjust the thermostat before he walked into the family room. Helen sat in a deep club chair, her bare feet on a matching ottoman. She was reading the latest James Patterson Alex Cross mystery.

Her head came up and she smiled. "I suppose you're looking for Hope? She's down on the beach," Helen continued before he could answer. "She's very nice, Theo. A lot better than some of the others I've seen you with."

He flashed a half-smile. "So, you like her, too?"

She stared at him with surprise. "You're not going to tell me to mind my business?"

"Not today, Miss Helen," he said, grinning.

"Invite her back tomorrow." She wasn't certain Theo heard her, because he was already out the door, heading in the direction of the beach.

# Seventeen

*She's gazing at you so tenderly, drowning you in sparkling conversation.*

—Aleksandr Pushkin

*Theo spied Hope* sitting on the sand. She'd taken off her shoes. Slowing his pace, he watched her as he closed the distance between them. Wisps of jet-black hair had escaped the twist at the back of her head and trailed over her nape and shoulder. She was so still she could have been a statue. Then she moved, cradling her hands in her lap. She appeared to be meditating. He stopped, prepared to retreat, when she turned her head and looked at him, smiling. He sat down beside her, close enough for their shoulders to touch.

"I hope you'll forgive me for not being the attentive host."

She turned and looked at him. "Why? Because you fell asleep?"

She had a wonderful voice—cloaking, sensual and seductive. "Yes."

"I probably would've joined you if I'd remained

on the chaise. That's the reason I came down here. I've been taking in the view."

Theo's gaze shifted from Hope's face to the expanse of ocean in front of him. "It is magnificent. The first time I came down here all I thought about was how the first Africans who stepped foot on this island must have felt seeing it for the first time. Were they frightened? Did it remind them of home? Did they ever believe they would make it back across to reunite with their families?"

Hope stared at Theo's profile. "I used to wonder the same thing whenever I summered here as a child. My great-grandparents died before I was born. However, Grandmomma told me that there was a time when a lot of McKinnon was jungle. The trees and underbrush were so thick that sunlight never touched the ground."

"How old were you when you began spending summers here?"

"My parents brought us down when we were toddlers. The first summer I remember staying without my parents was the year I turned nine. My two older brothers were involved in summer youth programs back in New Jersey, so they didn't have to stay. And my younger sister cried so much my parents took her back with them.

"This suited me because then I had Grandmomma and Grandpapa to myself. I'd become a regular farm girl. I got up early to gather eggs from the chicken, then eat with Grandpapa before he went out on his fishing boat. I'd help weed the vegetable garden, sit on the porch and shell peas, piece quilts, and listen to the old people tell their stories about 'yondah' times before I'd help my grandmother cook supper.

"Even though we were isolated, everyone managed to keep up with events going on in the world beyond McKinnon. While the country was fighting over civil rights and the war in Vietnam, the islanders went on with their lives just like their grandparents and great-grandparents. That was when there weren't too many whites left on McKinnon."

"When did most of them leave?"

"After the Civil War."

"Why then?"

"The plantation economic system had vanished. Former slave owners returned to the mainland, while the Gullah stayed."

"Do you understand Gullah?"

Hope smiled. "Yes. But I don't speak it well. My mother wouldn't let any of her children speak it."

Theo arched an eyebrow. "Why not?"

"She said it was too African." Her gaze met Theo's. "Tell me about your Gullah roots. How did you get to the West Coast?"

"My maternal grandfather, whom I don't remember, was from these parts. He got a job as a porter on the railroad and found himself heading west. The first time he saw California he thought he had come to the Promised Land. He quit the railroad, even though it was considered a good job in those days, and went to work in one of the newer hotels in San Francisco as a handyman. That's when he met my grandmother."

"She also worked at the hotel?"

Smiling, Theo shook his head. "No. She was a nurse. He was taken to a municipal hospital after he'd fallen down an elevator shaft, breaking his leg. She took a liking to him after he'd been placed on her ward. Once he was discharged, they began courting and married three months later."

"It sounds like a romance novel."

"She always said that a woman may love a lot of men, but will fall in love only once in her life."

"Is it the same for men, Theo?"

He shook his head. "I wouldn't know." And he didn't, because he'd never been in love. "Have you ever been in love, Hope?"

Why, she thought, did he make her name sound like a caress? A cynical smile twisted her mouth. "I thought I was."

"What happened?" he asked after a comfortable silence.

"He preferred someone else." Theo's head came around slowly, his expression mirroring incredulity.

She smiled. "What's the matter?"

"I can't believe he left *you?*"

Her expression sobered as she gave him a long, penetrating look. "No. I left *him.*" Changing the subject, Hope asked, "How was it growing up in southern California?"

Theo was perceptive enough to know that Hope had deftly redirected the topic of conversation away from her. And he did not have to have a doctorate in psychology to know that she had come to McKinnon to recover from a failed relationship.

"I didn't grow up in southern California."

"Where did you grow up?"

"In the Bay Area. I was born in Los Angeles. I was three weeks old when my mother left me with my grandmother to bond with her first grandchild. The bonding continued for the next thirty years."

"Are you saying your grandmother raised you?"

"Yes."

Hope detected a hint of censure in his tone. "Are you still angry with your mother?"

"She wasn't my mother, Hope. She happened to have been the woman who gave birth to me. My grandmother was mother, father, and everything else in between."

Hope's gaze filled with an emotion he did not want to feel: pity. The seconds ticked by until a full minute had elapsed.

"Tell me, Hope," he whispered softly, "what it is you're thinking?"

She blinked once. "What makes you think I'm thinking anything?"

"You have a way of tilting your head slightly when you're deep in thought."

"You noticed that?" It had been her mother who had first called her attention to that particular expression.

"I've noticed a lot of things about you."

"Which are?"

"You're forthcoming when it comes to giving advice, but reluctant to talk about yourself."

"You forget that I'm paid to give advice."

"Here on McKinnon?"

Her brow furrowed. "Touché, Theo."

He leaned closer so that her bare shoulder pressed against the sleeve of his shirt. "I'm not into tit for tat, so if I've insulted you, then please accept my apology."

She shook her head. "There's nothing to apologize for." Shifting slightly, she gave him a direct stare.

She was entranced by the silent sadness in his eyes, and she longed to put her arms around his neck and hold him.

Theo's left arm came up and curved around her waist. Hope leaned into him. The motion was so natural, as if he had executed it hundreds of times before. Her right arm slipped around his waist, and they sat silently, motionlessly, and watched the tide come in and deposit its riches on the sand before it retreated. Somewhere between the time when the sun sank lower on the horizon and streaks of orange crisscrossed the sky, Hope trustingly laid her head on Theo's shoulder, closed her eyes, and slept.

*Theo was still sitting* on the sand with his arm around Hope when his siblings returned from the movies. Noelle walked over and sat down beside him. His free arm went around her shoulders.

"How was the movie?" They had gone to see part three in *The Lord of the Rings* trilogy: *The Return of the King*.

"Even better the second time. I think I want to read the books."

Theo stared down at Noelle smiling up at him. "Are you certain?" She nodded. "The next time we go into Savannah we'll stop in a bookstore and buy them. I remember seeing them in a four-book slip-case."

"What's the fourth book?" she asked.

"*The Hobbit.* It's the first book that sets up the trilogy."

"Do you think I can finish four books before we go back to California?"

"I don't know. Don't put that kind of pressure

on yourself, Noelle. It's all right if you don't finish them until after we return." Theo knew his sister was anxious about the upcoming school year because she'd made the honor roll despite the upheaval going on in her young life. "You're going to do all right, sweetheart."

Noelle giggled. "I'm not your sweetheart," she said close to his ear.

"If you're not, then who is?"

She cupped a hand over his ear. "Miss Hope."

Theo decided to play along with his sister. "But she didn't say that she'd be my sweetheart."

"Did you ask her?"

"No," he whispered back.

"Then, why don't you ask her?"

Lowering his head, he dropped a kiss on her braided head. "Maybe I will."

"Don't take too long, big brother, or you're going to lose her."

He chuckled softly. "When did you get so smart?"

"I don't know," Noelle said, shrugging a slender shoulder. "You're smart and Christian and Brandon are smart."

Hope felt like a voyeur listening to the conversation between Theo and his sister, but she was loathe to stir and end the easy camaraderie between the two. She had been hard-pressed not to laugh when Noelle had asked her brother if he had asked her to be his sweetheart, and that made her think about what if. What if Theo had been her lover instead of Kendall? Would he have deceived her with another woman? After all, his reputation for dating a lot of women was always fodder for the supermarket tabloids.

Tiring of the subterfuge, she moaned softly and opened her eyes. Tilting her chin, she smiled up at Theo. "I'm sorry I used you for a pillow."

"There's nothing to apologize for."

Noelle peered around Theo, smiling. "He's a good pillow, isn't he?"

Hope returned her smile. "The best."

Theo dropped his arms, stood up in one graceful motion, and stretched. "I don't know about you guys, but I'm ready for dessert." He pulled Hope and Noelle up with a minimum of effort, then bent over to pick up Hope's shoes.

"Race you back to the house," Noelle called out as she sprinted up the hill toward the house.

Hope looked at Theo then began running, with him only steps behind her. She gulped a lungful of air and put her head down, increasing her pace. She ran not to keep up but to win.

Theo couldn't believe Hope was outrunning him despite the fact that he had longer legs. She was not only shapely but she was also in shape. His competitive instincts kicked in, and he quickened his pace. He and Hope made it to the patio at the same time, Noelle several steps ahead of them.

He dropped her shoes, curved an arm around Hope's waist and lifted her high off her feet. He swung her around several times as she pleaded with him to put her down. He did, but not before he brushed his mouth over hers. The teasing stopped the instant they swallowed each other's breath.

Holding onto his neck, her head level with his, Hope stared at him. "Please." Her breasts were crushed against his chest, the nipples hardening within seconds. His gaze shifted downward as he complied, her body still in contact with his. Her bare feet touched the still warm concrete. She felt every muscle, curve and dip in his physique. Electricity snaked through her body with a shiver of wanting.

"Please what, Hope?"

Her gaze never wavered. She was certain he could feel her heartbeat drumming against the expanse of his chest. "Let me go."

"I will even though I don't want to." He dropped his arms, bent over and picked up her shoes. His fingers caught her right ankle and he put the shoe on her foot, forcing her to place a hand on his shoulder to keep her balance. He repeated the motion with the left shoe. Theo straightened, smiling. "By golly, they fit," he teased in a very proper British accent.

Resting her head on his chest, Hope laughed until her eyes filled with tears. "You know you're a little crazy?"

"Aren't we all a little crazy, Dr. Sutton?"

She sighed and nodded. "You're right about that."

"Let's go inside before Chris and Brandon get jealous."

"What do they have to be jealous about?"

His expression stilled, becoming serious. "I'm the one with the smart, pretty girl."

"Would it make a difference if I wasn't smart or pretty?"

"No, Hope. It's not outside that matters, but in here." He pointed to her heart.

A warning voice whispered in her head that she had to stop him. Now. "What is it you want from me, Theo?"

"Anything and everything you're willing to give me."

"And what do I get in return?"

"Anything and everything you want."

"What if I want something you're unable to give me?"

"I wouldn't know what that something is until you tell me."

"I can't tell you, because I'm not certain whether it is what I really want or need."

"Try me," he said, challenging her.

"Later," she countered softly.

"When?"

She smiled up at him, and for the first time he noticed the slight dimple in her chin. "At the end of the summer."

Theo pushed out his lower lip, the expression reminding her of a petulant little boy, even though there was no trace of a boy in the very adult Theodore Howell. "I'll be leaving before the end of the summer."

Hope affected a seductive moue. "Then I'll tell you before you leave."

"I never thought you'd be a tease."

"I'm not, but what I am is honest. The day before you leave McKinnon Island, I will tell you what it is I want."

"I'm going to hold you to that promise."

Reaching for her hand, he held it in a firm grip, leading her into the house.

# Eighteen

*And I shall have some peace there, for peace comes*
*dropping slow, dropping from the veils of the morning*
*to where the cricket sings.*

—W. B. Yeats

**Ezra Smith watched** the play of emotions cross the face of the woman sitting at the opposite end of the rowboat. He had known Rebecca Owens a week and was completely enchanted with her. At first he'd thought it was her delicate beauty, but after spending several days together he realized it was her enthusiasm, her thirst for knowledge, her intense need to know more and more.

She had come to his sister-in-law to learn to weave baskets from dried sweetgrass and palmetto strips, and subsequently had become his companion and his friend. She pulled her fingers from the water, shaking them. Pinpoints of light piercing the thick overgrowth of trees glinted off the diamonds on her delicate left hand. The rings were a constant reminder that she was committed to another man.

Rebecca opened her eyes at the sound of a loud

crack. A flock of squawking birds flew overhead. The sound echoed loudly in the early morning quiet, then the area surrounding the swamp settled back to a shrouded eeriness punctuated by the *slip-slap* sound of oars slicing through the murky water.

She spied a graceful white bird with a long neck and plumage perched on a fallen tree limb. "What's that?"

Ezra glanced over his shoulder. "A heron."

"Beautiful."

"Yes."

He was looking not at the bird but at Rebecca. She had chosen to wear a long-sleeved white linen shirt, jeans, and a pair of leather boots for their boat trip to an abandoned slave cemetery at the northern-most tip of the island, and he found her casual attire more provocative than if she'd worn a bikini. The denim fabric defined every curve of her compact body.

Palmetto trees and ancient oak draped in Spanish moss, lined the bank of the swamp, closing in around them as the water narrowed until it was little more than a meandering stream. The elderly man who had given him directions had warned him to look out for snakes—water moccasins in particular—and for the earth that moved under his feet. It had taken several minutes for Ezra to interpret that to mean quicksand. Steering toward the bank, he pulled the oars into the boat, then jumped out.

From the bottom of the boat he retrieved a large, ornately carved wooden cane, then he curved an arm around Rebecca's waist and hoisted her out of the boat. The entwined serpents on the walking stick, also known as a "conjure stick," symbolized the magic and religion coiled around every facet of life of the sea islanders. His conjure stick was for snakes and quicksand. He planned to tap the ground before he placed one foot in front of the other.

"Stay behind me at all times," he warned, as he turned and headed in an easterly direction.

Rebecca stared at the back of Ezra's head. At sixty-two, he still had all of his hair. Streaks of silver shimmered in a mane as pale as moonlight, the color incongruent against his deeply tanned brown skin. He wasn't the type of man she would have found herself physically attracted to, except for his intelligence. He was a brilliant historian.

"How far is it?" she asked after ten minutes.

There was no road, only narrow foot trails where the forest had yet to reclaim the land. There came an occasional rustling in overhead trees and brushes, but except for the heron, she hadn't caught a glimpse of any wildlife. The cloying smell of flowers mingled with decaying foliage and animal waste.

Ezra stopped, pointing. "It's just up ahead. See where the woods thin out a little."

She nodded. Massive oak trees formed a natural canopy, shutting out the rays of the hot sun. Ezra started up again, and she followed until they stood outside the rusty gates to a cemetery. There were gravestones covered with mold, moss and mildew. She was fascinated by the number of bottles, cups and shells around the graves.

She waited outside while Ezra pulled a digital camera from the pocket on his denim shirt and began taking pictures. The longer she waited, the more uncomfortable she became. She hadn't visited a cemetery since burying her sister. Her parents went back every year on the anniversary of their youngest daughter's death, but she refused to join them.

The sun rose higher, along with the heat and humidity, and forty minutes later Ezra was finished. He had seen and photographed enough. Some of the items left at the graves were interesting, most were familiar, but there were others he'd never seen before.

He smiled at Rebecca. "Are you ready to go back?"

She flashed a dimpled smile. "Yes."

"May I offer you breakfast before I take you back home?"

Her smile widened until it was a full grin. "Yes, thank you."

The return trip to where they'd left the boat was accomplished in half the time it had taken to reach the cemetery. Rebecca got in and sat down while Ezra pushed off the bank and got in with a nimbleness that belied his age. By the time they were underway, the swamp was alive with movement and sound. A large water snake came within several feet of the rowboat, swimming in the direction from which they'd just come.

"Why was the cemetery filled with so much litter?" She had to say something, anything to keep her mind off of what lurked under the slow-moving boat.

Ezra smiled, steering the boat toward the opposite bank. "It's not litter, it's grave decorations. Broken bottles and other ornaments in an African-American cemetery are expressions of religion and magic. Offerings to the deceased are much like the ancient pharaohs, wherein the dead must be given whatever they may need for the next world, lest the spirit come back. And woe to one who steals anything from a grave, even a broken mirror, because bad luck will follow him."

"It sounds more like magic than religion."

"Gullahs practiced their West African beliefs in relative isolation until the 1840s. After that the Baptist religion dominated the culture. However, the abundance of Moslem practices on the Georgia coast in the 1930s indicate the importation of people from northern Nigeria or the Western Sudan. I interviewed a woman on Sapelo Island who told of the regular ritual prayers of her great-grandfather on his prayer rug. Despite Christianity, superstitions still govern the lives of sea island natives from birth to death."

Resting her elbows on her knees, Rebecca leaned forward. "What are some of them?"

"The left eye jumping means bad news, the right one means good news. If someone wears a dime on their body, and it turns black, then it is a sure sign that one has been conjured or root-worked, and when you hear an owl hoot that means someone is going to die. You never sweep up and throw out your trash after dark, or someone will die. Never leave hair in your comb or brush. Burn it, because someone can use it to cast a spell on you. The same goes for nail clippings."

"That sounds ridiculous."

"It may sound ridiculous to you, but it is very real to some. I spoke to a woman who'd moved to Little Rock from Savannah to escape the evil influences that she said would drive her crazy. To her the curse put on her by a jealous neighbor was so real that it defied Western psychiatric practices.

"Dr. Ramsay Mallette, a former professor of psychiatry at the Medical University of South Carolina in Charleston, trained his residents to perform root magic to reverse the hexes placed on patients whose fear of death was paralyzing. He showed a videotape of the healing procedure, complete with the instruments of conjure that produced recovery, as a demonstration of the power of belief."

Rebecca's gaze did not waver. "What do you believe, Ezra?"

"It has nothing to do with what I believe, Rebecca. I only report what I see and hear. A woman who'd had her hex reversed told me, 'She wuk a root on me so strong dat she put a big snake in muh bed, and uh could feel tings moobin in tru muh body. I could feel duh snake runnin all tru me.'" His inflection was pure Gullah.

"Hey, that was good."

Ezra wiggled his eyebrows, grinning. "You understood me?"

"Yes." There was no mistaking her delight.

"Let's see if you understand this: 'Day clean broad.'"

She shook her head. "I can't figure that one out."

"Broad daylight. Placing an adjective after the noun it modifies is an example of word order that makes the Gullah language colorful and distinctive. For example: 'a child bad,' 'tree high,' or 'I not see him.' Opening a sentence with a subject and repeating it with a pronoun is attributed to African syntax. So is the frequent repetition of words or phrases. 'I go,' 'I went,' 'I shall go' may also be said in the same phrase. Suppose a woman tells her doctor, 'I bees sick,' she connotes both that she is, and has been, sick."

"Are the differences between sea island peoples that discriminating?"

"Yes, but they are subtle. Although early rice planters along this coast were aware that Africans were as diverse as Europeans, they molded them into a cohesive workforce, ignoring ethnic differences and discouraging native customs. For survival, slaves had to repress differences and create a common Gullah culture."

*Ezra maneuvered into the driveway* behind Rebecca's Mercedes and shifted into park, but he did not shut off the engine. Turning toward her, he stared at her profile. It had been a long time since he'd enjoyed a woman's company. Usually they bored him—to tears. But Rebecca was different.

Ezra rested his arm over the back of her seat. "Will I see you tomorrow?"

"I don't think so. I plan to sleep in this weekend."

He nodded. "If that's the case, then I'll use the time to input my notes into my computer. Call me when you're ready for another field trip."

Leaning over, she brushed a light kiss on his cheek. "I will. Thanks for everything. Good night, Ezra."

He inclined his head, smiling. "Good night, Rebecca."

She hesitated, waiting for him to come around and open her door, but when he didn't, she got out of his truck unassisted. Spending more than twelve hours with Ezra Smith had changed both of them. In the past they had only discussed his research, but today that had changed. As they'd strolled a historic section of Hilton Head, he'd talked about growing up within sight of the Mississippi River, his mother, father, and his brother, Thomas, who was born the day after he'd celebrated his eighth birthday. He'd also talked about the young woman who had captured his heart in the first grade and their elopement.

Pushing open the door, Rebecca got out of his vehicle and made her way up the porch to her summerhouse. She had come to discover what she wanted and what she should do with her life.

It took less than half an hour for her to brush her teeth, wash her face, and take a bath. Not bothering to dry off, she lay facedown on the bed. A hint of a cooling ocean breeze filtering through the screens swept over her nude body. Like the simplicity of the little beachfront house, the intense heat no longer bothered her.

The cell phone on the bedside table rang. She rolled over and reached for it. Her home number showed in the display. "Hello."

"Hi."

"Hello, Lee."

"How are you, Rebecca?"

After their last telephone conversation, she had promised herself she would be civil to him. "I'm doing well."

"I'm glad to hear that. What have you been doing?"

She told him about picking sweetgrass and palmetto leaves, then visiting the slave burial ground, unaware of the rising excitement in her voice.

Lee chuckled softly. "It sounds as if you're enjoying yourself."

"I am. I never realized how rich our heritage is. You must come down and see for yourself." There was silence. "Lee?"

"I'm here, Becky."

"Did you hear what I said?"

There was another moment of silence before he said, "Yes, I did. Do you really want me to visit?"

"Of course I do."

"I'll let you know," he said slowly, as if monitoring each word.

"When?"

"I'll call you."

She did not know why, but she felt so alone. She'd invited her husband to join her on her magical island and his reply was, *I'll let you know.*

Her jaw hardened. "Call me before you come, so I can pick you up at the ferry." Pressing the End button, she terminated the call.

"You spiteful bastard!" she screamed. His decision not to commit to coming to McKinnon was his way of paying her back. She had extended the olive branch, and he had rejected her peace offering. It would serve him right if she had an affair. How would he feel if she slept with another man? She scrolled down the cell phone's directory and pushed the Talk button.

"Ezra?"

"Yes."

"Rebecca."

"What's the matter?"

She closed her eyes. "Nothing. It's just that I don't want to be alone right now."

"Did you have a fight with your husband?"

"Not really."

"Yes or no, Rebecca?"

Why, she thought, did he draw her name out into three distinct syllables? "No."

"I'll be over."

Her eyes filled with tears. "Thank you."

She ended the call and scrambled off the bed to find something to wear. By the time she heard the sound of the engine to Ezra's truck, she had carried two kitchen chairs out to the porch and set on a table, a bottle of chilled white wine and a plate of tiny Parmesan and black olive shortbreads with parsley pesto and goat cheese.

She stood motionless, watching him mount the steps leading to the porch. The lingering rays of a setting sun turned him into a statue of molten gold. A trembling smile flitted over her lips when he extended his arms. She moved into his strong and protective embrace.

Ezra closed his eyes, inhaling the scent of her hair and body. Everything that was Rebecca seeped into him, leaving her indelible imprint on his heart— forever. He did not know what had precipitated Rebecca's telephone call, but that no longer mattered. He buried his face in her flower-scented, curly hair. "I'm here."

Rebecca raised her chin, smiling up at him. "Thank you for being here." She threaded her fingers through his. "Please sit down."

Waiting until she was seated, Ezra took the remaining chair, barely glancing at the small table set with a bottle of wine, glasses and a platter of hors d'oeuvres. "What are we celebrating?"

"Friendship."

Crossing one knee over the other, Ezra stared

out at the beach. Rebecca did not want to be alone, and he wanted more from her than friendship.

"Do you think we can be friends, Rebecca?" Turning his head, he saw her wide-eyed expression. "Your reason for calling me, inviting me here was not because you need a friend. I'm certain you have enough of those back home."

"Oh, but I don't," she said quickly.

He lifted a dark eyebrow. "Whether you do or don't is irrelevant, because of our situation."

"What situation?"

"You're a married woman." What he did not say was a wealthy married woman.

"What does my being married have anything to do with us? With our being friends?"

Ezra closed his eyes for several seconds, sighing. "I like you, Rebecca. And—"

"And I like you, too," she said, interrupting him.

He shook his head, unable to believe her naïveté. "You've misinterpreted my liking." The soft sound of the water washing up on the beach and the incessant chirping of crickets filled the silence between them. He continued, "I've seen a lot and known a lot of women in my sixty-two years. I've had students come on to me, women who were young enough to be my daughter, but I never entertained them because my reputation and position with the university were more important than a quick lay. And that was what they would've become—a quick lay.

"I view you as one of my students, Rebecca—but with a difference. You're not enrolled in any of my classes, and we're not at the university. You, I would sleep with." He ignored her soft inhalation. "You called me not because you needed someone to talk to but because you want someone to sleep with. That cannot happen. Not when you're still wearing your rings and not when you haven't legally left your husband." He uncrossed his legs. "I know nothing about your private life, and I don't want to know. But if you want a friend, then that's what I'll be, and not a participant in what young folks refer to as a late-night booty call."

Rebecca was glad the semidarkness hid the flush in her cheeks. Only pride kept her from jumping up and going into the house. He knew. How did he know?

"You're right." Her voice was so soft that he had to lean closer to hear what she was saying. "I called you because I was angry with my husband. He had an affair with a woman two years ago, and I don't think I've ever really forgiven him. I wanted Lee to come and spend a few days with me, but he wouldn't give me an answer. That's when I called you."

Shifting his chair and reaching out, Ezra captured her fingers, holding them in a firm grip. "You don't need to complicate your marriage any further by engaging in an extramarital affair. If we did sleep together, it would be with disastrous results."

Her gaze searched his face. "Why would you say that?"

His expression was a mask of stone. "Think of what you would lose."

"What?"

"Do you have children?"

She nodded. "Yes. I have a son and daughter."

"How old are they?"

"Twelve and fourteen."

"Sleeping with me would put you at risk for losing your children." A momentary look of discomfort crossed her face at the possibility. "I'm too old to engage in a summer fling, Rebecca. If we're going to share our bodies, then it must be for keeps. I refuse to give you my heart and then permit you to walk away from me without fighting for you. I'm saying all of this to make you aware of your reputation and what you stand to lose with a messy divorce and custody battle."

"Who said anything about divorce?"

He leaned closer. "Oh, but there would be a divorce, because I would not let you go back to doing whatever it was you did before you came to McKinnon Island. Let's settle it right here, right now. Are we going to be friends or lovers?"

Rebecca felt as if her composure was under attack. His question had set off all types of alarm bells. She liked Ezra and loved Lee. Despite his infidelity, there had never been a time when she'd stopped loving him. Her face clouded with uneasiness. As much as she complained about her boring, sterile existence, it was all she'd known for the past sixteen years. There was no way she would ever leave her children.

A new sense of strength came to her, and she smiled. "Friends, Ezra." Much to her surprise, he smiled.

"That's what I was hoping you'd say." Rising slightly, he kissed her cheek. "Would you mind if I poured the wine?"

"Not at all."

Relaxing against the chair's slatted back, Rebecca closed her eyes, overwhelmed by the powerful relief filling her.

"Madam."

She opened her eyes and took the glass of wine from Ezra. They touched glasses, smiling at each other over the rims.

They finished off the bottle of wine and all of the hors d'oeuvres. The dark sky was littered with millions of stars and a quarter moon when they finally went into the house and lay across the double bed together, holding hands.

It was just before dawn when Ezra gathered Rebecca to his chest. She stirred, whispering her husband's name, but did not wake up. He lay in the small, hot room, asking himself why he was there, why he was in bed with a woman who had captured his heart with a single glance. The questions kept coming, and still he had no answers.

# Nineteen

*I lie here thinking of you.*
        —William Carlos Williams

Theo lay facedown on a blanket, savoring the heat of the sun on his bare back. He had spent the past half hour swimming with Christian, Brandon and Noelle. All had learned to swim, but of the three Noelle had been the first.

Christian put Brandon in a headlock before he released him and swam back to the beach. His chest rose and fell heavily as he sat down next to Theo. "Are you going back in?"

Theo shook his head, his gaze narrowing behind the lenses of his sunglasses. "Not today." He was exhausted after spending the night tossing restlessly, his mind filled with images of Hope.

Moving closer, Christian peered at him. "Are you all right, Big Brother?"

"Sure."

"You said that a little too quickly."

Theo smiled. "Why would you say that?"

"You haven't been yourself all week."

"Explain yourself, Little Brother."

Stretching out his legs, Christian leaned back on his elbows. "Brandon, Noelle and I have been talking."

Theo gave Christian a quick glance. "What about?"

"You."

"What about me?"

"Well . . ." His words trailed off.

Rolling over, Theo sat up. "Come on, Chris, spit it out."

"Well," he repeated, "we were talking about you and Miss Hope."

Theo went completely still. Was he that obvious? Had everyone noticed how he hadn't been able to take his gaze off her after they'd sat down to eat dessert late Sunday afternoon?

"What about me and Miss Hope?"

Christian flashed a wide grin. "You two look good together. Noelle told us that you had your arm around her when we came back from the movies. She also said you were going to ask her to be your sweetheart."

"Noelle talks too much."

"Did you ask her?" Christian asked after a moment of silence.

"Ask her what?"

"If she wanted to be with you."

"Is that the same as asking someone to be your girlfriend?"

Christian bobbed his head. "Yeah!"

"No." Theo's expression was deadpan.

"Why not, Theo?"

"Because it's not like that. I invited her to dinner and she came. And, that's it."

"If I was older I'd ask her out."

"Are you saying I should ask her out?"

"Hell, yeah!"

"What is it you like about her?"

Christian lifted his shoulders. "Everything. She's pretty and she can cook. That strawberry shortcake she made was mad good."

"You're right about the cake. It was working."

"Are you going to ask her out?"

Theo stared at Christian. In just two weeks the sun had darkened his skin several shades even though he had put on sunblock. "Why the sudden interest with me and Hope getting together?"

"You could use a little fun. All you do is write."

"I enjoy writing."

"There's got to be more than just you writing."

"Where are you going with this, Chris?"

"We talked—"

"We?" Theo cut him off.

"Brandon, Noelle and me. We think it's pretty cool that you brought us here. Well . . . we think it's pretty cool that you took us in after Momma and Dad died. You didn't have to do it."

"I promised your mother I would."

"You didn't have to keep the promise. We wouldn't be the first kids to go into foster homes."

"That would've never happened."

"I'm not saying it couldn't happen. You gave up a lot for us. I've realized that since coming to McKinnon."

"What else have you learned, wise little grasshopper?"

"Be serious, Theo."

He sobered. "Okay, Chris."

"You're a good brother, and you deserve to have a woman and some kids."

"I'm not looking for a wife and kids."

"Why not?"

"I don't want a wife and I don't need kids."

"What's going to happen when you're mad old?"

"I can't think about that until I'm 'mad' old."

"Come on, Theo."

Theo's expression changed as he stared at his brother. "I am serious."

Christian returned the glare, then pushed to his feet, mumbling under his breath. He walked several feet, stopped, but did not turn around. "You're just like Momma."

Theo turned his attention back to the two in the water, Christian's words echoing in his head. There was no mistaking his frustration.

Pushing to his feet, Theo walked down to the water and dove under an incoming wave. He swam until he tired. By the time he returned to the beach, Noelle and Brandon had disappeared. It was when he stood under the spray of the shower that he decided to take Christian's advice. He would ask Hope to go out with him.

*"Did you talk to him?"*

Christian saw the expectant look on Noelle's face. She'd convinced him to talk to Theo even though he hadn't wanted to do it. "Yes."

"What did he say?" Brandon asked. He took off his glasses and wiped the lenses on the hem of his T-shirt.

"He said he was going to call her."

Noelle frowned at Christian. "I don't believe him."

Brandon put his glasses back on. "Why are you guys so revved up on hooking Theo up with Miss Hope? If he wanted to go out with her, he would've done it already."

"Wrong," Christian spat. "I'm with Noelle. I don't think he's going to do anything."

Noelle leaned closer to her brothers. "Which means we're going to have to do something." Christian nodded, while Brandon shook his head. "We can get Miss Helen to help us."

"How?" the two boys said in unison.

Pulling back her narrow shoulders, she pursed her lips. "Let me handle this."

"He's going to have a cow if he finds out that we're plotting behind his back," Brandon warned.

"If he goes ballistic, then I'll say it was all my idea," Noelle said. "Wait here, and I'll be back."

Christian and Brandon stared at each other as their sister walked out of the family room, hoping their plan to hook their brother up with Hope Sutton would not backfire.

*Noelle found Helen* in the kitchen slicing cucumbers. "Miss Helen, do you mind if we have company for dinner tomorrow?"

Helen's bright blue eyes crinkled in a smile. "Of course not. Who did you want to invite?"

"Miss Hope."

Her smile vanished quickly. "Did you ask Theo?"

Noelle chewed on her lower lip. "I didn't think we had to ask him. Because didn't you say if she comes again she won't be a guest?"

"Yes, I did." Helen's expression brightened. "Invite her. If Theo says anything, then I'll tell him I wanted her to come."

Noelle hugged Helen, then kissed her cheek. "Thanks."

She raced out of the kitchen and returned to the family room. "It's on!" Her eyes glittered like polished onyx. "Chris, I need you to drive me over to Miss Hope's house."

Brandon crossed his arms over his chest. "If this mission blows up, then I'm going to disavow any knowledge."

Christian pushed to his feet. "Punk!"

"Yeah, I'd rather be a punk than have Theo in my face."

"Our big brother has gone soft," Christian stated with a newfound bravado. "All he's interested in is finishing his scripts."

"Let him finish the scripts before we push a woman in his face," Brandon argued softly.

"Chris, I'm waiting," Noelle whined.

They walked out of the house and stopped. The Lexus was missing. That meant Theo had taken it.

Christian stared at his sister. "What do you want to do?"

"Do you want to walk?"

"How far?"

"Not too far. Let's ask Brandon if he wants to come with us."

Puffing out his cheeks, Christian blew out his breath. "Okay."

*Hope walked into* the McKinnon Island post office. Her eyes narrowed behind the lenses of her sunglasses when she spied the tall figure of Theo at the counter. He was mailing an overnight package.

Charles completed Theo's transaction, then looked up. "Hey, Hope."

Theo turned and stared at Hope standing behind him. He flashed a dazzling smile. "Good afternoon."

Nodding to Theo, she said, "Good afternoon to you, too." She took the bundle of letters and magazines Charles placed on the counter. "Thanks."

Charles winked at Hope. "See you next week." She made it a habit to pick up her mail every Wednesday.

Theo fell into step with her as she walked out of the post office. "How have you been?"

Hope gave him a sidelong glance. "Wonderful. How about yourself?"

"Relieved. I just mailed off the pilot script."

"Congratulations."

"Thank you. How's your writing project?"

"Good. I've begun the first chapter."

"How many chapters have you projected?"

"Twelve."

He whistled softly. "That's a lot."

They moved outdoors under a porch. "How's your family?"

"Thankfully, everyone's well. They've been asking about you."

"Really?"

Theo angled his head. "Really. In fact, Chris, Brandon and Noelle have decided to get into the matchmaking business. They think I'm old, write too much, and because I don't have any fun, they believe we should 'hook up.'"

"You're not old," she said, deciding to ignore his reference to their "hooking up."

"Tell that to teenagers. To them anyone over thirty is old. And once you hit forty, then you're ready for an assisted living facility." Reaching out, Theo caught Hope's arm. "I'd be honored if you would have dinner with me tomorrow evening."

Her body stiffened in shock. "Are you asking me out to refute your siblings' assessment that you're an old workaholic?" Much to her surprise, he threw back his head and laughed.

"No. I'm asking you out because I enjoy your company."

"I enjoy talking to you, too. But did you tell them you were going to ask me out on a date?"

"No." He gave her a tender smile.

She returned his smile. "Do you realize how lucky you are, Theo? You have family who love you. They have one another, yet they're concerned because they don't want you to grow old alone."

"What they don't realize is that I'm alone by choice."

"Teenagers don't want to understand that concept. At their age they are the quintessential party animals."

"You're right. But you didn't answer my question. Will you have dinner with me?"

Going out with Theo signaled a beginning, a step into the dating scene. "Yes, Theo. I'll go out to dinner with you."

Behind the dark lenses of his sunglasses, Theo let his gaze travel slowly over her. "If it's all right with you, I'll pick you up at six-thirty."

She nodded. "Where are we dining?"

"I'll make reservations at a restaurant in Savannah."

"I'll be ready." She pulled her arm from his loose grip, smiling. "I'll see you tomorrow."

"Tomorrow," he repeated, watching her as she walked to her car.

Hope parked her car and reached for the stack of mail on the passenger seat. As soon as she stepped out, she saw the Anderson children standing on her porch. The first thing that came to mind was that something had happened to Theo, but she dismissed it because she'd just left him at the post office.

She smiled slowly as she mounted the stairs. "Good afternoon."

Christian moved forward. "Good afternoon, Miss Hope. We're here because Miss Helen would like you to come to dinner tomorrow."

"That is, if you don't have other plans," Noelle added quickly.

Hope noticed they'd said Miss Helen and not Theo. "I'm sorry, but I do have something planned for tomorrow."

Head lowered, Brandon asked, "How about tonight?"

Noelle walked over and stood next to Christian. "Please, Miss Hope."

She stared at the three teens, trying not to laugh. There was desperation in Noelle's voice, and Brandon was hard-pressed to meet her gaze. "Does Theo know I'm invited for dinner?"

Sighing, Christian stared out over her head. "We may as well tell you."

"Tell me what?"

He looked sheepish. "We're trying to get you and our brother together."

Hope's lips twitched in amusement. "Does he know this?" All three nodded. "Why do you think Theo needs your help?"

Noelle's eyes were misty. "All he does is write. And I know he likes you, because he told me he did."

"He's getting old and he's going to need someone to take care of him." It was Christian's turn to offer his rationale.

She wanted to tell them that Theo wasn't old. And even when he did get old he still would not have a problem attracting women. The Anderson children inviting her to dinner without Theo's knowledge validated his claim that his brothers and sister did have boundary issues.

"How do you think Theo would react if he knew you guys were here hatching a plot to set him up with me?"

Brandon stared at his brother, then his sister. "I'm certain he wouldn't like it."

Hope decided it was better not to tell them that she and Theo had plans to see each other the following evening. "I won't tell if you won't. But, on the other hand, if your brother likes me, then I'm certain he will ask me out."

Noelle gave her a skeptical look. "Are you sure?"

Hope smiled at her. "Very sure."

"My brother is really cool."

"I'm sure he is."

"Does that mean you like him?"

"Yes, I like him." Christian and Brandon, grinning from ear to ear, exchanged high fives.

"Does that mean you're coming for dinner, Miss Hope?"

"Not tonight, Noelle."

"When?"

Hope tugged gently on the girl's braided hair. "Perhaps we can all get together Sunday afternoon. If it doesn't rain, then I'll cook outdoors."

Her answer seemed to satisfy the trio. She stood on the porch watching them as they made their way down to the beach. Within minutes they became smaller and smaller until they disappeared.

She did not envy Theo. Not only were his charges willful but they were also determined to get him a girlfriend. And she knew they would be formidable opponents if they decided a woman wasn't worthy of their brother.

Well, she wasn't too worried about the Anderson siblings, because her association with Theo would not extend beyond the summer. She had come to McKinnon to write and heal, not become involved with a man.

# Twenty

*My soul is full of longing for the secret of the sea, and the heart of the great ocean sends a thrilling pulse through me.*

—Henry Wadsworth Longfellow

Hope stepped out onto the porch. Turning to her right, she saw Theo sitting on the rocker, hands dangling over the curved arms. There was something about the way the diffused light shadowed his face that reminded her of a scene from a classic Orson Welles film. The sound of the screen door hitting the frame caught his attention and brought him to his feet.

She smiled. "How long have you been waiting?"

Theo slipped his hands into the pockets of his black linen slacks. He hadn't realized it before, but he loved the sound of Hope's voice. It was low, husky, and sensual.

"I got here a little after six."

"Why didn't you ring the bell?"

"I didn't want to rush you. Sitting here and staring at the ocean is wonderful for the soul. I believe Longfellow said it best: 'My soul is full of longing for the secret of the sea, and the heart of the great ocean sends a thrilling pulse through me.' "

Smiling, Hope closed the distance between them. "You and my sister would get along famously. She loves poetry."

Theo removed his hands from his pockets and began snapping his fingers. "I used to spend so many hours hanging out in Bay Area coffeehouses listening to poetry readings that I finally got a job in one."

"There once was a little coffeehouse along Factor's Walk that hosted poetry readings."

"What happened to it?"

"It closed down, then reopened as a club for a predominantly college crowd. The weekend entertainment usually features up-and-coming bands."

Theo shook his head. "Too loud."

She gave him a saucy look. "I've heard it said that 'if it's too loud, then you're too old.' "

He glared at her under lowered lids. "You got old jokes, too."

"No. I'm probably right behind you."

"How old are you?"

"Thirty-eight."

Hope shivered despite the summer heat, her gaze moving slowly over Theo's clean-shaven profile. They shared a smile as he led her to his vehicle. Hiking up the hem of her dress, she stepped up into the SUV after he opened the door for her. She was seated and belted-in when he slipped behind the wheel beside her.

Theo started up the Lexus and drove toward the ferry landing for the 6:55 sailing.

\* \* \*

*Theo slipped* into his suit jacket after he'd maneuvered into the parking lot at Elizabeth and Thirty-seventh. The restaurant was housed in a bleached-beige Palladian-style mansion. He waited for the maitre d' to seat Hope before he sat opposite her.

"I've heard the food is excellent."

She lifted an eyebrow. "Have you eaten here before?"

"No. But my agent recommends it highly. Jeff may exaggerate about a lot of things, but I have to give him credit when it comes to his dining recommendations. So far, he's never been wrong."

Staring at Theo through lowered lids, Hope said, "I'm certain he's pleased having you as his client."

"We are a good team." His statement lacked modesty.

"How long has he represented you?"

"He's my first and only agent."

The sommelier handed Theo the wine list, and he and Hope selected a blush to complement entrées of pecan-crusted chicken and cinnamon-spiced shrimp. They raised their glasses in a toast.

Hope touched her glass to Theo's. "To McKinnon Island."

"McKinnon Island," he repeated.

She took a sip of the chilled wine. It was excellent. She put down the glass. "You should've won an Oscar for your last script."

Theo lifted a broad shoulder under his jacket. "It doesn't matter much whether I do or don't win. Just being nominated is reward enough."

"How many scripts do you write a year?"

"It varies." He took another sip of wine. "I've done as many as six. One year I completed only one."

"All originals?"

"No. Some of them are adapted from novels or short stories. The two Academy Award nominations were original screenplays."

"Can you tell me about your television project?"

Theo reached across the space of the table and held her hands. "Can I trust you not to disclose what I'm going to tell you?"

She leaned forward. "Yes."

The word slipped off her lips just as a bright flash of light blinded her. She blinked, attempting to clear her vision. Theo had released her fingers and was on his feet. She glimpsed the back of a short man as he scurried away.

Hope glanced up to find Theo frowning down at her. "Who was that?" she asked.

He shook his head and sat down. "I don't know."

Their waiter came over to the table. "I'm sorry, Mr. Howell, Miss."

Theo waved him away. "It's all right." The man backed away from the table. Theo directed his attention to Hope, noting her expression. She wasn't pleased. "Did being photographed upset you?"

She closed her eyes for several seconds. "I'm more annoyed than upset. People usually ask permission before they take my picture." She had made it a practice to keep her private life private. No one knew she had been dating Kendall except family members and close friends.

"Do you give consent?"

Sighing, she nodded. "Usually I do."

"How has your life changed since you've become a celebrity?"

"I don't see myself as a celebrity."

"How do you see yourself?"

"More as a public figure." She gave Theo a long, penetrating stare. "You're the celebrity."

He lowered his head and smiled, the gesture reminding her of Brandon. "No, I'm not. The difference between you and I is where we live. The paparazzi are as thick in L.A. as a swarm of hornets. They make their name and money from taking photographs of the suspecting and unsuspecting. At first it bothered me, then I learned to ignore them, because the tabloids are going to print what they want. Smut and gossip sell."

"You're saying that you don't care if someone photographs you?"

"It's not that I don't care. I've chosen a career that at times is high profile, and I've learned to accept all of the advantages and disadvantages that go along with it. As long as they don't invade my privacy or slander me, I could care less."

"Two years ago there were photos of you in *People, Entertainment Weekly,* and film footage of you on E! Entertainment Television." What she did not say was that each time he'd been photographed it had been with a different woman.

"Pre-Oscar hype," he said disdainfully.

The waiter set their entrées on the table. She concentrated on eating her chicken and wilted spinach. She watched Theo watching her each time she glanced up. Whenever their gazes met, both shared a secret smile.

Theo put down his water goblet and dabbed his mouth with the cloth napkin. "Have you thought about going into television?"

Hope touched the corners of her mouth with her napkin. "No."

"How about radio?"

"I've been offered a spot at an Atlanta-based talk radio station."

Theo leaned back in his chair and crossed his arms over his chest. "Which one?"

"WLKV."

"I know the program manager."

"Derrick Landry?"

He nodded. "I met Derrick about ten years ago. He was in television at that time. He wanted me to do scripts for daytime soaps, but I turned him down because I preferred screenplays." Lowering his arms, Theo leaned over the table. "Would you like me to put in a good word for you?"

Hope pulled her lower lip between her teeth, wondering how much she should tell Theo about her medical dilemma. She then decided to be truthful. "That won't be necessary because, I have the job."

He straightened. "When do you start?"

"I'm not certain."

"You have the position, yet you don't know when you're going to start?"

"I have a medical problem I have to resolve before I relocate to Atlanta." Her gaze shifted and met his. "I have endometriosis."

He frowned. "What's that?"

She explained the symptoms of the disease.

"Don't you . . . isn't there an alternative to you having a hysterectomy?"

Hope would've laughed at his expression if the subject matter hadn't been so serious. It was a combination of shock and confusion. "Yes."

"What is it?"

A smiled played at the corners of her mouth. "Have a baby."

He silently mouthed the three words. "You mean get pregnant?"

"I believe that's the same as having a baby, Theo."

Theo decided to ignore her flippant retort. "When were you first diagnosed?"

"About seven weeks ago. I'm scheduled to return to the doctor early October. He has to reevaluate me and determine if I'll have to undergo a procedure to remove the lesions."

"This procedure would not be a hysterectomy?"

"No."

"Do you want children, Hope?"

The flickering light from a candle on the table threw shadows over her face. She glanced down. "Yes, I do."

"Why haven't you had a child?"

Sighing softly, she said, "There are a few reasons. I'm not married and I haven't met the man I'd want to father my children."

"Are you saying that you'd *have* to be married before you'd consider bearing a child?"

She gave him a level look. "I'm saying that I'd *prefer* to be married before I have a child. If not married, then at least engaged."

Theo shook his head. "I can't believe some man hasn't made you his wife."

"What's not to believe? I could say the same thing about you," Hope countered. "Why isn't there a Mrs. Theodore Howell?"

"There's no Mrs. Howell because all the women

I date are girls. Los Angeles is filled with twenty-, thirty-, and sometimes forty-something-year-old *girls*."

"Perhaps you should consider relocating."

"Where would I go?"

"New York, Atlanta, Chicago, Denver. You'd have lots of options."

Amusement flickered in his eyes. "Big Apple Diva, 'Lanta Hottie, Chi-town Sweetie, and Mile High Honey. You really think I'd find the love of my life in one of these cities?"

"Only if you are really looking for a wife, Theo."

He shook his head. "The truth is that I'm not looking because I don't need a wife, nor do I want children."

"Why not, Big Poppa? Are you having too much fun to settle down?"

"I *had* fun." He winked at her. "This Big Poppa has sworn off *girls* for the next five years to take care of my brothers and sister."

Hope laughed. "Will you be able to survive your sacrifice?"

"You don't think I can do it, do you?"

She sobered. There was something in Theo's eyes that dared her to challenge his declaration that he would devote the next five years of his life to his siblings. "I don't know you well enough to judge whether you can or can't."

Reaching into his jacket's breast pocket, Theo withdrew a pen. He picked up the paper napkin next to his wineglass. "Are you online?"

"Yes. Why?"

He handed her the napkin and pen. "Write down your e-mail address. I'll e-mail you the day Noelle enters college to let you know if I succeed."

Hope shook her head. "You're kidding."

"Write, Hope," he urged softly.

She wrote her e-mail address on the napkin, then handed it and the pen to Theo. He stared at what she had written before he folded the square of paper and secreted it in his pocket. He printed his e-mail address on another napkin and slid it across the table. Hope put it in her purse.

The waiter returned with dessert menus, and they both ordered sorbet. Their conversation shifted to less personal topics. Two hours after they'd entered the restaurant, they left, knowing a little bit more about the other.

The ferryboat ride back to McKinnon Island was accomplished in silence as they leaned against the rail, watching streaks of red and orange fade against the encroaching navy blue sky. The silence was not broken until Theo stood with Hope on her porch, holding hands.

"Can we do it again?"

Tilting her chin, she smiled up at him. "Yes."

"When?" His breath whispered over her mouth.

"E-mail me and I'll let you know."

Theo chuckled deep in his throat. "I'll do just that." Dipping his head, he brushed a soft kiss over her parted lips. "Thank you for a wonderful evening."

She smiled in the shadowy darkness. "You're quite welcome." He released her hands and walked down the stairs. "Theo." He stopped but did not turn around. "You and your family are welcome to come for Sunday dinner."

He glanced over his shoulder, smiling. "Thank you."

Hope stood in the same spot, watching him

drive away. The red taillights disappeared from view, and she still had not moved.

"How is it going, Sophie Lady?" asked a familiar feminine voice.

Hope spun around. Rebecca had come up without making a sound. "Good." She smiled at her neighbor. "How are you doing with your basket-weaving lessons?"

Rebecca made her way up the stairs and leaned against the porch column. "Slow. I've been touring McKinnon with Janie's brother-in-law. He's spent the past two years gathering research on the culture of the Sea Islands, and I've volunteered to be his research assistant."

Hope gestured to her. "Come sit down." Rebecca took the chaise. "Would you like something cool to drink?"

Flashing a set of dimples in her deeply tanned face, Rebecca shook her head. "No, thank you. I'll explode if I have another drop of liquid. Janie and Thomas had a little something at their house to celebrate Ezra's birthday, and I overindulged on champagne."

Hope flipped two switches next to the door, turning on the porch lamps and the ceiling fan. She slipped off her heels, sat on the rocker, and rested her bare feet on a footstool. Rebecca looked nothing like the woman who had come to McKinnon Island nearly three weeks before. Her hair was longer, lighter, her face darker, and she had changed her designer labels for a pair of white, cropped pants and a blue-and-white striped tank top that screamed Gap.

Rebecca closed her eyes. "It's kind of nice being

just slightly drunk." She waved a hand. "No cares, no worries, no nothing."

"How much did you drink?"

Rebecca opened her eyes. "I lost count after the third glass."

Hope whistled softly. Her neighbor's Mercedes sedan was parked in the driveway. "Did you drive home?"

"Ezra drove me back." She gave a lopsided grin, raised her arms, and wiggled her fingers. "I'm free . . ." Her words trailed off as her cell phone rang. She pulled it from her pocket. "Hello." Her expression was impassive. "Yes, Lee. Have them bring their swimsuits. Call me when you reach the landing, and I'll meet you." She ended the call and smiled at Hope. "My children are coming down Friday afternoon."

Leaning over, Hope patted her hand. "That's wonderful, Rebecca."

"They'll probably complain that there's nothing for them to do, but I don't care. I just want to see them, hug them."

"You can take them to the playhouse to see *West Side Story.*"

Giggling, Rebecca kicked her feet. "I'll take them to The Fish Net and introduce them to 'chitlins.' Will you come with us?"

Hope's laughter joined her giggles. "You're beginning to sound like a real down home girl. And to answer your question about coming with you, I have to decline."

"But I want them to meet you."

Hope knew Rebecca needed time alone with her family to reconnect. "I can meet them Sunday. I've invited Theo and his family for Sunday dinner. You're welcome to come, too. I plan to cook outdoors and serve everyone on the beach."

Rebecca clapped her hands. "That sounds wonderful. Can I bring anything?"

Hope stared at Rebecca. Despite being a wife and mother to two adolescent children, she was still very much a child herself. Her need to please others and be accepted made her so vulnerable to disappointment.

"Bring anything you want, Sophie Lady."

Rebecca gave a mysterious grin. "How are you doing with Theo?"

"What do you mean about how am I doing?"

There was a sharp edge in Hope's tone, but Rebecca chose to ignore it. "He seems like a nice guy."

"That's because he *is* a nice guy."

"So?"

"So, what are you getting at?"

The giddiness in Rebecca vanished, and in its place was a woman who suddenly appeared in complete control of herself and her emotions. "I asked you a simple question, and your barking at me made it sound as if I'd asked you if you were sleeping with him."

Hope closed her eyes and blew out her breath. "You're right, Rebecca." She opened her eyes, meeting her neighbor's narrowed stare. "I had no right to snap at you." Placing a hand over her mouth, she leaned back on the rocker. "Theo's great," she said through her fingers, "but right now I'm not really into men. At least not to sleep with one right now."

Rebecca moved off the chaise, sat down on the

footstool, and rested Hope's bare feet in her lap. "What happened, girlfriend?"

Hope lowered her hand and clasped her fingers together to stop their trembling. After she'd told her sister about Kendall, she had promised herself that she would never repeat what she had witnessed to another person. It would remain a secret between three people: Marissa, Kendall, and herself. Since she had come to McKinnon Island, the image of Kendall with another man had begun to fade, and she did not want to revive it by retelling the tale to Rebecca.

Rebecca sucked her teeth. "You're a fraud, Dr. Hope. You can give everyone else advice, but you don't practice what you preach. How many times have you told your readers to talk it out with someone? That talking was the first step in healing thyself. What's the matter, Hope? Did you really think you'd be exempt from whatever else we mere mortals go through because you're the great Dr. Hope?"

Hope glared at Rebecca. "You don't understand!"

"What's not to understand? Your man hurt you! Just like *my* man hurt *me!*"

For Rebecca it had been easy. It was easy for women whose husbands or lovers preferred another woman. But everything changed when men preferred a same-sex or bisexual relationship.

"The difference is your husband slept with another woman." Hope's voice was barely audible.

Rebecca's luminous eyes widened in astonishment as she brought her hands up to cradle her cheeks. "Oh shit!" she whispered. She lowered Hope's feet, rose slightly and hugged her. "I'm sorry, girlfriend. I had no right to say what I did."

Hope hugged her back. "You said what you

needed to say. And you're right about me. I have answers for everyone but myself."

"Did you leave him?"

"Yes."

"What are you going to do now?"

Hope flashed a cynical smile. "I'm going to spend the summer on McKinnon Island as planned. Hopefully I'll discover who I am, what I want, and what I need to do before I leave."

Nodding, Rebecca reclaimed the chaise. "Now you sound like me."

"That's because we're not all that different."

The two women sat on the porch, talking for hours. They told each other about their childhood, friends they had made and lost, and of the men who'd made them who they were. They talked until the sky brightened with the dawn of a new day, then fell asleep where they lay.

Hope and Rebecca had come to McKinnon Island as strangers and neighbors, but before the sun rose again they had become friends who had unburdened their hearts and bared their souls to each other.

# Twenty-one

*We've made a great mess of love.*

—D. H. Lawrence

*Rebecca spied Kyle and Ashlee* as soon as the ferryboat docked at the McKinnon Island landing. Both looked as if they'd grown several inches, especially her son. He now was as tall as his sister.

Kyle waved to her and she returned the wave. The gangplank was lowered, and they raced toward her. She stood motionless. Something in her brain would not tell her legs to move, so she stood there waiting for her children to come to her. Ashlee reached her first, her arms going around her neck. Her daughter's face blurred as tears filled Rebecca's eyes.

"Baby. Oh, my baby," she sobbed in Ashlee's curly hair.

"Mama, please don't cry." Ashlee's voice quivered.

Pulling back, Rebecca wiped at her tears, smiling. "I'm crying because I'm so happy to see you guys."

Kyle, who often said that kissing his mother was stupid, leaned over and kissed her cheek. "Hi, Mom."

Tilting her head, Rebecca stared up at him. "What on earth is your grandmother feeding you?" Not only had he shot up but he had also put on weight.

"I've been working out with Dad at the gym," he said proudly.

Rebecca winked at him. "You look good."

"Thanks, Mom."

Her children may have changed in appearance, but Ashlee still called her Mama, while Kyle preferred Mom. The day he'd turned ten he'd declared Mama sounded too childish for a preteen boy.

Ashlee curved an arm around her mother's waist. "You look very pretty, Mama. I like your hair."

Running a hand through her hair, Rebecca pushed sun-streaked curls off her forehead and ears. She could not remember the last time she had missed her weekly salon appointment. But then again, there was no one on McKinnon Island she had to impress. Not her husband or his business associates, her mother-in-law, or the wives who held monthly golf outings followed by luncheons at their husbands' country club.

"Thank you, Ashlee."

She saw Lee behind the wheel of his silver BMW X5 as he drove off the ferryboat; a slight flutter settled in her chest, and she wondered if he, like their children, had changed. Less than a minute later he stood in front of her. Her question was answered.

He had changed. There were flecks of gray in his close-cropped hair, and he was slimmer than he'd been the last time she'd seen him. Despite the changes, he was more handsome and imposing than he had ever been.

She smiled, her dimples deepening in her tanned cheeks. "Welcome to McKinnon Island, darling."

Lee's dark eyes took in everything about his wife in one sweeping glance. She had gained weight and was deeply tanned. She was so ardently beautiful that he found it hard to breathe. He loved her more than he could ever imagine loving a woman.

He pulled her to his chest, lowered his head, and kissed her. He wasn't disappointed when her lips parted, permitting him to taste her. His body reacted quickly, drawing a moan from Rebecca.

"I've missed you, baby." His hot breath feathered over her mouth.

Rebecca broke the kiss, her eyes sweeping over her husband's face. "I've missed you, too."

He smiled. "I'm going to hang out here for awhile before I catch a later ferryboat back to Hilton Head." He had driven from Charleston to Savannah, then picked up the ferryboat to McKinnon Island.

She stared at Lee. When he'd called to say that he was bringing Kyle and Ashlee, she had thought he would also stay the weekend. A tight smile masked her disappointment. "Well, let's get back to the house. Then we'll decide what you want to see or do."

Lee's gaze swept over the parking lot. "Where's your car?"

"I left it back at the house."

"You walked?" There was no mistaking his surprise. Anyone familiar with Rebecca knew she never walked anywhere. Not even to a house a block away.

"It's not that far."

Reaching for Rebecca's hand, Lee directed her to his vehicle, Ashlee and Kyle following. Once she was seated and belted in, she said, "Pull out and turn left. Follow the road until you get to an intersection, then turn right onto Beach Road. I'm staying in the next to the last house."

The joy Rebecca had felt when Lee had held her and kissed her had vanished with his statement that he did not plan to spend the weekend on the island. Why, she asked herself, had he bothered to come? Her parents could have driven their grandchildren down.

"Look!" Kyle shouted from the rear seat. "What is that?"

Turning, Rebecca looked out the side window. A large hairy animal with tusks and a snout ambled into the thick woods. "That's a feral hog."

"Yuck!" Ashlee spat out. "I'll never eat pork again."

Lee smiled as he drove slowly over an unpaved road lined on both sides with twisted live oaks. The scene unfolding before him was both fascinating and frightening. McKinnon Island, one of the smaller, less populated Sea Islands, appeared to have stopped in time. He slowed to ten miles an hour in an attempt to take in everything around him. He saw a sign advertising Palmetto Haven—a future gated community slated for completion the following summer. The developer had yet to lay the foundation for the new homes.

"How many new developments are projected to go up here?"

Rebecca stared at her husband's profile. "One—for now. Give it a few years and this place will never look the same."

He turned onto Beach Road. Small, bungalow-type structures were on his right, and the ocean on his left. His wife had selected an ideal setting to spend the summer. He spotted her car and maneuvered into the driveway behind it.

Kyle leaned over the passenger-side seat, staring at the house. "It looks small, Mom."

Rebecca unsnapped her seat belt. "It is small."

Doors opened and everyone got out of the SUV. Rebecca walked up the porch and unlocked the front door, while Lee took two canvas bags from the cargo area. Open windows and oscillating fans in every room had cooled the house considerably. Rebecca had decided to purchase the fans because she knew her family was not used to sleeping in the heat.

Ashlee stood in the middle of the living room, a stunned expression freezing her features. "Where's the air-conditioning?"

Rebecca sat down on a love seat and crossed her legs. "There is no air-conditioning." She enunciated each word as her gaze shifted from her daughter to her son. "Let me know now if you want to stay. Otherwise you can go back to Charleston with your father."

Ashlee flopped down on an armchair and pushed out her lower lip. "I'll stay," she mumbled.

Kyle stared at his mother. It was apparent she was angry, because vertical lines had appeared between her eyes. "I'll stay, too."

"Please don't make it sound as if you're doing me

a favor. I've missed you guys more than you'll ever know, but if you don't want to stay, then I'll understand."

Taking three strides, Kyle sat down next to his mother. "I want to stay, Mom. Really."

She smiled and touched his cheek. "Thank you."

"Do we get our own rooms?"

"Yes, Kyle, you'll have your own room." Rebecca stood up. "Let me show you your bedrooms." They followed her to the rear of the house. "Ashlee, this one is yours."

Ashlee's disappointment about not staying in a centrally cooled house vanished as she walked into a small room with a large brass bed covered with a colorful patchwork quilt. A rag rug next to the bed covered uneven floorboards, while a large crock pitcher in a matching bowl rested on a drop-leaf table in a corner. Her smile was dazzling.

"I like it. This looks like something from *Little House on the Prairie.*"

Rebecca left Ashlee in her room and led Kyle to the smallest of the bedrooms. It claimed a charm that was unique to the space. There was only enough room for a wrought-iron bed, rocking chair, and a highboy. A table lamp claimed a spot on the floor next to the bed, and large nails driven in the walls served as a makeshift closet. None of the rooms had closets except for a pantry off the kitchen. The air circulating from an oscillating fan lifted the sheers at the tall, narrow windows.

Kyle smiled at his mother. "The room's fine, Mom. It's not like I'm going to spend a lot of time in here except to sleep."

Satisfaction pursed Rebecca's mouth. Her daughter complained about not having air-conditioning but did not mind sleeping in a room that was smaller than her bedroom's walk-in closet, while Kyle could care less where he slept as long as he had a bed.

She patted Kyle's shoulder. "We're going to have to work out a schedule for sharing the bathroom."

"No problem, Mom."

Lee crowded into the small space and put Kyle's bag on the rocker. He glanced at his watch, then his wife. "Is there a place on the island where we can get an early lunch?"

"I know the perfect place." She would take her family to The Fish Net.

Rebecca sat on the porch next to Lee, her gaze fixed on her son and daughter as they waded in the surf. They had yet to change into their swimsuits.

Eating lunch at The Fish Net had been a pleasurable experience for her and her children. Ashlee and Kyle had been amenable to sampling dishes they'd never eaten before, but not Lee. He'd complained that the restaurant was too small and noisy, there were too many dishes cooked with pork, and that he couldn't understand a word the servers were saying. She had held her tongue, because his complaint made her aware of how opinionated she'd been before coming to the island.

"I want to buy this house." The notion she had been entertaining for more than a week was finally verbalized.

Lee shifted on the kitchen chair and stared at his wife. "You what?"

"You heard what I said, Lee."

His eyes narrowed. "You want me to spend my

money on this place? It's one step up from shack status. It should be condemned."

Rebecca sat up straighter, her confidence increasing. She had changed—inside and out—since coming to McKinnon Island. She was no longer the Rebecca Leighton-Owens Lee knew, but someone who was aware of who she was and what she wanted for herself and her children.

"If you'd listened, you would've heard me say that *I* want to buy this house. You, of all people, should know that I have my own money." She had been sole beneficiary of her maternal grandparents' life insurance policies. After they'd died, Rebecca had put the money in tax-free municipal bonds.

"But . . . but why would you want to buy property that will eventually be condemned once developers come with cash in hand to longtime residents the way they've done on the other Sea Islands?"

"That's just it, Lee. I don't want this island to look like all of the other Sea Islands."

She told him about volunteering as research assistant to Ezra as he toured and gathered information on McKinnon Island. She stepped out of her role as wife and mother into that of teacher as she told him of a culture unique only to the Sea Island African-American. The passion in her voice matched the deep color in her face. Her hazel eyes glowed with an excitement that hadn't been there since she'd come face-to-face with Lee Owens for the first time during her college freshman year.

"Why can't McKinnon Island become another Williamsburg, Virginia, Lee? Why can't we preserve our culture for future generations?"

"But it's not your culture, Becky. You're nothing

like these people—these Gullahs who are more African than they are American."

"What are we, Lee?"

"Americans."

"Wrong! You're deluding yourself. We *are* African-Americans. As long as we look like we do, we will never be Americans. Not in this country. You and I are only Americans once we leave these shores. Our passports read United States. The world views us as Americans, while America identifies us as African-Americans."

Lee stared at Rebecca as if she were a stranger. She was talking about being African, yet the Massachusetts Leightons claimed more Euro-American blood than the South Carolina Owenses.

"Where are you going with this, Rebecca?" he asked. There was a gentle softness in his voice.

She leaned closer. "I want to preserve the Gullah culture."

"How?"

"By setting up a not-for-profit McKinnon Island historical preservation society, and purchasing abandoned or vacant properties and restoring them. I don't want the Gullah language, basket weaving and quilt making skills to die with this generation like the oyster industry did in the 1950s on Daufuskie Island after industries along the Savannah River polluted many of the marshes and creeks there. The health officials closed most of the valuable oyster beds, so many folks left the island. Of course, the exodus impacted on many of the businesses."

"Which impacted on the island's economy," Lee added. Eyes wide, Rebecca nodded. "What do you want from me?"

Rising, Rebecca moved over and sat on her husband's lap. His arms went around her waist. "I want nothing from you but your support."

He buried his face in her curly hair. He wanted to support her, but he also did not want to lose her. Setting up a preservation foundation and hosting fund-raisers for her cause would take her away from her home and her children.

"If I tell you that I can't give you my support, will you change your mind?"

Easing back, Rebecca stared at him for several seconds before slipping off his lap. She stood over him, her eyes widening until he could see their golden depths. "You can't or you won't?"

He met her direct stare. "I can't. Not now, Rebecca."

She folded her hands on her hips. "When, Lee?"

"Give me time."

"How much time do you want?" she shot back.

Lee stood up, his hands going to her shoulders. "I'll let you know before the end of the summer."

Rebecca's forehead furrowed in a frown. "Why the wait? Why can't you give your answer now?"

His fingers tightened on the cotton T-shirt over her delicate shoulders. "Because I don't want to lose you now," he said softly.

"What do you mean? You're not going to lose me."

He lowered his head. "I am losing you, baby. Every day we spend apart, we grow apart."

"That's not true, and you know it."

Lee stared out over her head, certain Rebecca could hear his heart pounding in his chest, smell his fear. "I don't know why I keep thinking that you're punishing me for cheating on you."

"I've forgiven you. What you have to do is find the strength to forgive yourself. I needed some time away from Charleston to see myself for who I am, and for who I've become. What I found out was that I didn't like myself. I used to be Rebecca Owens, wife to Lee, mother to Ashlee and Kyle."

"What are you now?"

"I'm still Rebecca, wife and mother, but I also have another reason for getting up every morning other than to make breakfast. Growing up in Lowell, I always felt disconnected from black people. Whenever I wanted to see more than fifty black folks at one time, I had to go to Boston. That's why before I graduated high school I decided to apply to historically black colleges.

"I cried the first time I walked into this shack as you call it, because it was nothing like I was used to back in Charleston or even Lowell. But after going out with Ezra and listening to him interview native islanders, people whose African descendants were brought to the Sea Islands to work the rice and cotton plantations to make their European owners fat and wealthy, I felt nothing but shame. All you have to do is take a look at several of the large plantation properties with the tiny outbuildings that made up the slave quarters, and you'll never complain again about not having air-conditioning.

"Now real estate developers are looking at McKinnon as the perfect place for exclusive resorts, private roads, spas, golf courses, tennis courts, and riding stables. All of these things mean two words: big profits. They profited off us four hundred years ago when the first African was brought to these shores, and even though I am not Gullah I will fight and make certain they will not rape our people again. They cannot turn McKinnon Island into another Hilton Head. Daufuskie, as well as Edisto, Wadmalaw and Johns Islands, are the latest to lose to developers. There's a famous Gullah proverb that says: 'If oonuh ent now weh oonuh dah gwine, oonuh should kno weh oonuh come f'um.' "

Lee saw tears in his wife's eyes. "What does it mean?"

"If you don't know where you're going, you should know where you come from."

A muscle quivered at his clean-shaven jaw. "Do you know where you're going, Becky?" His voice was calm, his gaze unwavering.

She blinked once. "Yes, I do, Lee. I know where I'm going with or without you."

He stiffened as if she had struck him, his hands falling away from her body. "I'm going to ask the kids if they want to go back to Charleston with me."

Her heart lurched in her chest, making it difficult for her to breathe. "You can't," she said, once she recovered her voice.

The joy she'd felt when seeing her husband again after a three-week absence dissipated like wisps of moist breath on a frigid day. "Why are you doing this, Lee? Do you resent me so much that you'd try to drive a wedge between me and my children?"

"Why do you keep saying they're your children, Rebecca? When are they ever going to be *our* children?"

Her nostrils flared in fury, and in that instant she hated Lee more than she had when she'd found out that he had been sleeping with another woman. "You low-down, controlling son of a bitch."

Rebecca's angry retort hardened Lee's features. His near-black eyes seemed as flat as his cheekbones. "Have you listened to what you've been saying, Rebecca? You haven't mentioned Ezra Smith's name once, you've mentioned it at least a dozen times. You're not taken with a cause, but with a man."

Turning on his heel, he stalked down the porch and to the beach. Rebecca could not hear what he was saying to Kyle and Ashlee, but whatever it was, they did not agree. They shook their heads at him. They stood close together, watching their father retreat to where he'd left his sport-utility vehicle.

He started up the engine, backed out of the driveway and drove away in the direction of the landing for the ferry. Ashlee and Kyle returned to the porch, their questioning gazes fixed on their mother's face.

Kyle was the first one to break the silence. "Is Dad okay?"

Turning her head slowly, Rebecca stared at him. "I believe he will be."

Ashlee wound her arm through her mother's. "He said he'll be back tomorrow night to pick us up."

"I think he's mad because we didn't want to go back with him," Kyle explained.

Rebecca smiled. "He'll get over it." She pressed her palms together. "We can either spend the rest of the afternoon here, or go into Savannah to do some shopping and sightseeing. It's your call."

"Savannah," Kyle and Ashlee chorused.

Rebecca nodded. "Okay. Tomorrow afternoon my neighbor is having a cookout, and we're invited. There will be kids there who are about your ages for you to hang out with." She smiled. "As soon as you change out of those wet clothes, we'll be off."

She reclaimed her chair on the porch and waited for her son and daughter to change their clothes. She and Lee had disagreed, but this time it did not bother her. There had been a time when she never would have challenged her husband, but that was in the past. Now, all she looked forward to was *her* future—with or without Lee Baxter Owens.

# Twenty-two

*Speak softly; sun going down. Out of sight. Come near me now.*

—Kenneth Patchen

Hope had been up for hours, basting, slicing, dicing, mixing, and sautéing, when the clang of the cowbell joined the slapping sound of a whisk beating egg yolks. She put the whisk aside and went to answer the bell. Rebecca stood on the porch cradling two large foil-covered pans to her chest. Her curly hair was held off her forehead by a headband covered with black grosgrain ribbon. She looked cool in a pale blue, loose-fitting sundress and a pair of matching leather sandals. Her attire and petite figure made her appear a lot younger than her actual years.

Hope opened the door, smiling. "Good morning. Please, come in."

Rebecca walked in and sniffed the air. "Mmm-mmm. Something smells good. What are you cooking?"

"You must smell the sweet potato pies. I just took them out of the oven."

"I made brownies. One pan is double chocolate without nuts, and the other is covered with chopped peanuts, filberts, pecans, walnuts, and macadamia."

Hope walked back to the kitchen, Rebecca following. "I suppose no one is going to count calories today."

"I've stopped monitoring everything I put in my mouth since coming here." Rebecca placed the pans on a countertop next to the sink.

Wagging her net-covered head, Hope sucked her teeth loudly. "It's always the skinny ones who are on a constant diet. Right now I'm hovering around one sixty, and it's the thinnest I've been in years."

"One sixty looks good on you because you're tall. When I was pregnant with Kyle I went from one twelve to one fifty-seven, and I couldn't see my toes or bend over. At five-two I looked like the Michelin man."

Hope went back to whisking eggs for homemade ice cream. "Did your children come down?"

Rebecca sat on a high stool, watching Hope as she poured a portion of hot liquid into the beaten egg mixture before she stirred it back into the saucepan over a double boiler. "Yes, they did. They got up a little while ago. We hung out rather late last night in Savannah."

"They've never been to Savannah?"

"No."

"I'm looking forward to meeting them and your husband."

"Lee isn't coming to eat. He'll be back sometime tonight to pick up Ashlee and Kyle. They're committed to working one more week at the summer day camp." She closed her eyes in an attempt to keep her emotions in check. "I think I fucked up."

Hope lifted her eyebrows at the expletive. She never would have guessed that her very proper, straitlaced neighbor would ever say *that* four-letter word aloud. "What about?" she asked as she strained the thickened mixture into a large bowl.

Rebecca's hands shook slightly as she told Hope about her confrontation with her husband. "I said things to him I didn't mean to say. They just came out because he more or less accused me of being involved with Ezra."

"Are you?" Hope's voice was low and coaxing.

A rush of color darkened Rebecca's cheeks. "Of course not," she replied quickly. "I'm not saying I'm not attracted to him, but I am not involved with him the way you think."

"How do you know what I'm thinking?"

"I don't, Hope. He's a brilliant historian, and he has helped me see things I never would've seen before if I hadn't met him. He's helped me open my eyes to a different kind of world where people don't measure their importance by the make of their cars, bank balances, or the number of carats on their wrists, fingers, or necks."

Hope stared at her neighbor as a chill of silence surrounded them. "Are you certain you don't want to set up a preservation foundation out of guilt? Because you feel sorry for the poor McKinnon Island Gullah who probably will never have one-tenth of what you have unless they sell their land and precious legacy to a greedy developer?

"Do you actually think these people will welcome you with open arms once you drive up to their door in your Mercedes with a Rolex on your wrist, Manolo Blahnik on your feet, and wearing enough bling-bling for a Harry Winston print ad? I may be Dr. Hope to the outside world, but to longtime islanders I'm still Queenie Robinson's grandbaby girl. And that's all I ever want to be here on McKinnon.

"But, on the other hand, I like what you're proposing, Rebecca, and if you want my support, then you have it. I'm certain Janie and Thomas Smith will volunteer to help, because they're committed to preserving Gullah culture. If you need other names, then I'll give them to you."

The tense lines in Rebecca's face relaxed as she breathed in shallow, quick gasps. "You think it will work?"

"Why shouldn't it work? All you have to do is use Williamsburg as your model, and it's guaranteed to work. I believe there are two abandoned plantations that should be purchased before the developers get to them."

"We're going to need money—and a lot of it." The words tumbled from Rebecca's lips.

"How much do you think you're going to need?"

"I don't know."

"I suggest you talk to Janie and Thomas. They should be able to give you an idea of how much it cost them to restore their property."

Pressing her palms together, Rebecca did not want to acknowledge the inevitable. She would have to go back to Lee, apologize, and then ask for his help. After all, he was president of a bank and had direct contact with businesspeople who could possibly invest in a venture to preserve McKinnon Island's Gullah culture.

"I'll ask them, and I will also ask my husband."

Hope measured the vanilla mixture into three bowls, adding honey and pecans to one, and pistachios and dried cherries to the second. She did not add anything to the third, knowing some people preferred their dessert without the fruit or nuts.

"I thought you said your husband refused to support you."

A mysterious smile curved Rebecca's mouth. "Lee is president of a bank, and at this juncture in my life I'm not above seducing my husband to get exactly what I want. And what I want is to set up the McKinnon Island Historical Society before the end of the year."

"Well damn, Sophie Lady, you're something else," Hope drawled, as she gave Rebecca a high five handshake.

Nodding her head, Rebecca smiled. "I won't be the first woman to do it, and I'm certain I won't be the last."

*Hope had showered* and pulled a white, man-tailored shirt over a pair of black capris when the cowbell clanged for the second time that day. Slipping her feet into a pair of mules, she made her way to the door. Theo and his family had arrived. Opening the screen door, she stepped out onto the porch.

"Good afternoon. Welcome. I've planned for us to eat on the beach." Rebecca had helped her carry a long wooden picnic table with two matching benches down to the beach. A tent with a canopy of sailcloth suspended from four poles provided protection from the rays of the sun in an overcast sky. A gas grill sat a few feet away.

Noelle nudged Brandon. "I told you we were eating on the beach."

Helen smiled at Hope. "Do you need my help with anything?"

Hope pulled her gaze away from Theo's seemingly amused one. "I'm going to need some muscle to carry several boxes to the beach." Christian, Brandon and Theo stepped forward.

Helen reached for Noelle's hand. "We'll just sit around and eat while the jocks work." Her quip failed to elicit a smile from Noelle.

Theo took charge when he said, "Chris, unload the SUV and set up everything under the tent. Brandon, you and I will help Miss Hope."

"You didn't have to bring anything," Hope said, staring at Theo.

He lifted a pair of broad shoulders under a white T-shirt. "Don't look at me. It was Helen." The older woman rolled her eyes at Theo before she walked into the house, Noelle and Brandon following her.

Theo took a step, bringing him inches from Hope. "Did you get my e-mail?"

Her gaze lingered on his smiling mouth. "No. When did you send it?"

"This morning."

She blinked. "I didn't check my e-mail this morning."

"Bummer," he said softly. Reaching up, he touched the damp hair grazing her shoulders. "I like your hair when you wear it down." His gaze moved with agonizing slowness from her eyes, to her shoulders, and came to rest on her chest.

"Thank you." The two words were a husky, breathless whisper.

"No, Hope. Thank *you*."

Hope felt a tingling in the pit of her stomach. Theo disturbed and soothed her at the same time. His womanizing reputation kept her at a distance, while he radiated a sensual masculinity she found herself powerless to resist.

"Rebecca and her children will be joining us," she said, deftly directing the topic away from herself.

Theo's smile widened. "Good. The kids can hang out together." His smile was still in place as he followed Hope into the house.

*The five teenagers* eyed one another as Rebecca made the introductions. Christian's expression was impassive, as was Noelle's. Brandon and Ashlee shared a smile, while Kyle appeared totally bored, even though he was being given the opportunity to interact with someone other than his sister.

Hope leaned closer to Theo as they stood at the grill, basting slabs of spareribs and chicken with a spicy barbecue sauce. "Teenagers," she said under her breath.

He grunted under his breath. "They're extraterrestrials."

"They're not quite that bad," she countered, giving him a sidelong glance.

Lowering his head, he pressed his mouth to her ear. "Noelle got her period for the first time yesterday, and all she does is mope."

"Has she complained of cramps?"

"Cramps and a headache."

"Take these." She handed him a pair of tongs. "I'll fix her a tea that should help."

Theo took the tongs, but not before he curved an arm around Hope's shoulders and kissed her forehead. "Thank you."

She smiled up at him. "You're welcome."

*Four hours later,* Noelle sat on the sand with her brothers, Ashlee and Kyle, singing the lyrics to the *Bad Boys II* soundtrack. The teenagers had paired off: Noelle with Kyle, and Ashlee with Brandon. As the eldest, Christian had become the unofficial chaperone for the group.

There had been more than enough food for everyone. Hope had prepared potato salad, barbecued and fried spareribs, barbecued chicken, crab cakes with a black bean sauce, crispy fried popcorn shrimp and catfish fritters, a large pot of turnip and mustard greens, sweet potato pie, and homemade ice cream. Helen's contribution had been a carrot salad with golden raisins and a large bowl of watermelon balls. It had taken three and a half hours to sample every dish set out on the eight-foot-long picnic table. After eating, everyone had decided to wait before sampling dessert. All had pitched in to carry food inside where Hope, Rebecca and Helen had stored the leftovers in the refrigerator. Theo, Christian and Brandon had returned the grill, picnic table and benches to the shed behind the house.

"You cooked too much, Hope," Helen complained as she eased down onto one of three quilts spread out on the sand under the tent.

"I agree," Rebecca moaned, "but it's not her fault

that we ate too much." Following Helen, she, too, stretched out on a quilt, leaving Hope and Theo to take the remaining one.

"Amen to that," added Theo. He glanced over at Noelle. She sang, eyes closed, her lithe body moving to a rocking tempo. He smiled at Hope. "It appears as if your magical brew worked."

"It works for me. I'll give you some to take home for her. Was she prepared for this?"

Theo nodded. "Her mother had prepared her. Noelle told Helen, who in turn told me. I have to admit that it freaked me out. She's only thirteen— two years younger than Mary when she got pregnant with me."

Hope placed her hand over Theo's fisted one. "Don't get crazy about it. In other words, don't smother her the way my brothers did my sister and I. Having older brothers can be a good thing, but it can also be a curse."

"They chased away all of your potential boyfriends?"

"Not me, but my sister's. I didn't date until college."

"What did you do? Spend all of your time studying?"

"No." She stared at the waves washing up on the sand. "Not too many guys wanted to be seen with a big girl. I'm really proud of today's young women who have come to accept their curvaceous bodies. Not focusing on how they look helps them to like who they are."

Theo turned on his side and stared at Hope. "Those guys were fools. I would've dated you."

Hope affected a smile and shook her head. "No

you wouldn't have, Theo. I'm not your type. Every woman you've ever been photographed with could double as a high-fashion model."

Frowning, his jaw hardened. "You don't know me well enough to say what I'd like or not like."

"You're right," she conceded. "In fact, I don't know you at all."

He smiled, and attractive lines fanned out around his eyes. "At last we can agree on something." He glanced at his watch. "What I propose is starting today, June twenty-second, we get to know each other better."

Hope shook her head. "It's not going to work."

"Because you say it won't."

The smoldering flame she saw in his dark eyes startled her. "You want us to sleep together?" Her query was a hushed whisper.

Theo leaned closer. "Only if you want."

Hope felt as if her emotions were under direct attack. Could she sleep with the infamous Theodore Howell, then walk away from him at the end of the summer? Banish him from her mind as if he had been a stranger? The reckless part of her crooned yes, while the voice of reason shouted a resounding no.

"I did not come to McKinnon to sleep with a man."

"Nor did I come here to sleep with a woman."

She smiled. His getting to know her did not necessarily translate into intimacy. That was something she could agree to. "Okay, Theo. We begin today."

Theo held Hope's hand. He hadn't lied to her when he'd said he hadn't come to McKinnon Island to sleep with a woman, but he also hadn't been completely truthful about wanting to sleep with her.

Erotic dreams disturbed his sleep. He fantasized about making love to her in ways that would bring them both pleasure and satisfaction. It was on these mornings that he awoke more tired than he had been before going to bed. It was on these mornings that he went swimming before he began his morning writing ritual. And it was on these mornings that he forced himself not to go to Hope's house, ring the cowbell, and ask if he could come in.

Hope closed her eyes, enjoying the comforting protection of her hand in Theo's. The gesture was tender and possessive. A peace she had never experienced swept over her. She felt good, and at that moment all was right in her world.

Helen and Rebecca had fallen asleep where they lay, while the younger Andersons and Owens interacted with each other as if they had known each other for years instead of hours. Rebecca's son and daughter were tall and gangly with delicate features, dark eyes, and curly black hair. There was no doubt they looked like their father.

Christian left the group and came over to where Theo lay with Hope. "Theo, is it all right if we go into town for a little while?"

Theo glanced at the watch strapped to his wrist. It was after six. "Did you ask Miss Rebecca?"

"Yes, I did. She said it was okay."

Theo gave him a narrowed stare. "Where are you going?"

"Not far."

"How far is not far?"

"I want to show them the old Sullivan plantation and a few other spooky places."

Theo wagged his forefinger. "Drive carefully, Chris.

Stay in the vehicle. I don't want you guys wandering around in the dark, or get bitten by something." He slipped the small phone off his waistband and handed it to his brother. "Don't conveniently turn it off, mister."

"I won't." Christian raced back to the beach. Seconds later, all of the teenagers scrambled off the sand and raced to the Lexus. The four adults on the beach watched the sport-utility vehicle as it headed toward town.

"You're doing quite well in the daddy role," Hope said softly to Theo.

He lifted his eyebrows. "What would you give me on the daddy scale of one to ten?"

"At least a high seven or low eight."

"That high?"

She nodded. "Yes."

"Are you interviewing for the position?" he asked, remembering her telling him she could alleviate her medical condition if she had a child.

Her jaw dropped slightly before she recovered enough to ask, "Why? Are you applying for the position?"

A silence swelled between them, like a thick fog hugging the shoreline. Theo had changed since coming to McKinnon Island. In Los Angeles he had always been on guard, measuring every word lest he be misquoted. But now he had figuratively put his foot in his mouth.

"Maybe yes, maybe no," he crooned.

A flash of humor crossed Hope's face, and she pushed to her feet. "I'm going for a walk."

Theo waited several seconds, stood up, and then joined her. He reached for her hand as they walked slowly, leaving impressions of their bare feet on the wet sand before the incoming tide washed them away. A rising wind had swept away the clouds, leaving the sky a deep indigo blue with a strangely colored orange-red sun.

"This place is like a Garden of Eden." There was no mistaking the awe in Theo's voice. "Clean air, unpolluted water, and no traffic jams."

Hope glanced at his distinctive profile. A hint of a beard shadowed his jaw. "Travel brochures say it's remote, primitive, and unspoiled. That translates into a virtual paradise."

"Brandon and Noelle have been hounding me to buy a place here."

"They like it that much?"

"Yes. The day we came I was prepared for constant bitching and moaning, but they surprised me. I think they like not having a curfew. They stay up as late as they want, sleep as late as they want, and spend most of their time hanging out on the beach."

What, she thought, was it about McKinnon Island that made newcomers consider settling here? "Are you thinking of building a house?"

He shook his head. "No. I'd rather buy an old place and fix it up. I prefer living in a house with a porch or veranda. There's something to be said for sitting on a porch at the end of the day, watching the sun set."

"That's what the old folk here do."

"I suppose the Gullah in me surfaces every now and then."

Theo spied something on the sand ahead of them. He stopped, bent over, and nudged a small sea turtle. It moved, wobbly, before it swam with the outgoing tide.

They walked along the beach to the property line where Theo and his family were spending the summer, then turned and retraced their steps. The sun had dipped lower in the sky, leaving feathery streaks of fiery red across a deep blue canvas.

Without warning, Theo stopped and cradled Hope's face between his palms. His warm, moist breath swept over her mouth before he covered her mouth with his. She pressed closer, inhaling his clean scent mingling with cologne.

The feel of Theo's firm mouth pressed to hers, the solid crush of his chest against her breasts melted her resistance and tore down the shield she had erected with Kendall's duplicity. She returned his kiss, parting her lips to his probing tongue. She had asked him what he wanted, and he'd said anything and everything she was willing to give him. The instant their tongues met and dueled, she was willing to lie with Theo and offer him the passion roaring through her like a twister touching down and sweeping up everything in its path. She would give him her passion, but not her heart.

Pushing against his shoulder, she ended the kiss. She was breathing as if she had run a long, grueling race. "Why did you do that?"

He stared at her under lowered lids. "If you'd read your e-mail, then you'd know why."

"I'll be certain to read it once I get back to the house."

"Good."

Hand in hand they continued their walk as if the kiss had not happened. They returned to the house to find that Rebecca and Helen had dismantled the tent, folded the blankets and retreated to the porch.

Helen sat in the rocking chair and rocked in a slow, measured motion. "How was your walk?" A knowing smile curved her mouth when she saw Theo cradling Hope's hand.

"Good," Hope and Theo chorused.

Theo saw the Lexus parked behind Hope's car. "Where are the kids?"

"Inside eating dessert," Rebecca said from her reclining position on the chaise. "All I can say is that they must have bottomless pits masquerading as stomachs. Did you see how much they ate?" Helen and Theo exchanged knowing looks. They were quite familiar with feeding three ravenous adolescents.

The sound of an engine caught Rebecca's attention. She sat up. Lee was back. Waving her hand, she caught his attention. "Lee, over here."

Lee Owens walked over to the neighboring house ablaze with bright lights. He had driven from Charleston to Savannah in record time and picked up the ferryboat minutes before it was scheduled to leave the landing.

Hope stared at the man walking up the porch steps. There was no doubt he was Rebecca's counterpart. Although simply dressed, the cut of his clothes was exquisite. A pair of double-pleated tobacco-brown linen gabardine slacks fell at the proper break above a pair of imported leather slip-ons. The left cuff of his long-sleeved shirt claimed an embroidered initial monogram. Although he hadn't worn a jacket or tie, he still appeared what he was—a wealthy man.

Rebecca moved off the chaise and stood next to her husband. The top of her head reached his shoulder. She slipped her hand in his. "Lee, I'd like to introduce you to my friends. Theodore Howell, Helen

Bryant, and Hope Sutton. Theo's brothers and sister are in the house with Ashlee and Kyle. Theo, Helen, Hope, this is Lee Owens, my husband."

Everyone took turns shaking hands. Waiting until introductions were concluded, Hope smiled at Lee. "May I offer you something to eat or drink?"

His expression was solemn. "No, thank you. Perhaps the next time I come. I hadn't planned on staying."

Rebecca successfully concealed her disappointment behind a forced smile. "I'll get the kids."

There was an uncomfortable silence after Rebecca went inside to inform her children that their father was waiting for them. Several minutes later the screen door opened, and Ashlee, Kyle, Brandon, Noelle, Christian, and Rebecca crowded out onto the porch.

Ashlee kissed her father's cheek as he curved an arm around her waist. "Daddy, can we please, please, *please* come back after we finish with camp?"

Lee stared at his daughter's hopeful look. "I'll let you know after your mother and I talk."

"What's there to talk about, Daddy?"

"Ashlee." Rebecca's voice, though soft, was firm.

Pushing out her lower lip, Ashlee stomped off the porch, walking quickly toward her father's SUV. Seconds later, Kyle stomped after her.

Rebecca forced a smile she did not feel. "Thank you, Hope, for everything." She hugged her. She waved to the others. "Good night." A chorus of good nights followed her.

A war of emotions raged within her. She had never known Lee to be so rude. Waiting until she was out of earshot of the people on Hope's porch, she turned and faced her husband.

"Don't you ever do that again!"

"Do what?"

"Be rude to my friends."

He stared down his nose at her. "Friends, Rebecca?"

"Yes, friends."

"You haven't been here a month, and already you're calling them friends."

Rebecca's hands curled into tight fists, and she put them behind her back to keep from slapping him. "Take my children home. Then I want you to bring them back Friday. I'll call my mother and have her pack enough clothes to last them until I bring them back before school starts." Turning her back on Lee, she walked over to the SUV and hugged and kissed Ashlee. "I'll see you Friday, baby." She repeated the motion with Kyle. "Stay well until I see you again."

Kyle tightened his grip on his mother's waist and glared at his father over her head. "See you soon, Mom."

Lee cursed to himself. He had made the second most grievous mistake of his life since marrying Rebecca. The first one had been to cheat on her, and the second one was to insult her in front of their children. There was no mistaking the hostility in his son's eyes. Lee feared he was losing his wife. Rebecca's divorcing him was not an option. That was something he refused to entertain.

He moved closer to Rebecca as Kyle and Ashlee got into the truck, slamming the doors harder than necessary. "I'll call you." She nodded. "I'll bring them back Friday." Rebecca nodded again. Then she turned on her heel, walked to the porch, opened the front door and closed it softly behind her.

Lee closed his eyes and drew in a deep breath before he let it out in an audible sigh. He had to right the wrongs. Somehow he had to save his marriage. He opened his eyes, rounded the BMW and slipped behind the wheel.

He glanced up in the rearview mirror at his son and daughter. They sat motionless, sulking, arms folded over their chests. "I want you to help your grandmother pack what you'll need for the next four weeks."

Ashlee and Kyle looked at each other and smiled.

# Twenty-three

*Your air inhaling what you exhale I'd like to be that.*
                                          —James Laughlin

Lee's arrival signaled the end of what had become a relaxed and festive gathering. New friendships had been forged between Ashlee and Kyle and the Anderson children; the outing had also changed Hope, because she had decided it was useless to fight her growing feelings for Theo.

She stood on the porch watching and waving as he backed out of the driveway. Helen lowered her window and returned her wave. The red taillights disappeared, and Hope backpedaled to the rocker, falling onto its cushioned softness. Exhaustion descended on her like a comforting blanket, and, closing her eyes, she fell asleep.

*The soft patter* of a rain shower washing the earth with its cooling, clean scent woke Hope. She peered at the dark sky, unable to discern whether it was day or night. She pushed off the rocker, went into the house, undressed, lay across her bed and went back to sleep.

*Hope woke up* totally disoriented but rested. Forcing herself to leave the bed, she walked to the bathroom to shower and brush her teeth.

The lukewarm water revived her, and as she moisturized her body and pulled on an oversized T-shirt and shorts her travel clock chimed the hour. It was already one in the afternoon. Fortifying herself with a cup of tea and a bowl of sliced peaches, watermelon, and green grapes, she settled down in the office/bedroom to read her e-mail. As soon as she signed on she remembered that she hadn't read Theo's e-mail. She perused her new mail: one from Lana, two from Marissa, one from Bill, and two from Theo.

She read Lana's first:

> *Jonathan and I decided we're going to try to have a baby. I know you think we're crazy to have changed our minds, but after talking to you about your endometriosis I decided to take the same advice I gave you. We been screwing like rabbits. All I can say is baby-making is big fun!*

"All I can say is that you're crazy, girlfriend," she said as she reread her friend's message.

Hope then clicked on the first of her sister's messages:

> *Big Sis, I had the worst fight with Trey when my acceptance letter from Fairleigh Dickinson arrived the other day. The man went buck wild! If he'd*

been smoking that crack sh—t, then I could've understood his reaction, but you know he won't touch drugs. So, I let him rave and rant about his ability to take care of his family until I got sick and tired of him beating his gums, then I leaned in real close and told him I was going to take my kids and stay with Mama and Daddy until he learned to respect my decisions. I called Junior and had him pick me up with the twins. When Trey saw Junior he knew he was going to get a serious beat-down if he said another word. He just stood there looking crushed and pitiful. The twins took drama to another level when they held onto Trey's legs, screaming that they wanted to stay with their daddy. Of course the neighbors came out of their homes to see what was going on, so I had to put a cussin' on them, too. Miss Ruby sucked her teeth so hard that her dentures slipped out and fell in the bushes. Junior and the twins laughed so hard they couldn't stand up. Even Trey was laughing. However, that did not change anything, because I'm now at Mama's. If you need to contact me in an emergency, then call me on my cell. Hugs, Lil Sis

Hope clicked on Marissa's second message:

I didn't know that Mama and Daddy had planned to spend a few days in Atlantic City before heading down to Cape May for a week. I will be here at least until they return. Trey came by and tried to talk me into coming back home. I wouldn't even open the door. Once the clown realizes I'm serious about going back to school, then we'll talk. Smooches, Lil Sis

Hope shook her head. Marissa and Trey had more drama in their lives than a daytime soap opera. She would call her sister later that evening.

She clicked on Bill's message:

> *Printed out your chapter introductions. Love what you've done with them. Let me know your tentative completion date. Would like to project a late spring publication. Hope you are enjoying yourself. Bill*

Theo's was next:

> *Your air inhaling what you exhale I'd like to be that.*
> —*James Laughlin.*

Her smile was dazzling. That was why he'd kissed her on the beach.

She clicked again:

> *I lie here thinking of you.*
> —*William Carlos Williams*

Hope swallowed the lump that formed in her throat. It was taking only two lines of poetry to strip away the last barrier she had erected to keep a man out of her life.

She returned his e-mails with the only line of poetry she could remember:

> *A sad sort of rain today, and I inside alone.*
> —*Margaret Newlin*

The next ten minutes were spent typing replies to Lana and Bill. She typed three words to Marissa:

*I'll call you.*

Before she signed off, an instant message appeared on the upper-left-hand screen. It was from Theo:

> *Flickwriter: One day I wrote her name upon the strand, but came the waves and washed it away.*
> —Edmund Spenser

Hope stared at what he'd typed. Was he reminding her of the day when he would leave McKinnon to return to California? Her fingers were poised on the keys.

> *HelpDoc: We must enjoy what we have now before the end of the summer.*
> *Flickwriter: What do we have now, Hope?*
> *HelpDoc: Friendship.*
> *Flickwriter: Friendship is ok. But . . .*
> *HelpDoc: You want more than friendship?*
> *Flickwriter:* ☺

She smiled.

> *HelpDoc: What do you want?*
> *Flickwriter: I'd have to show you.*
> *HelpDoc: Will I like it?*
> *Flickwriter: I'm hoping you will. I know I will like it.*
> *HelpDoc: Show me, Theo.*
> *Flickwriter: I'll see you around six. Bye.*
> *HelpDoc: Bye.*

She logged off and closed her eyes. When she opened them, she knew she was ready. Ready for

Theo and what each would offer the other before summer's end.

*The cowbell clanged,* bringing Hope to the door. Theo stood on the other side of the screen door, grasping the handles to a picnic basket in his left hand. Instead of his customary white, he wore a long-sleeved navy blue T-shirt with a pair of jeans and running shoes. His clean-shaven jaw and close-cut hair indicated he had recently visited a barber.

Turning the latch, she opened the door. "Please come in."

Theo shook his head. "No. Please come out. We're going to picnic out here."

"But . . . it's raining."

His eyes crinkled in a smile. "It's been raining all day. We will picnic on your porch."

A steady falling rain, one hundred percent humidity, and a haze had blanketed McKinnon Island. It was on days like this that everyone and everything appeared to move in slow motion.

"Let me put on shoes and I'll be right back." She returned to her bedroom and slipped her bare feet into a pair of black ballet-type slippers. She'd dressed for the damp weather: a loose-fitting, off-white cotton sweater over a pair of black leggings.

She returned to the porch to find Theo setting the small bistro table, reminiscent of those found in ice cream parlors, with china, silver, and stemware. "Would you like help?"

He glanced up. "No, thank you. Just sit down and relax."

She sat on one of the two chairs at the table, watching him empty the basket. Small containers labeled with their contents crowded every available space. She smiled when he set out two votive candles and lit them.

"A little ambience," he said in a quiet voice.

What Theo did not know was that he was all the ambience Hope needed. There was something about him that was calming and soothing. With him she did not have to pretend she was other than who she was. She wondered whether those he interacted with in California saw the same Theo Howell she had come to know on McKinnon Island, South Carolina, or an entirely different person who had learned to play the Tinseltown game so well that he was able to hide his true self.

She smiled up at him. "Would you mind if I add to the ambience?"

The light from the flickering candles flattered his dark, sun-browned face. "Not at all."

Rising, she went over to the radio sitting atop the table between the rocker and chaise, and turned it on. The sound of light music filled the air. Theo went completely still as she closed the distance between them, his gaze following her every motion.

"Nice," he whispered close to her ear. Curving an arm around her waist, he pulled out a chair and seated her.

Hope mumbled a soft thank you and smiled. She wasn't disappointed when he returned it with a sensual one of his own. He sat opposite her, opening the lids to containers filled with shrimp and pasta salad, guacamole and tortilla chips, cole slaw, deviled eggs with capers, and a bottle of chilled champagne.

"Very nice."

He inclined his head. "Thank you." He deftly

popped the cork on the bottle of champagne, filled the glasses, then handed her one.

Hope raised her flute. "To McKinnon Island."

Theo shook his head. "No, Hope. We toasted McKinnon already. This one is to us."

She touched her flute to his. "To us," she repeated before taking a small sip. The champagne was excellent. "Very nice."

He lifted an eyebrow. "I'm glad you approve."

Her expression changed, becoming sober. "Did you do all this," she waved her hand over the table, "to get my approval?"

Theo lowered his glass and glared at her. "No. Why must you analyze everything? Can't you just accept things for what they are?"

Hope gave him a long, penetrating look, then nodded. "You're right, Theo. There are times when I don't know how to separate Hope from Dr. Hope."

"Shouldn't it be easier for you here than in New York?"

"It should, but sometimes it isn't."

"Why?"

Hope stared down at her plate with unseeing eyes. "Because when I'm Dr. Hope I have all the answers. But as Hope . . ." Her words trailed off.

Theo reached across the table and cradled her left hand in his larger one. "What about Hope?"

Her head came up. "Hope is no different from those who write to Dr. Hope for answers. My personal life is as, or more, screwed up than theirs." Her gold-brown gaze was steady. "For three years I dated a man, who proposed marriage a couple of months ago. I went to his place to tell him that I'd marry him, but found him in a compromising position with another man. I can't believe I never saw it coming. In other words, I was completely clueless."

She found it odd that Theo's expression didn't change with her disclosure.

He tightened his grip on her fingers. "I hope you aren't blaming yourself because he's a switch-hitter."

"There are times when it's hard not to."

"Your ex-boyfriend's penchant for sleeping with both sexes has nothing to do with your inability to satisfy him sexually."

Her gaze narrowed. "How would you know?"

Theo angled his head. "I've taken actresses to parties who *only* prefer women, but they don't want their adoring public to know this because it would limit them. Therefore, their secret had become our secret. Coming out of the closet is very risky in Hollyweird."

Hope laughed, her dark mood lifting. "Is that what it is, Theo? Hollyweird?"

He nodded. "You don't want to know just how weird it can be. I've seen things that would make Caligula blush."

"Damn-n-n," she drawled, shaking her head. "It's weird, yet you won't leave it."

"Wrong, Hope. I left it six months ago when I assumed guardianship of my brothers and sister."

"Don't you miss the glitter?"

Theo released Hope's fingers. Leaning back in his chair, he gave her a direct stare. "Hell, no."

She smiled at his response. "You've left Hollywood. Where do you go now?"

"I told you the kids want to live here."

"There hasn't been a high school on McKinnon

in more than twenty years, which means they'll have to go to Hilton Head Island."

"I could always have them home-schooled."

"What about football games, senior proms? You wouldn't want them to miss out on that."

"You're right." He picked up his glass and gave her a tender smile. "May I repeat the toast?" Not waiting for an answer, he said, "To us."

Reaching for her glass, Hope smiled. "To us," she repeated.

Sitting on the porch, staring out at a curtain of rain in the soft glow of candlelight was mysterious and romantic. Hope sampled the portions Theo had purchased from a Savannah gourmet shop. They were as pleasing to the eye as they were to the palate. She offset the spiciness of the guacamole with two glasses of champagne. The wine made her feel loose and uninhibited. Now she knew how Rebecca felt the night they talked well into the morning hours.

Without warning, Theo pushed back his chair and came around the table. He eased her to her feet, his arm around her waist. "May I have this dance?"

She tilted her chin and smiled. "Yes, you may."

Hope closed her eyes and sank into the comforting hardness of his chest. She felt the strong, steady pumping of his heart against her breasts. All of her senses were operating on high alert: smell, touch, sight and hearing. The only thing missing was taste. Her arms moved up and curved around his neck, bringing his head lower. Boldly, confidently, she touched her mouth to his. He tasted of champagne.

"Nice," she moaned softly. Theo deepened the

kiss, slanting his mouth over hers and sending spirals of desire through the lower portion of her body.

Theo's probing tongue parted her lips. It was his turn to groan. "Nicer," he murmured in the moist sweetness. He inhaled the scent that was exclusive to Hope, a scent that lingered on his clothes and skin long after they parted, a scent that sent currents of desire through him whenever he lay in bed.

It wasn't until he'd met Hope that he had come to the realization that he hadn't slept with a woman for more than six months. He'd tired of sharing his time with women who were for the moment. Perhaps turning forty had changed him in more ways than just celebrating a milestone birthday, or becoming a temporary father.

Hope ended the kiss and pressed her nose against the column of Theo's strong neck. She had to stop before she wouldn't be able to stop. A soft gasp escaped her as he swung her around and around in an intricate dance step. The song ended and they stumbled dizzily toward the chaise, falling heavily onto it, Hope atop him.

She went completely still. There was no mistaking the hardness pressing against her middle. The twin lamps flanking the front door provided enough illumination for her to see his expression. His steady gaze bore into her with a silent expectation that eliminated the need for speech. His gaze moved from her eyes, to her throat, and even lower to where her breasts were flattened against his chest.

Hope's body throbbed with a need she had not thought possible. The throbbing between her legs quickly became an ache that had to be assuaged. "Show me, Theo." Her voice was barely a whisper.

Tightening his grip around her waist, Theo shifted Hope until she straddled his thighs. He moved up against her, permitting her to feel what he was feeling—a runaway desire threatening to explode. He cupped her hips and pulled her closer.

"Hope," he whispered in her ear, rotating his hips until she felt the distinct outline of his erection.

Her reaction was so swift that she couldn't stop the rush of moisture bathing the folds between her thighs. She followed his lead, squirming and wiggling on his lap. She quickened her rocking motion as waves of desire swept over her, clouding her mind and body. Her heart hammered against her ribs as the hot ache between her legs erupted in a fireball of throbbing ecstasy that left her struggling for each gulp of precious breath.

She still had not recovered when Theo stood up and carried her into the house. Her trembling hands reached out for him as he lowered her to her bed. He stepped back and pulled his T-shirt over his head. His upper body stood out in stark relief in the glow of the lamp on the bedside table. He was broad shouldered with long arms, a flat belly and narrow hips. He had a swimmer's body.

Theo never took his gaze off Hope as he removed a condom from the pocket of his jeans before he pushed them down around his hips. He wanted to see her reaction to his naked body—see how much he wanted her, and had desired her from the first time he saw her.

Hope could not look away from his erection. Just seeing him aroused increased her desire for him.

"Relax, baby," he crooned, his hands sliding under her sweater. They feathered over her belly, up her rib cage, and over the silk fabric covering her breasts. The mere touch of his fingers on her bare skin made her arch off the mattress. Supporting his weight on an elbow, he brushed a kiss over her parted lips. "It's going to be good—for both of us."

She closed her eyes and let all of her senses take over. It was only when she heard his breathing falter after he'd removed her bra that she opened her eyes to see an expression of awe on his face.

Lowering his head, Theo placed small, nibbling kisses over her full breasts. His tongue circled the areola before his teeth closed over one nipple then the other. He undressed her slowly, deliberately, tasting every inch of flesh he bared.

His tongue traced a path from her belly to the moist curls. His fingers searched and found the distended, blood-engorged nub at the apex of her thighs, and then his mouth replaced his finger, worrying the flesh with his teeth. She screamed and arched her back, her breasts trembling violently above her rib cage.

"Please. Oh, please," she pleaded over and over as jolts of ecstasy shook her like a fragile leaf in the wind. "Don't tease me."

He moved up her body and kissed her. With one hand sandwiched between her thighs, he reached for the condom on the pillow beside her head. "I should tease you, because you've teased me from the first time I laid eyes on you." Smiling, he kissed her again.

He let go of her moist heat because he needed two hands to put on the condom. He slipped on the latex sheath, remembering her desire to have a child. He knew he wasn't ready for fatherhood: he did not want history to repeat itself. His greatest fear was to father a child and have that child grow up without him in his or her life.

Slowly his hands skimmed the sides of her body to her thighs. Resting his hands on her thighs, he spread them wider. He reached up and took Hope's right hand, guiding it to his penis.

He saw her staring up at him. "Let's do this together."

Hope's fingers closed around him, and she closed her eyes. She welcomed him into her body, sighing in pleasure. Theo began moving in a measured rhythm that made her gasp in sweet agony. His love-making was slow, unhurried, and she responded in kind.

She felt her defenses weakening as she opened not only her body for his possession but also her heart. A profound feeling of peace carried her to a place where she'd never been. The heat of his body coursed down the entire length of hers and curled her toes. Her skin grew hotter and hotter until her breath came in long, surrendering moans.

The passion radiating from the core of Hope's body pulled Theo into a vortex of whirling passion that hurtled him to a dimension that was both excit-ing and frightening. What, he thought, was there about her that made him forget all of the promises he'd ever made to himself? His claiming her body had become a raw act of possession. She had become his.

Their passions peaked simultaneously in a shud-dering explosion that left them shaking uncontrol-lably. Afterward, they lay together, savoring the aftermath of their lovemaking. Theo withdrew, gathered her to his chest, and held her until their respiration resumed a normal rate.

Hope savored the feeling of satisfaction that made it virtually impossible for her to move. She was awed not only by the magnitude of her own desire but also by the passion Theo had aroused in her. She wanted to kiss and taste his body like he'd done to hers. A smile softened her lips. Next time, she mused, as she closed her eyes.

*She woke with a start.* "It's okay, sweetheart," said Theo close to her ear. She was in bed, but the room was dark. "I just put everything away and locked the door."

"Aren't you going home?"

"Not unless you tell me to."

Hope reached out for him, her hand grazing his thigh. "Not tonight," she said, laughing softly. Her fingers closed around his flaccid penis. She slid down his body, lowered her head and took him into her mouth. He hardened, his breath coming quickly.

"No!" he gasped. But it was too late for protests as her mouth worked its magic.

It was later, after he had ejaculated inside her, that the enormity of what he had done swept over Theo. "I'm sorry, I'm sorry," he said over and over.

Hope savored the weight of the body pressing her down to the mattress. "Sorry for what?"

"I didn't use a rubber. It's . . . it's the first time that—" Her fingertips stopped his explanation.

"You can't get me pregnant."

He grasped her wrist, pulling her hand down as he tried to make out her expression in the darkened room. "Why?"

"I'm on the Pill."

Theo let out an audible sigh and reversed their positions. His fingers feathered up and down her spine. He kissed her mussed hair and smiled.

"Go back to sleep," he said softly.

She kissed his chin. "Good night."

"Good night, sweetheart."

# Twenty-four

*We are born to live in peace and freedom, giving and receiving, loving and being loved.*

—Iyanla Vanzant

 *"Don't get up."*

Hope noticed slivers of light coming through the curtains of the bedroom windows. "What time is it?"

"Almost five," Theo whispered. "I'm leaving." He kissed her forehead. "Will you come for dinner tonight?"

She nodded. "What time?"

"Six."

"Okay."

He kissed her again. "I'll see you later."

He was there, then he was gone. Hope turned over on her side and rested her head on an outstretched arm. Her mind burned with the memory of what she and Theo had offered each other.

The second time they had come together their lovemaking had been passionate, unrestrained, and totally uninhibited. This coupling had stripped away her insecurities, allowing her to give and receive love on equal terms. She rolled over and turned on the bedside lamp. After completing her morning toilette, she would write for several hours, call Marissa, then go to Savannah for a scheduled day of beauty. She had made the appointment because she was grossly overdue for a facial, manicure, pedicure, touch-up and a trim.

*Hope waved* to Brandon and Noelle as she maneuvered her car into a space next to the Lexus. She turned off the engine and reached for the large white box on the passenger seat. Brandon wasn't wearing his glasses, and his resemblance to Theo was uncanny. Instead of their usual shorts, T-shirts, and bare feet, he and his sister had on clothes that would be more appropriate for school. It was the first time she had seen them wear footwear other than sandals or running shoes.

"Hi, Miss Hope."

She handed him the box. "Hello, Brandon. Here's a little something for dessert."

Noelle moved closer and touched her hair. "Your hair looks beautiful."

She smiled. "Thank you."

The stylist had relaxed her new growth and cut her ends before blowing it out and bumping the ends. Each time Hope moved her head, layers of coal-black hair rippled as if they had taken on a life of their own.

Noelle slipped her hand in Hope's. "Come inside. Theo has a surprise for you."

Brandon glared at his sister. "Big mouth. You weren't supposed to say anything."

"My bad," Noelle said, wincing.

Hope squeezed her fingers gently. "I promise to act surprised." She followed them into the house, wondering what the surprise could be. As soon as she saw Helen, Christian and Theo, she knew they would not dine at home.

"Miss Hope brought dessert," Brandon announced loudly. He gave the box to Helen.

"I'll put it in the refrigerator for another time."

Hope stared at Theo staring back at her. He wore a pair of oatmeal-colored slacks with a matching jacket over a black silk T-shirt. "Where are we going?"

He gave her a mysterious smile. "It's a surprise." Closing the distance between them, he kissed her cheek. "You look very nice."

Noelle nodded. "Isn't her hair the bomb, Theo? Maybe when I take my braids out I'll have it styled like Miss Hope's."

"We'll talk about it." He turned to Christian. "You're the designated driver tonight."

"Woo-woo," Christian said, grinning. "Somebody plans to get lit up tonight."

Theo looked at him under lowered lids. "Let's go, mister."

After everyone was settled in the SUV, Christian backed out of the driveway and drove toward the ferryboat landing. Helen sat beside him, while Hope and Theo flanked Noelle in the rear seat. Brandon sat in the cargo area for the short ride. The ferryboat was waiting when they arrived, and at exactly 6:55 it sailed.

A light breeze lifted Hope's black-and-white striped silk dress around her legs as she stood at the rail with Theo, feeling the heat of his gaze on her face. The rain had stopped and the sultry heat had returned.

"What are you celebrating?" she asked in a quiet voice.

"My pilot was accepted, and network executives want a total of thirteen scripts."

Turning, she smiled at him. "That's wonderful news. Congratulations."

His smile was modest. "Thank you."

She turned back to stare at the water. "You never told me what it's about." Theo would have told her if not for the stranger taking their photograph.

Theo rested his arms on the railing. "It's a dramatic series about a group of highly successful businesspeople who become targets of a government investigation after one is deliberately set up by a rival group. It opens with him being charged with bribing an elected official to approve a construction contract."

"Are the lead characters black?"

"Yes." There was a hint of pride in his voice.

"Why cable and not regular network television?"

"Some of the episodes are a little too graphic for regular programming."

Hope glanced at his profile. "Language?"

He glanced down at her. "Language, sexual content, and occasionally violence."

"When is it scheduled to debut?"

"Next February."

She nodded. "I'll be certain to watch it."

Noelle joined them at the rail, and Hope curved an arm around her shoulders. She was rewarded with a warm smile as Noelle returned the hug. The ferryboat reached Savannah and they traded one boat for another, boarding one of the old-fashioned river-boats for dinner on the Savannah River.

Theo ordered two bottles of sparkling cider, and everyone raised their glasses several times in congratulatory toasts. Live music from a combo added to the festivities. Brandon and Christian sang along with some of the songs, adding their own hip-hop base-line beats.

Hope laughed at their antics, which seemed to amuse Helen. "It's apparent you don't have a lot of experience with teenagers."

"I don't. My sister's and brothers' children haven't reached that age."

Helen crossed her chest. "I pray for them." She smiled at her employer. "Theo has no idea how many novenas I've said for him."

He winked at his housekeeper. "The power of prayer is amazing."

"Miss Helen, are you going to miss Chris and me when we leave for college?"

Her blue eyes misted. "Of course I will, Brandon."

"Don't rush it, Little Brother," Theo warned, smiling. "You guys still have another year."

"That's true," Christian added, "but it will come fast."

"Have you selected a college, Chris?" Hope asked.

Chris glanced at Theo. "That depends on where we live. If we move here, then I'll probably apply to schools in North Carolina or Georgia. I'm kind of partial to Duke."

Hope looked at Brandon. "What about you?"

"I'd probably apply to the University of Virginia or Georgetown because of their political science programs."

"Why don't you both go to the same college?" Noelle asked.

Theo touched Noelle's braided hair. "I told them it would be all right if they decided not to go to the same college."

He had suggested it more for Christian than for Brandon. It was apparent that Brandon was intellectually gifted, and despite being a year younger than Christian, he still achieved higher grades. Attending different colleges would eliminate what had become an inconspicuous competition between brothers.

The musicians played a slow number from the early sixties, and Theo extended his hand to Helen. "May I have this dance?"

She blushed to the roots of her silver hair. "Oh, Theo."

Christian touched her shoulder. "It's your kind of music, Miss Helen."

She rolled her eyes at him. "What would you know about my kind of music?"

Theo stood up and pulled back her chair. Everyone clapped as he led her out to the dance floor. Brandon rose to his feet, offering his hand to Hope. "Miss Hope, may I have this dance?"

She gave him a perplexed look. "But it's not my kind of music."

"Neither is it mine," Brandon countered, refusing to be denied.

Hope pushed back her chair and took his hand. "I do like a persistent man."

Noelle and Christian touched fists after their

brothers exchanged partners, Brandon and Miss Helen dancing with at least three feet of space between them, while Theo held Hope so close they could have been one.

The celebrating continued when the riverboat docked and Theo suggested they go to a restaurant known for their ice cream concoctions. Conversation was nonexistent as the amount of ice cream decreased and waistlines increased. Theo patted his belly and smothered a yawn. He smiled at Christian. "Now you see why you're the designated driver."

Christian flashed a brilliant, white-tooth smile. "Everyone knows old folks have to take a nap after they eat."

Theo bit back a smile. "I thought I warned you about old folk jokes. I'm going to be the first to give you back your words once you're forty with a wife and a couple of knuckleheaded kids giving you grief when they break curfew, rear-end the car, and invite all of the neighborhood thugs to hang out at your house the minute you darken the door."

Shaking his head, Christian said, "You're forty, and you don't have a wife or kids, so what you say won't matter."

Theo's expression was a mask of stone. "I don't need kids. I have you guys."

"We're not your kids, Theo." Brandon had decided to contribute to the conversation.

"You're our brother," Noelle added.

Christian folded his arms over his chest. "You need your own kids." He stared at Hope. "Shouldn't he have his own children?"

Shaking her head, she held up a hand. "Please,

don't drag me into this. Theo has the right to decide whether he chooses to become a father."

Noelle tugged on Hope's arm. "What about you, Miss Hope? Don't you want a baby? If you and Theo got married and had a baby, then I'd be an aunt. You can always count on me to babysit for you."

Theo hit the table with the palm of his hand. "Night court is adjourned. All rise."

Christian and Brandon exchanged a knowing smile. It was apparent they had gotten to their older brother. It was just a matter of time before they would wear him down completely. They'd had years of practice with Mary Anderson.

Helen fell asleep before the ferryboat sailed away from the Savannah landing, Noelle a few minutes later. Brandon and Christian stood at the rail, pointing out constellations in the night sky.

Theo cradled his sister's head to his chest, while his free arm curved around Hope's shoulder. "I'd like to apologize for Chris and Brandon's meddling." His mouth was pressed to her ear.

"There's nothing to apologize for," she whispered. "They're just looking out for you."

"Their not-so-subtle attempt at matchmaking doesn't bother you?"

"No, Theo. They're just kids."

"Kids on a mission."

She grasped the long fingers hanging over her shoulder, squeezing them gently. "In a couple of months they'll be back in school, and then you'll be off the hot seat."

*A couple of months,* Theo mused. Everything and everyone would change by summer's end. He hoped to complete at least script number five, and although he wanted to purchase property on McKinnon Island, he knew realistically he would not be able to finalize a closing before returning to Los Angeles.

In a couple of months Hope would close up her summer home and return to New York and whatever awaited her there. He closed his eyes as a foreign emotion swept over him. Sleeping with her had changed him; in the past it had been he who had always walked away from a woman. The tables were reversed now, though, for he did not want to acknowledge what had become so apparent. He had fallen in love with Hope.

*The ferryboat docked* at the McKinnon Island landing and Theo changed seats with Christian. He dropped everyone off, then drove Hope to her little house on Beach Road. They stood on the porch, arms around each other.

Hope broke the silence. "Thank you for a wonderful evening. I really enjoyed your family."

He smiled down at her. "They like you, Hope."

She returned his smile. "That's because I like them."

"I like you—a lot."

She dropped her gaze, staring at his throat before glancing up again. "Thank you, Theo." Rising on tiptoe, she brushed a light kiss over his mouth. "Good night."

His arms fell away from her body. "Good night, sweetheart. I'll call you tomorrow."

Hope nodded. She unlocked her door, opened it, and closed it softly behind her. She stood, listening for the sound of an engine. She waited for several minutes before opening the door. Theo hadn't moved. She smiled and held out her hand. He placed his hand in hers, and she pulled him into the living room. He followed her to her bedroom, and once there they began a dance of desire that ended when their bodies were in exquisite harmony with one another.

# Twenty-five

Chance says, come here, chance say, can you bear to part?

—Hilda Doolittle

 "How long has it been since McKinnon Island's Sophie Ladies shared afternoon tea?"

Hope smiled over the rim of her cup. "At least a month."

Rebecca flashed her attractive dimples. "We've been bad, Hope."

"Speak for yourself, Rebecca. I've been here practically every afternoon. You're the one who has been traipsing all over the island."

"Traipsing, campaigning, and weaving baskets. I'm close to finishing my first one."

"Is Janie amenable to helping you set up the preservation project?"

"She is willing to co-chair it with me." Rebecca glanced at her watch before she took another sip of her blackberry currant tea. "Lee and the kids should be here soon. He called me once he boarded the three o'clock Hilton Head ferry. Ashlee and Kyle are really excited because they can't wait to reconnect with Theo's family." She peered closely at her neighbor. "Speaking of Theo."

"What about him?" Hope asked softly.

"I came back late one night and noticed his Lexus parked in your driveway."

"How late?"

"I know it was after midnight."

"*Mrs.* Cinderella, you know you shouldn't be out after the clock strikes twelve," she teased.

Rebecca blushed. "Don't change the topic, girlfriend. What's up with you and Theo?"

Hope took a deep breath and let it out slowly. She and Marissa talked several times each week, and not once had she mentioned Theo to her sister. "We've been sleeping together."

"Sleeping together or making love?"

"Is there a difference?"

Rebecca looked startled. "Of course there's a difference. Ezra and I slept together without making love."

"Theo and I sleep together, and we also make love."

Pressing her palms together, Rebecca wrinkled her delicate nose. "Good for you. I think he's perfect for you."

Hope wanted to believe he was perfect, too, but she held her tongue. Theo came to her house every night, and they'd lie in bed discussing his scripts. His knowledge of the human psyche was uncanny once he developed a character. He revealed that in college he had majored in English with a minor in psychology, which had served him well once he'd entered film school.

But whenever they did not talk about his work, they made love. Each encounter was different, more exciting, and satisfying. In Theodore Howell she had found her sexual counterpart, her physical and intellectual soul mate.

The sound of an approaching vehicle brought Rebecca to her feet. Hands on her slim hips, she watched her husband maneuver into the driveway behind her car. Ashlee and Kyle were out of the BMW before Lee shut off the engine. They raced up the porch and hugged their mother.

"I can't believe it. This was the longest week of my life," Ashlee moaned.

Rebecca kissed her son and daughter. "What do you want to do?"

"Can we go over to see Brandon and Noelle?" Kyle asked.

"You can't just drop by someone's house without calling first."

"But they said we could come over when we came back," Kyle insisted.

Lifting her shoulders, Rebecca stared at Hope. "What do I do?" she mouthed, sotto voce.

"I'll call Theo," Hope volunteered. "Why don't you invite them over for dinner? You can have something simple on the beach."

Rebecca nodded, smiling. "That's a wonderful idea. I have hamburgers and franks in the refrigerator." Reaching into the pocket of her slacks, she handed Hope her cell phone. "Call him."

Hope dialed the number to the house, and Theo's deep voice came through the wire. "Hello."

"Hello back to you. I'm calling because Rebecca's children are here and they're asking to hang out with

Brandon and the others. She thought everyone could get together at her place for dinner."

"What time does she want them to come over?"

Hope covered the tiny mouthpiece with her thumb. "What time should they come?"

"Now!" Kyle and Ashlee chorused.

Rebecca and Hope shared a smile. She moved her thumb. "Now, Theo."

"Let me round them up, and we'll be over in a bit."

"See you later." She pressed the End button, terminating the call. She handed Rebecca her phone. "They're coming. Let me check my refrigerator to see what I can contribute."

"That's not necessary," Rebecca said in protest. "I went to the market yesterday and bought enough groceries to last a week." Even though she had spoken to Hope, her gaze was fixed on her husband, who had mounted the porch, carrying several bags under his arms.

"You can never have enough food with teenagers."

Lee put down the bags and kissed his wife. Smiling, he extended a hand to Hope. "Hello again."

She shook his hand and smiled. "Welcome back to McKinnon Island."

He returned her smile. "Thank you. And, you're right about adolescent appetites. My mother used to say it was cheaper to clothe and shoe me than feed me."

Hope nodded. "Shoes may be the exception nowadays, especially with the price of so-called designer sneakers. I refuse to comprehend a one-hundred-fifty-dollar-plus price tag when the kid will need another pair in three months. On that note, I'm going to check my refrigerator. And, before I forget, you're more than welcome to use the gas grill."

"Thanks," Rebecca called out to Hope's retreating figure.

Ashlee tapped her mother's arm to get her attention. "Can we go swimming before we eat?"

"Yes, but don't go out too far."

"Daddy, can you please bring my bag in. I need my bathing suit."

Lee hesitated, his gaze fixed on his wife's face. "I've missed you, Becky."

Rebecca nodded before she turned away from him. She did not want Lee to see the longing in her gaze; he missed her and she missed him. She'd noticed that one piece of luggage on the porch belonged to Lee. When he'd called to tell her he was coming back to McKinnon, she had not asked whether he planned to stay. But seeing the bag indicated he would stay—even if only for the weekend.

"Perhaps you want to change out of your suit into something less formal, Lee."

He stared at the back of her head. Her hair was longer; it was the length it had been when he'd first met her. The way he liked it. "You're right." Picking up the bags, he waited for her to open the door.

"Give me your bag." Rebecca took the supple leather satchel anchored under his arm and walked in the direction of her bedroom. Lee hadn't moved. "Your children are waiting for you so they can change," she said over her shoulder.

Lee lifted his eyebrows and smiled. It was the first time in a very long time that Rebecca had referred to their son and daughter as his children. He did not want to make too much of it, but he hoped this weekend would signal a change in their relationship. He'd willingly give up all of his material possessions to get his wife back.

*Rebecca and Lee* sat inches apart on the top porch step and watched the orange sphere sink lower on the horizon. She counted off the seconds, reaching eight hundred fifty-three before the sun disappeared completely. Nightfall had come to the island much like a curtain lowered slowly over a stage. The aroma of grilled food mingled with the omnipresent smell of saltwater.

Lee sandwiched his hands between his knees. "Kyle and Ashlee should be sleeping here instead of with strange people."

Rebecca closed her eyes and bit down on her lower lip. She opened her eyes and stared at her husband. "If you're looking to start an argument, Lee, then you're out of luck tonight. Theo and his family aren't strangers to me. And if I'm comfortable letting Kyle and Ashlee sleep over, then you should respect my decision."

Turning his head, he met her gaze. "I *don't* want to argue, Rebecca. We've done enough of that to last several lifetimes. I'm just saying that looking after three teenagers is enough without adding two more."

She placed a hand on Lee's bare knee. He had changed out of his suit into shorts, a T-shirt and sandals. "Theo and Helen are more than capable of looking after five kids." Rebecca saw something in Lee's gaze that disturbed her. Her face clouded with uneasiness. "What's wrong?"

"Theo Howell."

"What about him?"

"He doesn't have the best reputation—"

"When did you start believing Hollywood gossip?" she asked, interrupting him. "If Theo's reputation had been that unsavory, then a court never would've awarded him guardianship of his siblings. And you're a fine one to talk about someone's morality. If I'd chosen to air our dirty linen publicly, I don't believe Charlestonians would now hold you in such high esteem."

"Why are you bringing that up? I thought we had agreed to let the past remain in the past."

"I would if you'd stop thinking yourself above reproach. Three generations of bankers is not the panacea for social respectability. The only difference between you and the people who work at The Fish Net is money. You just happen to have more or better access to it."

"Are you calling me a snob?"

"No, Lee Owens. You're not sophisticated enough to be a snob. You're nothing but a fake-ass bougie Negro whose folks made a lot of money taking advantage of their people. Your grandfather offered loans to unsuspecting illiterate farmers, knowing they could not be repaid. When they defaulted he took their farms and their lives." Throwing back his head, Lee laughed loudly. Frowning, Rebecca asked, "What's so funny?"

He stopped laughing long enough to say, "You." He peered closely at her. "Negro? Do you know long it has been since I've heard that word?"

She frowned at him. "I could've called you another N word, but I promised myself I'd never use it because I was called that in Lowell by a bigoted, narrow-minded kid who had a bigoted, narrow-minded father."

Lee curved an arm around Rebecca's waist, shifting her to sit across his lap. He pressed his nose to her hair. "I can always count on you, darling, to remind me of where I came from. And you're right about my grandfather swindling poor, unsuspecting Negroes out of their property and life savings. I suppose you can say he paid for it, because it took less than six months for him to die from a very aggressive bone cancer."

Rebecca's arms circled his neck. "There is a way for you to make amends for your grandfather's ruthlessness."

"How?"

She lifted her chin. "Invest in my dream, Lee. I want you to provide the financial backing for the McKinnon Island Historical Society."

He went completely still. "You won't let it go, will you?"

"No, Lee. I won't let it go, because I don't *want* to let it go."

His eyes searched her face, reaching into her thoughts. There was something about Rebecca's expression that unnerved Lee. The woman he loved, who had given him a son and daughter, had acquired a regal strength that was commanding and frightening.

"I need to see what it is that has you so hellbent on risking our future over."

"You'll give me the money?"

Lee smiled. Rebecca reminded him so much of his daughter asking for money for a frivolous trinket because her friends had it. But his wife was not a girl. She was a woman, one who had assumed complete control of her life and her future since coming to McKinnon Island—a future that could exclude him.

"I'm not going to commit until you give me a formal proposal with all the budget projections. I also need specs from architects, zoning variances, and listings of abandoned properties and their owners. I need that and more before I approach a group of businesspeople who, I'm certain, would be willing to invest in your dream."

Rebecca's eyes sparkled with the eagerness of a child's on Christmas morning. Her arms tightened around Lee's neck. "Thank you," she whispered tearfully. "Thank you so very much, Lee."

Angling his head, he kissed her trembling lips. "No, darling. Thank you for being who you are." He deepened the kiss and was rewarded when she parted her lips, her tongue meeting his in a slow, sensual duel. He had only agreed because he did not want to lose Rebecca.

His hand searched under her blouse, closing over a firm breast. He smiled. She had gained weight in all of the right places. A groan escaped him when her nipple hardened against the sheer fabric of her bra.

Rebecca snuggled against his neck. "Let's take this inside before our neighbors see us."

Lee stood up with Rebecca in his arms. Minutes later they were in bed, their naked bodies writhing together in a timeless rhythm. Wordlessly, they reconciled in the most intimate way possible.

*Ezra joined his brother* and sister-in-law on the veranda for brunch. His joy in seeing Rebecca reclining gracefully on a chaise was short-lived when he saw a tall, slender, dark-skinned man hand her a cup of coffee before he rested a hand on her bare shoulder. The familiarity of the gesture was enough to let him know that the man was Rebecca's husband.

He forced a smile and joined the two couples. "Good morning." His voice sounded false even to his own ears.

Rebecca's head came around, and she smiled at the man who had become teacher, mentor and friend. "Good morning, Ezra."

Lee rose to his feet, but Ezra motioned to him. "Please, don't get up." He extended his right hand. "Ezra Smith."

Eyeing the man who'd had a profound effect on his wife, Lee smiled and shook the proffered hand. He had to admit that the historian was attractive and imposing. The richness of his gold-brown skin gave him the appearance of having a year-round tan.

"Lee Owens."

Ezra sat down on a chair and poured coffee from a silver pot into a porcelain cup, adding a small amount of heavy cream to the chicory-flavored brew. He took a sip, enjoying the fragrance and taste. He always looked forward to visiting McKinnon just to drink his sister-in-law's coffee.

Lowering the cup to a matching saucer, he stared at Rebecca. There was a tiny red bruise along the side of her neck not covered by the thick gold-streaked curls on her nape. There was no doubt Lee had marked his territory.

"Well, Lee, how do you like McKinnon?"

Resting his elbows on the arms of his chair, Lee

tented his fingers. "I like what I've seen of it," he answered honestly.

"Do you feel it's too primitive for someone who has lived all of his life in a cosmopolitan city?"

"Not at all. There was a time when Charleston could be thought of as primitive."

Janie, sensing a thread of hostility between the two men said, "Lee has agreed to provide financing for the McKinnon Island Historical Society once we get it established."

"Not me personally," Lee said quickly. "But as president of a bank I'm going to do everything within my power to help my wife realize her dream to turn McKinnon Island into another Colonial Williamsburg."

"It's a dream with incredible merit," Thomas stated emphatically. "I've given Rebecca the name of the historical architect Janie and I commissioned to plan the restoration of this property."

Rebecca's hazel eyes sparkled like polished citrines. "I want all of McKinnon Island to achieve historic landmark status like Newburyport, Massachusetts."

Ezra smiled at her. "That's possible, given some of the surviving authentic Gullah structures on the island."

Lee crossed a leg over the opposite knee. "The locals can take advantage of tourists coming to the island by setting up antique shops and boutiques to sell their baskets and quilts. And for those who would want to stay over, lodging accommodations can be provided at private guesthouses, or restored plantations can become B and Bs."

"Talk the talk, banker man," Thomas teased with

a wide grin. Lee pressed a fist to his mouth to suppress a laugh.

"How about eating establishments, Lee?" Janie asked.

"If the owners of The Fish Net aren't willing to set up a chain of restaurants throughout the island, then they're going to be in for some serious competition from the women who turn their homes into guesthouses."

Rebecca nodded. "I've witnessed that. Hope made the most delicious homemade ice cream, sweet potato pie, and fried spareribs I've ever eaten. In fact, it was the first time I'd ever eaten fried spareribs."

"I'm with you, Rebecca," Janie said. "Hope's grandmother, Queenie Robinson, earned the reputation of best cook on McKinnon. Whenever there was a church social, everyone sampled Miss Queenie's dishes first."

Lee spent the next two hours with the Smiths, listening as they extolled the importance of keeping the Gullah culture alive. They did not know he did not need much more convincing because his wife had done that the night before.

Pressing his palms together, he brought his fingertips to his lips and stared at her. He would do anything for her. All she had to do was ask.

# Twenty-six

*The cool kindliness of sheets, that soon smooth away trouble.*

—Rupert Brooke

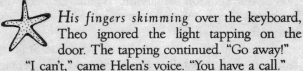 His fingers skimming over the keyboard, Theo ignored the light tapping on the door. The tapping continued. "Go away!"

"I can't," came Helen's voice. "You have a call."

"Tell whoever it is I'll call them back."

"It's Jeff. He says it's important."

"Okay!" Theo saved what he had typed and pushed back his chair. Damn his agent.

Crossing the room, Theo threw open the door and took the cordless phone from Helen. "Thanks." Waiting until she walked away, he closed the door softly. "What's up, Jeff?"

"I should ask you the same thing, lover boy."

A frown furrowed Theo's forehead. "What are you talking about?"

"I have a copy of the *Chatterer* in front of me, and you and Dr. Hope Sutton made the front page. The two of you look pretty cozy holding hands in a

Savannah restaurant. The caption reads, 'Did second loss at Oscar send scriptwriter Theo Howell into Dr. Hope's capable hands?' "

"Real cute," Theo snarled.

"Cute or not, please answer one question for me, Theo. When did you and the self-help diva start knocking boots?"

Theo clutched the phone so tightly that his fingers ached. "Watch your mouth, Jeff."

"I'm only asking because I need to know what to say when the media comes knocking."

"Tell them what you tell everyone when you don't want to be bothered—fuck off!"

"If I tell them that, then they're going to think I have something to hide."

"Well, I don't have anything to hide. I'm going to hang up because I still have a lot of work to do. Please don't call me again unless it is something really important."

Not giving his agent the chance to say another word, he ended the call. He left his bedroom office and replaced the telephone on a wall in the kitchen.

He stared at Helen staring back at him. "I'm going to see Hope."

She nodded, knowing instinctively that whatever it was he wanted to see Hope about had to be important for him to leave his writing project. Theo had maintained a ritual of rising early and working until the afternoon. Once the door opened, it remained open until the following morning.

His nightly ritual had changed, because he hadn't slept in his own bed in more than three weeks. She knew he had been sleeping with Hope, and she respected his discretion. She had begun saying novenas again for the second time since coming to work for Theo.

This time it was for Theo and Hope to see what was so apparent. They were in love with each other.

*Hope answered the door,* shocked to see Theo standing on her porch in the middle of the morning when he'd left her house at dawn. She opened the door wider and moved closer to him. A muscle flicked in his jaw.

"What's the matter?"

Reaching out, he took her hands and pulled her close. He lowered his head and spoke close to her ear, repeating his conversation with his agent. She stiffened in his embrace, her heart pumping wildly against his chest.

"I'm sorry," he apologized softly. "I'm so sorry—"

Her fingers halted his apology. "It's okay, Theo. It was only a photograph, and holding hands across a restaurant table cannot be construed as anything but that."

His brows flickered. "Didn't you tell me that you go to great lengths to keep your private life private?"

She smiled. "As a public figure I do, but didn't I tell you that you're the celebrity, and celebrities aren't expected to have private lives."

He ran his forefinger down the length of her nose, then dropped a light kiss on the end. "We can always hang out someplace other than Savannah. There's always St. Simons, or Sapelo Islands."

"Don't stress yourself over it, Theo. It's nice dressing up and going up to Savannah or Hilton Head to eat in fancy restaurants, but I still prefer places like The Fish Net. We have another four weeks to be together, and I don't want to spend that time agonizing over a photograph on the front page of a sleazy tabloid." She and Theo had less than a month, while Rebecca and her children would return to Charleston in three weeks. Her arms went around his waist. "Hanging out on McKinnon Island does have its advantages."

"Why would you say that?"

"You can't buy the *Chatterer* or any of the other more popular supermarket tabloids at the minimarket."

Theo smiled for the first time since answering his agent's call. "As the kids say, 'That's cool.' "

"It is cool." She rested her head between his neck and shoulder, shivering slightly when he tunneled his fingers through her hair and massaged her scalp.

"I don't want to think of leaving here," he whispered in her ear.

"You're probably going through a little premature separation anxiety."

"You're right."

Rebecca, along with several prominent residents of McKinnon Island, had gotten an injunction to halt the buying and selling of all properties, which had sabotaged his efforts to purchase a house. The Owens children, who spent more time at his summer place than at their own, had convinced his brothers and sister that they should relocate to Charleston.

Theo watched and carefully monitored the growing attraction between Brandon and Ashlee. Most times they sat apart from the others, talking and laughing. He had taken his youngest brother aside and counseled him about not going too far with the young girl. Brandon had appeared embarrassed by the lec-

ture, but he'd reassured his guardian that he would
never disrespect his new friend because Christian had
talked to him about the same thing.

Later that night Theo had sought out Christian
and praised him for his maturity; he'd also apologized for slapping him. Christian had shrugged off
the apology, saying he'd needed someone to knock
some sense into him. The brief encounter had ended
with them hugging while declaring they had to look
out for one another.

Theo brushed a kiss over Hope's forehead. "Are
you busy?"

She smiled. "A little. Why?"

Pulling back, he stared down at her. "I was thinking perhaps we could take a nap together. I didn't get
much sleep last night."

She lifted a waxed eyebrow. "Whose fault was
that, Theodore?"

"Yours."

"Not. You were the one who couldn't get
enough."

"That's because you had me on sexual lockdown
for a couple of days."

"That's because I had cramps and some breakthrough bleeding."

"Why didn't you tell me?" he asked when she
clamped her jaw tight and stared over his shoulder.

"Because there's no need to burden you with my
medical problems."

He swallowed a savage expletive. "For heaven's
sake, Hope, I'm sleeping with you!"

"And that's it!" she countered. "We're just sleeping together."

His eyes widened until she could see his near-black irises. Didn't she know he had fallen in love with her? That she was different from all of the other women he'd known?

"Do you still have cramps?"

She lifted her shoulders. "They come and go. I've increased my hormone dosage by another ten milligrams a day."

The fingers of his right hand circled her upper arm. "Come inside. We'll lie down together."

"What about your writing?"

"And what about it?" His tone was challenging.

"Nothing, Theo." She did not want to fight with him. The return of her menses and the spotting was an indication that the hormone therapy wasn't working. And that meant she did not have to wait until October for a prognosis. There was no doubt she would have to face a surgical procedure.

She walked with Theo to her bedroom. He pulled back the faded yellow patchwork quilt and sat down on the side of the bed. He held out his hand. "Come."

Slipping off her sandals, she lay down on the cool sheet and turned over on her side. Theo removed his running shoes and lay beside her in spoon fashion, his knees touching the backs of hers.

He pressed a kiss on her hair, inhaling the floral fragrance clinging to the heavy strands. "Everything is going to work out, sweetheart."

Hope closed her eyes, whispering her own silent prayer. "You sound so certain."

He laughed softly, the sound echoing in the silent room. "That's because I am."

They lay together, their chests rising and falling in unison until they fell asleep.

* * *

*The clanging of the bell* woke Hope, and when she rolled over she found herself alone in the bed. Pushing her hair off her forehead, she walked on bare feet to the front door. Rebecca stood on the porch, dressed in a revealing maillot. The high-cut legs and deep-V neckline displayed her petite body to its best advantage.

Hope smothered a yawn behind her hand as she opened the door. "Come in."

Rebecca took off her sunglasses and anchored them on the top of her head. "I came to ask you whether you wanted to go swimming. My children have deserted me."

"Where are they?"

"Over at Theo's. Whenever I go to either Savannah or Hilton Head to shop for groceries, I come back and drop them off over there. I forced them to stay with me one night, and they complained so much that I wanted to beat the shit out of them. And I would've done it if I weren't afraid of being charged with child abuse. They only stopped bitchin' when I threw a shoe at Ashlee, missing her by mere inches."

"Rebecca!"

She waved a hand. "My kids should know when I say no, it means no. Especially when I have PMS."

"So, you're one of those women who lose it before you get your period."

"Losing it is putting it mildly. I'm usually homicidal."

Hope gave her a cautious look. "You all right now?"

Rebecca flashed her dimpled smile. "I'm good.

It ended yesterday. I wanted to come over earlier, but I saw Theo's car."

Hope knew if she did not tell her neighbor about their photograph on the front page of the *Chatterer* she was bound to see it whenever she went to one of the major supermarket chains.

"Let's sit down. I have something to tell you."

Rebecca stared wide-eyed and listened as Hope related what Theo's agent had told him. "Have you ever been in a tabloid before?"

"No. And to my knowledge I don't believe my name has ever appeared in one."

"I don't know what to say. Theo has become a Hollywood icon not only because of his work but because we don't have that many black scriptwriters. I'm sure the photographer was surprised to get two prizes with one shot. He probably thought you were just another silicon-enhanced hoochie until he recognized you."

Hope's mouth dropped open. "What?"

"Any time Theo is photographed with a woman she looks as if she is hiding two midgets in her bodice." Rebecca registered Hope's shocked expression. "Come on, girlfriend, you have to know he's a breast man." She covered her modest cleavage with her hands. "He wouldn't even give these a passing glance."

"You think he's attracted to me because of my chest?"

"No. I think he's attracted to you because of three Bs."

"Three Bs?"

"You're brilliant, beautiful, and busty."

Hope tried not to laugh. "You're pushing it, *girl-*

*friend,* because I happen to have PMS right now. Another remark like that and you're in for an old-fashioned Harlem beat-down."

"I only speak the truth."

Hope pushed to her feet. "I'll be right back. Let me get my suit and I'll join you."

She'd had two unexpected visitors that morning, and she knew there was no way she could get back into the mood to resume writing. The day before, she had picked up a stack of letters for her "Straight Talk" column, and she had spent the afternoon reading them. Most she could answer off the top of her head, while others required more complex answers. She planned to spend the rest of the week answering letters before she picked up her book project.

*They swam for thirty minutes,* then retreated to the protective cover of the porch. Hope went into the house to prepare a pitcher of iced tea; she returned to the porch, and the Sophie Ladies had a late-afternoon tea party.

Rebecca was more talkative than usual as she brought her neighbor up to date on her preservation crusade. Hope noticed she rarely mentioned Ezra's name since Lee had begun spending his weekends on McKinnon Island.

She wiggled her toes, painted a shocking hot pink. "Did Theo tell you that Lee is contacting a Charleston real estate agent for him to look for properties in neighborhoods with good school districts?"

"No, he didn't."

A wave of annoyance swept over her. Theo had complained because she had not told him about the changes going on in her body, while he had conveniently neglected to tell her that he was considering relocating to Charleston.

"Oops!" Rebecca grimaced. "Did I say something I shouldn't have?"

"Of course not. Theo and I aren't joined at the hip, so there's no need for us to confide everything to each other."

"But you do have a relationship."

"We are sleeping together. That doesn't necessarily translate into a committed relationship."

Rebecca plucked a sprig of mint out of her glass. "Are you in love with Theo?"

Hope was too startled by the question to form a quick comeback. "I don't know, Rebecca, because I don't know what love feels like anymore. I thought I was in love with Kendall, but after leaving him I know in my heart that I wasn't. If I'd loved him, then I wouldn't have waited to give him an answer when he asked me to marry him."

"If Theo asked you to marry him, would you?"

"No, because that would never happen. I've heard him say that he has no intention of marrying or fathering children."

"Why?"

She shook her head. "I don't know."

"You've never asked him?"

"No."

"Why not, Hope?"

"Because it doesn't concern me."

"Do you want to marry and have children?"

A flicker of apprehension coursed through Hope, and she felt a momentary panic. She had always said she wanted to be married before she had a child, but since she had come to McKinnon Island she knew that prerequisite wasn't as crucial as she had originally thought.

"All I want is a baby." The last word came out in a sob. She clamped a hand over her mouth as her eyes filled with moisture. A shudder shook her as the tears fell.

Rebecca moved over and held her neighbor, rubbing her back until her trembling stopped. "Let it out, girlfriend," she crooned softly, losing her own battle with the tears filling her eyes.

The two women held each other, crying until spent. They passed the rest of the afternoon talking as they had done the night that now seemed so long ago, when it had actually only been weeks.

Most of their time together on McKinnon Island was behind them, and they knew it. They toasted each other with glasses of iced tea, swearing a solemn promise to enjoy whatever time they had left.

# Twenty-seven

*I am no good at love. I betray it with little sins.*
*—Noel Coward*

*Every minute Hope spent* with Rebecca and Theo was as precious to her as drops of water to a man dying of thirst in the desert.

All had established a ritual of having dinner together, Helen and Theo, Rebecca and Hope sharing cooking duties. Lee had shortened his workweek to three days. He usually arrived late Wednesday, and departed with the last ferryboat on Sunday.

The night before, the five adults had celebrated well into the night with potent concoctions after Theo announced he had completed his sixth script. He was two months ahead of schedule. Hope had completed more than half of her book and had downloaded enough letters to Bill for her "Straight Talk" column to run through the end of the year.

She lay facedown on a chaise on the patio at the rear of Theo's house, listening to the melodic voice of Phil Perry coming through the speakers of a portable stereo system. Lee and Rebecca had invited her to join them for a walk along the beach, but she had declined. It was to become the last weekend the Owenses would spend on the island. She closed her eyes, enjoying the heat of the waning sunlight on her back, when she heard Helen calling out to Theo that he had a telephone call.

Hope hadn't realized she had fallen asleep until she felt someone shake her. "Wake up, sweetheart."

She came awake immediately and sat up. Theo stood over her. There was a lethal calmness in his eyes that frightened her. "What's the matter?"

He reached for her upper arm. "Come with me. I have something to tell you."

Balking, she pulled back. "Tell me now."

"No, Hope. Not here."

Her sandals made little slip-slapping sounds on the patio's terra-cotta flooring as she followed Theo into the house. A blast of cold air swept over her. The contrast between the indoor and outdoor temperatures was at least twenty degrees.

Theo led her into a bedroom off a wing of the kitchen and closed the door. She knew with a quick glance that it was his bedroom. A computer and printer sat on a table in an alcove. Lacing his fingers through hers, he pulled her down to sit on a queen-size bed.

Theo stared at her, adding to her apprehension. "What do you want to tell me?" she asked.

"I just got some news that's . . . that's not going to bode well for you."

"What is it?" Her voice was trembling.

"Your name is back in the *Chatterer* again." He

squeezed her fingers in a comforting gesture. "The next issue has a story about your ex-boyfriend and his male lover. The lover claims the three of you have been involved in a ménage à trois."

Hope felt the roaring in her head and the constriction shutting off her breath before the room started spinning. Gurgling gasps came from her throat as she tried to speak. Theo's face shimmered before her eyes. She saw his mouth open but could not hear what he was saying to her. She did not remember what happened next, but suddenly her body was on fire. When everything cleared, she saw Helen staring down at her.

"Don't get up," Helen murmured softly. "You almost fainted."

"Is she going to be all right?" Rebecca's voice came from somewhere above her.

Theo placed his hand alongside her cheek. "Yes."

Hope swallowed in an attempt to moisten her throat. "Who told you?"

Leaning closer, Theo pressed his mouth to her ear. "Someone at the paper called my agent and told him the edition will be on the newsstands tomorrow."

Hope blinked back tears. "It's all a lie, Theo."

He gave her a long, penetrating look. "I know that."

"You believe me." Her lids fluttered wildly. "You're probably the only one other than my sister." Sitting up, she pulled a cloth from her forehead and stared directly at Helen. "I dated a man for three years, not knowing he was bisexual until I walked in on him and another man the day I planned to tell him that I would marry him."

The older woman gasped loudly. Theo glanced over his shoulder. Rebecca and Helen were huddled together. "Please leave us." The two women turned and walked out of the bedroom, closing the door firmly behind them. He released Hope and sat on a chair several feet from the bed.

"How are you feeling?"

"Better." She swung her legs over the side of the bed.

"Where are you going?"

"I have to make a telephone call."

"Use mine." He reached for a small phone on a table next to the chair, and handed it to her.

She flipped open the top and dialed. The call was answered after the second ring.

"This is KC."

The runaway pounding of her heart echoed in her ears. "This is Hope."

"Hey, baby. How are you?"

Hope's gaze was fixed on Theo's impassive expression. "This is not a social call, KC. I'm calling you to tell you that your business is in the street."

"What are you talking about?" His voice had lost its velvet softness.

"It appears that your lover went to the *Chatterer* about his relationship with you. I don't care how many men you sleep with, but what I don't want is to be brought into it—especially not in the tabloids. Tell your lover that he'd better get the paper to retract the story about me being a participant in a ménage à trois or I'll sue him and that rag he gave the story to for so much money that he won't be able to buy even a single sheet of toilet paper to wipe his ass." She pressed a button and ended the call. Her hands were shaking when she handed Theo back the phone. "Thank you." Lifting her chin, she met his tortured gaze. "I want to go home."

He inclined his head. "Come, I'll take you."

Hope fought against the tears she refused to let fall as Theo led her through the house and out the front door to his vehicle. There was complete silence as he drove down Beach Road to her house. She got out without waiting for him to help her. A jumble of confused thoughts and emotions made her feel as if she was swimming underwater in the dark.

Theo was beside her as she unlocked the front door. "Good night, Theo."

He rested a hand on her shoulder. "I'm not leaving, Hope."

She shook her head from side to side. "Please. I need to be alone." A cynical smile twisted her mouth. "You don't have to worry about me. I'm not going to do anything stupid."

His hand slipped down her spine. "Let me stay with you. Just for a little while."

"Why, Theo?"

He kissed her hair. "Because I care about you."

She smiled in spite of her predicament. "Okay. But just for a little while, because I have to make a few more phone calls." She had to call and leave voice mail messages for her attorney, Bill, and then she needed to speak to her parents. They had to be informed of the craziness going on in her life.

She and Theo lay across the bed together, holding hands. There was no need for conversation; there was nothing they could say that would counter the lewd gossip printed in the *Chatterer*.

"Do you know him?" Theo asked after a long, comfortable silence.

"Who?" Her voice was raspy, as if she had been yelling for hours.

"The piece of shit who gave the story to the rag?"

"No. Why did you ask?"

"No reason."

"You have a reason, Theo." Turning her head, she stared at his stoic expression. "You're not thinking what I'm thinking?"

"What am I thinking, Hope?"

She rose on an elbow. "I don't want anything to happen to that piece of shit until I settle this legally. If I'm not able to refute his accusations, then I'm finished professionally. I'll lose my column and possibly the radio position. And, I can forget about a private practice. I could make the rounds on the television talk show circuit. Imagine the hype I could generate by becoming a guest on *Maury, Jerry Springer, Montel Williams, Ricki Lake,* or *Jenny Jones* where the topic is, Are you involved in a straight, bi, or homosexual triangle?"

"Stop it, Hope!"

A tense silence enveloped the room as they glared at each other. She closed her eyes, and the tightness around her mouth eased. "It's either joke about it or cry about it." She looked at him. "And I'd rather laugh than cry."

"There's nothing wrong with crying, sweetheart."

"I only cry about things I can't control."

Theo wanted to tell her that what would appear in the *Chatterer* in a few hours was worth crying about because it was beyond her control. As soon as the paper was placed in the racks, the tongues would begin wagging.

*Hope sat in the dark* after Theo left. The darkness comforted and protected her so she could see not what was real but whatever fantasy she conjured up.

But she knew she could not spend her life in darkness, hiding from the real world. And despite her fear of what was about to happen, she reached over and turned on the bedside lamp. She slipped off the bed and walked to the other bedroom. Her hands were steady when she removed her cell phone from its charger. The tension was gone from her face when she opened her planner and dialed the number to her attorney's office. Following the prompts, she left an abbreviated version of what Theo had told her about the upcoming article and her cell phone number.

She dialed her editor's home number, and he picked up after the third ring. "Talk to me."

Hope smiled at his unorthodox greeting. "Bill, this is Hope."

He chuckled. "You never have to identify yourself, because your voice gives you away. I got your e-mail attachments the other day, and the bundles of letters were delivered today. You don't have to send them overnight. Regular mail will do."

"Overnight mail is special handling, regular isn't."

"Save your money, Hope, and buy a shredder."

"I will." After she answered all of the letters, newspaper personnel shredded them. Although she answered thousands of letters throughout the year, only a small percentage made the column.

"Why the call, Hope?" It was on a rare occasion that she called his home.

"I'm calling to warn you that I might be front page news in tomorrow's *Chatterer.*"

"Oh, damn! What crap do they have on you?"

She told him about seeing her ex-boyfriend and his lover together, and the lover's story about a sexual triangle. Each time she repeated the story, she gathered more strength.

William Casey Cullen let loose with a stream of expletives that forced Hope to hold the phone away from her ear. "Do you have the lover's name?" he asked once he recovered from his tirade.

"No."

"Can you get it?"

"I don't know."

There was a pause before Bill's voice came through the tiny earpiece. "I know someone who used to work for that rag. He still owes me a favor. Let me see what I can do on this end. It's too late to stop the sale of the paper, but that doesn't mean they won't pay for printing lies."

"It's more than lies, Bill. It's slander."

"I hope you called your lawyer."

"I called him first."

"Good for you. Don't worry, beautiful. You're going to beat this."

"Thanks for the vote of confidence. But . . ." Her words trailed off.

"But what?"

"What about my column?"

"What about it?"

"How will this affect my position with your paper?"

"If you're asking whether you still have a job, then the answer is yes. What happened to everyone is innocent until proven guilty?"

She smiled. "You're right. I am innocent."

"You don't have to try and convince me. I'm going to make a few calls, and I'll let you know what I come up with. Do you have a number at your house, or do you want me to call you on your cell?"

"The cell."

"Good. Talk to you later."

"Thank you, Bill."

"Don't thank me yet."

She smiled. "Good night, Bill."

He blew a kiss through the wire. "Later, Hope."

She was smiling when she dialed her parents' number. It was her mother who answered. Hope greeted her as she normally would, then asked that her father get on the extension. Patrick and Flora were silent as she told them about her breakup with Kendall and everything that had followed.

"Why didn't you say something before, Hope?" Patrick asked angrily.

"There was nothing to say, Daddy. What do you say to a man who prefers a same-sex relationship?"

"I just realized I have another use for those golf clubs you gave me."

"Daddy, no!"

"Patrick!"

Hope and her mother screamed at the same time.

"Junior, Bobby and me will handle this, Hope." There was a distinctive click when Patrick hung up.

Hope felt weak, as if she were going to faint

again. "Mama, please talk to Daddy. If he goes after Kendall, then I'll never clear my reputation."

"No worry, baby. I'll talk to him."

"You better talk to Bobby. You know he's the one who will thump, then talk afterwards."

"No one is going to hurt anyone. What I want you to do is sue the hell out of that paper for printing those lies."

She smiled. "I intend to do just that."

"When are you coming back?"

"The end of September."

"Will you be able to conduct your business from down there?"

"Yes."

"I'm going to pray for you, baby."

"Thank you, Mama. I love you."

"Love you, too."

Hope pressed a button. She had made her three calls, and now what she had to do was wait—wait for her attorney to call her back, and wait for the onslaught of negative reaction to the tabloid article.

*Theo hit the Talk button,* listening for the ringing on the other end. He sat up straighter when he heard a male voice.

"This is KC."

"KC, this is TH."

"I don't know a TH."

"Don't hang up," Theo warned softly, "because you will know me soon enough."

"What do you want?"

"This is about Hope Sutton."

"Look, man, I don't want to get into that with you."

"You won't," Theo snapped, "if you just answer my question."

"I'm going to hang up."

"I wouldn't do that if I were you."

"Who the *fuck* do you think you are?"

"If you hang up on me, then you'll find out who I am real quick. All I need from you is a name. The name of your lover."

"He's not my lover."

"What?"

"I saw Otis a few times, but it didn't work out."

"Does this Otis have a last name?"

"Pratt."

"Does Mr. Otis Pratt have an address?"

"What are you going to do?"

"That's none of your business, KC."

"If anything happens to him, then the police are going to come looking for me. That spiteful bitch has done enough damage. Once that article hits, I'm done."

"You should've thought about that when you took up with him. An address and phone number, KC." Theo wrote down the information Hope's ex gave him, smiling.

"I don't know if he's still there. It's his sister's place. He bounces around quite a bit, looking for someone to take him in. He's what I call a homo ho."

"Thanks for the information. Good luck."

Theo was still smiling when he dialed the number of a friend in San Francisco. He liked the old adage that it's not *what* you know but *who* you know. Jay had once lived on the streets for five years. He'd entered a rehab clinic and eventually taken over his father's trucking business.

Jay's daughter answered the call. "Daddy, it's Mr. Howell."

Less than a minute later Jay's soft voice came through the line. "What's up, friend?"

Theo explained Hope's situation and why he needed his friend's help. "All I need is for him to recant what will appear in tomorrow's paper."

"Consider it done," Jay said without hesitation. "What's your connection with the lady, Theo?"

"I like her."

"Just like?"

"Okay, Jay. I think I'm in love with her."

"Think or know?"

"I'm still confused." And his confusion stemmed from the fact that at forty years of age, he still had not accepted his mother's rejection.

"Once you clear up the confusion, send me a wedding invitation. If a former drug-addicted male prostitute can clean up his act, marry, and have a couple of beautiful, normal kids, you can, my friend."

"You're right about that, my friend."

Theo rang off, then headed for his bathroom to shower. It would be the first night in nearly six weeks that he would not share Hope's bed. Perhaps he needed to be alone with his thoughts to see things more clearly. He was scheduled to leave McKinnon Island in two weeks, and he knew his relationship with Hope had to be resolved.

# Twenty-eight

*One day I wrote her name upon the strand, but came
the waves and washed it away.*

—Edmund Spenser

Hope whispered a prayer of thanks that
she was cloistered on McKinnon Island,
because once the article was released about
the ménage à trois, newshounds would descend on
the newspaper like a swarm of hornets, or sniff
around her Harlem apartment like predators hunting
prey.

The soft chiming of her phone greeted her early
Friday morning. She squinted at the display. "Hey,
Lil Sis."

"I just found out this morning what that freaky,
punk-ass bitch did."

"Who told you?"

"Mama. She wants everyone to meet tomorrow
morning at her place for breakfast. I believe she's trying to diffuse Daddy and Bobby. Both are off the
chain."

"Marissa, please tell them not to do anything that

will jeopardize what will definitely become a slander
suit."

"As much as I'd like to get my licks in, I'm going
to agree with you, Hope."

"Please get the others to agree."

"Don't worry, Big Sis, I'm on your side with this
one. But I need to ask you one question."

"What's that?"

"Are you and Theo Howell a couple?"

"No. We're friends." Friends who happen to be
sleeping together, she added silently.

"That's too bad, because he's a helluva lot better
than what you just kicked to the curb. Is he really as
hot as his photographs?"

"Hotter."

"Ouch! I'm afraid of you."

Smiling, Hope sat up and swung her legs over
the side of the bed. "Keep me posted on the family
gathering."

"I will. Love you, Hope."

"Love you back, Rissa."

She left the bed knowing she had to fortify herself for what was to come: the media's dissection of
her sex life.

*Hope sat on the porch*, eyes closed, with an open
book on her lap. She caught the scent of a familiar
perfume and slowly opened her eyes. Rebecca stood
several feet away. A floral print, strapless sundress
accented her slim waist before it flared out around
her hips and legs.

"Hi, girlfriend."

Rebecca forced a smile. "Hi, girlfriend. I'll leave
if you don't want company."

Hope extended her hand. "Please stay, Rebecca." She hadn't seen her neighbor since the night Theo had gotten the call from his agent.

Rebecca took the chaise. "I wanted to come over earlier, but Lee said you probably needed to be alone to get your head together."

"He's right."

"Are you together?"

Lowering her head, Hope affected a sad smile. "As together as I'm ever going to be. My attorney has contacted the *Chatterer*, my editor at the paper has reassured me that I still have a job, while a prospective position with an Atlanta radio show has been placed on hold until I clear up what they're considering an image problem."

"Buttheads!"

Her head came up. "I'm trying to understand their position. They want to hire me because they're selling an image that's squeaky clean and morally above reproach. Americans like to believe they're so tolerant and open-minded, when in reality they're the most uptight, amoral, hypocritical people on the planet.

"People become instant millionaires selling sex on the big and small screens, and in magazines, yet the ordinary Joe and Jane are prosecuted for solicitation or loitering if they use the street corner. I don't have an issue with any consenting adult's sexual predilection as long as it's conducted in privacy. If Kendall had told me when we first met that he'd fantasized about a sexual encounter with a man, I never would've slept with him."

"The question is would you have remained his friend?"

"Yes, I would," Hope said after a pregnant pause. "Every woman should have at least one male friend."

"Like Theo?"

Two pairs of golden eyes measured the other. "Yes, Rebecca, like Theo."

"What's going to happen to the two of you?"

Hope turned her head and stared at the beach. "Theo is scheduled to return to L.A. in another eight days, and I'm going to stay here until the end of September."

"That's not what I mean, and you know it."

"You're talking in riddles."

Rebecca shifted on the chaise, moving closer to where Hope sat on the rocker. "I asked you this question before, and I'm going to ask you again. Are you in love with him?"

Hope sank lower into the cushioned seat. Her gaze shifted to the candy-apple-red polish on her groomed toes. "I've asked myself the same question over and over since the first night we slept together, and the answer is always no. No, because I don't want to lose my heart again. No, because I keep telling myself that I can never trust a man completely. And no because what I want most Theo isn't willing to give me. He doesn't want children."

"Would you consider marrying him and becoming stepmother to his brothers and sister?"

Hope repeated Rebecca's question to herself. There were thousands of women who were unable to bear a child yet had earned the status of mother once they adopted one.

"I'm not opposed to becoming a stepmother."

"You didn't answer my question, Hope."

She glared at Rebecca. "You remind me of a little

poodle I had that used to snap at me whenever I tried petting her. Muzzle it, Rebecca!"

Blushing furiously, Rebecca pulled her lower lip between her teeth. "I'm sorry. I guess I'm on edge because I'm leaving in a couple of hours, and tomorrow I'll celebrate my fortieth birthday without my new friends. My parents and in-laws have planned a special dinner for me."

"Congratulations!" Hope reached over and hugged her soon-to-be ex-neighbor.

Rebecca swiped at her tears with her fingertips. "I suppose I'm freaking out for nothing. Women turn forty every day."

"That's true, but not every forty-year-old woman has embarked on what you're about to undertake. I'm the one with the Gullah roots, yet you're the one who has assumed responsibility for preserving the culture."

The moisture in Rebecca's eyes turned them into shimmering jewels. "I couldn't have done it without you. It all started when you introduced me to Janie Smith."

"I hope we're not going to lose touch with one another."

"Heavens no. You're always welcome to stay with me if you ever come to Charleston. And of course we'll see each other next summer. You have my address and phone numbers. I expect to hear from you."

"Of course you will," Hope promised.

Rebecca stood up, and Hope rose with her. "I have to get back and finish packing."

Hope extended her arms, and she wasn't disappointed when Rebecca hugged her. "Good luck, Sophie Lady."

Rebecca sniffled. "Good luck to you, too, Sophie Lady."

They pulled apart. Hope stood motionless, watching her friend until she disappeared from view. Then she walked into her house and closed and locked the door.

*Rebecca nodded to Helen.* "I'd like to see Theo for a few minutes."

"He's writing, but I don't think he'd mind being interrupted."

"Tell him I only need a few minutes."

Helen walked away, leaving Rebecca standing in the middle of the living room. Her children had said their good-byes to the Andersons the night before. What had surprised the adults had been the tears. Noelle, Kyle, Ashlee and Brandon had wept openly, while Christian hadn't bothered to come out of his bedroom.

"Rebecca."

She turned and smiled at Theo. It was the first time she had seen him unshaven. "I just came to say good-bye."

He took several steps. "I thought we did that last night."

She clasped her hands together to stop their trembling. "We did. But I wanted to talk to you about something."

His gaze narrowed. "Talk."

"It's about Hope."

"What about her?"

"She's hurting, Theo. She needs you."

He lifted a black, curving eyebrow. "Did she say she needed me?"

"No. She'd never say that."

"I've done all that I can to help her. What she'll have to do is wait."

Rebecca's nostrils flared with fury. "I don't believe you."

"What is it you don't believe, Rebecca?"

"How can she fall in love with someone like you?" Turning on her heel, she ran out of the house, Theo steps behind her.

He caught her arm, spinning her around to face him. "What the hell are you talking about?"

"Nothing at all, Mr. Holly-wood! Now, take your hand off me."

Theo dropped his hand, watching as Rebecca got into her Mercedes and sped away amid a spray of gravel and a cloud of dust.

He stood in the same spot for a long time—long enough for the sun to penetrate the shirt on his back and burn his flesh. He replayed her accusation over and over in his head: *How can she fall in love with someone like you?*

He did not want to believe that Hope loved him. Nothing in the way she related to him indicated anything deeper than a mutual fondness for him. They'd slept together, but a lot of people slept together without falling in love.

He shook his head. Rebecca was wrong. Hope did not love him.

*Hope went online.* She had two new e-mails, both from Theo. She clicked on the first.

> *Flickwriter: Hope you're well. I decided to give you*
> *a little space to sort out your dilemma.*
> *Let me know if you need a shoulder.*

> Flickwriter: We will be celebrating our last Sunday
>                on McKinnon. You're invited to dinner.
>                Please try to come.

Hope clicked on Reply.

> HelpDoc: I'm better, thank you. Thank you for
>               understanding that I do need space at
>               this time. I'll let you know if I need your
>               shoulder.

She clicked on Reply to his second e-mail.

> HelpDoc: I'm going to decline your invitation for
>               Sunday. Thank you for asking.

Then she signed off.

It was not the first time that Hope cursed not
having a television in the house. At least she would
be able to view the news without having to rely on
her sister to give her updates on what had now
become a scandalous exposé of Dr. Hope's love life.

Marissa repeated the commentary over the
phone as she viewed *Access Hollywood, E! True
Hollywood Story,* and *Entertainment Tonight.* A
shock jock referred to her as Dr. Dope, who
should've known better than to engage in kinky sex
while masquerading as America's moral conscience.

Lana called to tell her that the press had camped
out in front of Hope's Harlem brownstone after
William Cullen informed them that she worked from
home.

Someone from WLKV-Atlanta leaked the news
that the owners of the radio station had withdrawn

their offer to hire Dr. Hope for a late-night talk segment.

Her attorney informed her that Kendall Clarke had gone into hiding, and that he could not move forward with the suit until he surfaced. His testimony was crucial to refuting his lover's slanderous article.

She hadn't left the house in nearly a week, but she knew she could not continue to hide out much longer. The larder in her pantry was dwindling rapidly. She wondered how many on McKinnon were privy to what the outside world had found so intriguing.

*Hope got up early* Saturday morning with the intention of going to Savannah to shop, but she was thwarted when she walked out of the house to find Theo sitting on the porch. "What are you doing here?"

Theo came slowly to his feet and turned to face her. She gasped. The lower portion of his face was covered with a short black beard. He pushed his hands into the pockets of his jeans. "I came to see you because you didn't come to me."

"Why would I come to you?"

He angled his head. "I thought we were friends, Hope. And where I come from, friends look out for each other."

"You've looked out for me."

"I came to tell you some good news."

Her heart thudded. "What about?"

"Your ex-boyfriend's lover has recanted his story."

She took a step. "How do you know this?"

"I have my sources. All I'll say is the headline

for next week's *Chatterer* will read: I Lied about Dr. Hope."

She covered her mouth with trembling hands and fell against Theo. If he hadn't caught her, she would have fallen. She couldn't believe it. Did not want to believe it. It had taken one week for her world to be turned upside down and then righted.

Tears of joy filled her eyes but did not fall. "Tell me, Theo. I need to know."

He led her over to the chaise, sat, and then eased her down to sit between his outstretched legs. "His name is Otis Pratt. He's nothing more than a predator. He manages to find a way to get himself invited to upscale social events, where he spots his target, then goes in for the kill. It doesn't matter if they are men or women. He will usually steal from women and blackmail men. It appears your ex-boyfriend refused to pay him to keep his mouth shut about his bisexuality, so he decided he could make more money by selling his story to the *Chatterer* for five thousand dollars."

"Five thousand dollars! He ruined my reputation for a stinking five thousand!"

Theo shrugged a shoulder. "People have killed others for less."

"What else did your 'source' tell you?"

"Nothing else," he lied smoothly.

Jay's East Coast people had found Otis Pratt strolling out of a luxury apartment building on Central Park South. It had taken less than five minutes of several well-aimed blows to the midsection for Otis to regurgitate not only his dinner but also all of his scams. A *Chatterer* reporter had been present, tape recorder in hand, when Otis had recanted his story.

Otis's next visitors had been from the NYPD, who'd handcuffed him and read him his rights.

She smiled up at him. "How can I thank you, friend?"

He flashed a lecherous smile. "I can think of a few ways."

Curving her arms around his neck, Hope kissed him. Not the wildly passionate kisses they'd shared before but a warm, soft, healing kiss. "I'm going to miss you so much," she whispered against his lips.

Theo stared at her under lowered lids. "Not as much as I'm going to miss you. Will you come see the kids before we leave?"

"I can't." Biting down on her lower lip, she blinked back tears. "It would get sloppy, Theo. And that's not how I want them to remember me."

His dark gaze moved slowly over her face, committing it to memory. "This is how I want to remember you." Lowering his head, he kissed her. His mouth moved down the column of her neck. "And like this." His marauding mouth tasted every inch of bared flesh until Hope moaned under the onslaught.

"Come inside," she gasped.

Theo stood up, cradling her to his chest. He carried her into the house and to the bed where he had given her his heart. They took their time undressing each other, but being apart for more than a week increased their hunger for the other.

He loved her with his body and his soul. Her soft moans and sighs as he pushed into her yielding flesh ignited a fire that refused to go out. He mapped her body with his tongue, sweeping away the memory of any other man who had glimpsed or touched her flesh. His hands sculpted the fullness of her breasts, hips. He breathed in the very essence that made Hope who she was, and when she cried out for release, he increased his thrusts until they reached the pinnacle of ecstasy that held them captive before hurtling them down into an abyss of passion that lingered well beyond their coupling.

Theo felt Hope withdraw before he eased out of her warm body. She turned her back. "Good-bye, Theo."

He sat there, staring at the flawless skin of her back and hips, the curve of her spine. He slipped off the bed. She was making it easy for him. "Good-bye, Hope."

Hope listened to Theo pull on his clothes, and when silence enveloped the room, she turned over. He was gone.

"I love you," she whispered as tears spilled over and dotted the pillow under her head.

# Twenty-nine

*I seem to have loved you in numberless forms, num-*
*berless times.*

—Rabindranath Tagore

Flickwriter: Are you ready?
HelpDoc: Yes, I am. I'm ready for any and
    everything.
Flickwriter: What time is the procedure?
HelpDoc: I'm scheduled for seven. However, I have
    to be at the hospital at 5:30.
Flickwriter: I'll be pulling for you.
HelpDoc: Thanks.
Flickwriter: I'll check in with you tomorrow after
    you come home.
HelpDoc: Thanks, again.
Flickwriter: ☺
HelpDoc: ☺

Hope signed off, smiling. She and Theo usually
"talked" every day via instant messages or by e-mails.
The three-hour time difference made telephone calls
a bit more difficult.

She stared at the clock. It was midnight on the East Coast. In another five hours she would check into an Upper East Side hospital for a procedure to remove the lesions in her uterus.

Walking over to her bed, she knelt on the floor, covered her face with her hands and did something she hadn't done in a very long time. She prayed.

*"Hope. Wake up, honey."*

Hope struggled to open her eyes, but her lids seemed weighted. She heard the steady beeps from the machines monitoring her vitals. She tried again to wake up.

"Hope, sweetheart."

Her lids fluttered. The voice was familiar. "Yess-ss," she slurred.

"Wake up, darling."

"Theo?" She felt the firm softness of his mouth on her parched lips and then his hand closing over hers.

"Yes."

"What are you doing here?"

"I came to make certain you're really okay."

A dreamy smile curved her mouth. "Thanks."

This time when her eyes opened, they did not close. It really was Theo. The last time she'd seen him he'd worn a beard. Now he was clean-shaven. Her fingertips touched his chin.

"I shaved it right after I got through instant messaging you last night."

She smiled. "Why?"

He returned her smile. "When you told me you were ready for any and everything, I took that as a sign that you'd be willing to put up with me and the rest of my neurotic household for the next forty or fifty years."

"Are you asking me to marry you, Theodore Howell?"

"Yes, I am."

"Why?"

"Because I love you. I already asked your parents' permission."

"What did they say?"

"Ask them yourself."

Theo motioned to Patrick and Flora to come closer. Hope smiled at her parents. "What did you say, Daddy?"

"I told him that he'd better be good to my baby—"

"No, he didn't," Flora interrupted. "He said yes."

Hope closed her eyes. "And what did you say, Mama?"

Flora flashed Theo a wide grin. "I told him of course."

Reaching into the pocket of his slacks, Theo withdrew a ring and slipped it on Hope's left hand.

She peered closely at it. "It's beautiful."

"You're beautiful," he crooned, bending over and kissing her again before he sat down on a chair beside her bed. "I'm going to close on a little place in Charleston the beginning of November. We'll be living four blocks from Lee and Rebecca."

"That's wonderful."

"Where do you want to get married?"

Sighing, she closed her eyes again. "McKinnon Island."

"I was hoping you'd say that."

"I have something to tell you, Theo."

"What is it?"

"I love you."

He chuckled softly. "I know."

"How did you know?"

"Rebecca told me."

Hope opened her eyes. "I never told her I loved you."

"Maybe it was women's intuition?"

"Maybe it was. Help me sit up. I need to get out of this place. I have to plan a wedding."

"When do you want to marry?"

"Anytime around Christmas."

Theo's smile was dazzling. "On the beach?"

"Yes."

Theo sat her up, and she curved her arms around his neck, holding him tightly. When he'd left McKinnon Island, he'd realized he had left a small part of himself there. And that was the woman he held to his heart. She had taught him that love was quiet and patient.

Flora pulled her husband's sleeve and led him out of the room. "Let them have their time together before the family descends on him."

Patrick rolled his eyes upward. "You don't think Junior and Bobby are going to do the same thing to him that they did to Trey?"

Flora laid her head on her husband's shoulder. "I doubt it. Theo may be smooth as peanut butter, but something tells me he can hold his own with those two thugs you call sons."

"I'll have you know my boys aren't thugs, Flora Robinson-Sutton. I just brought them up to take care of their sisters."

"And they have," she crooned softly. "Just like you've taken care of me."

Patrick patted her hand. "I would do nothing less for my Gullah Queen."

Flora stared at him, then whispered something in his ear.

"What did you say?"

She gave him a sassy smile. "Learn Gullah, city man."

Both were laughing as they went into the waiting room to wait for their future son-in-law to bring their firstborn baby girl home.

# Epilogue

*Love is a secret feeding fire that gives all creatures being.*

—*Anonymous*

Hope sagged against the wall. She couldn't believe it. It couldn't have happened so quickly. She hadn't seen her period in November, which meant she was about six weeks along.

"What is it?" came Marissa's voice behind the closed door.

"I'm going to do it again."

"How many times do you have to do it? Either you are or you aren't. Open the damn door and let me see." Hope opened the door. Marissa crowded into the tiny bathroom. She took the wand from her sister's hand, her eyes widening. "You are! You're pregnant!"

"Shh-hh! Don't say anything."

Marissa clapped her hands over her mouth and screamed through her fingers. "When are you going to tell Theo?"

"After we're married, of course."

"Which should happen in exactly twenty minutes. Come and get dressed. It's bad luck to keep your groom waiting."

Hope followed Marissa out of the bathroom and into the room where she'd slept and made love with Theo four months before. She smiled at her sisters-in-law and Rebecca.

"Are you all right?" Rebecca asked.

"I'm wonderful."

And she was. She was marrying a man she loved, a man whose child was growing beneath her heart. She had stayed in New Jersey with her parents while she'd recuperated, then moved to Charleston after Theo had closed on what he'd called his little house. The house had six bedrooms, eight baths, a three-car garage, an in-ground pool, and a tennis court set on six acres. She'd been reunited with Helen, Christian, Brandon and Noelle in what had become a tearful, festive celebration.

Every other weekend the house was either empty or filled with children when the Andersons and the younger Owenses alternated sleepovers. It was on the weekends, when the house was empty, that Hope and Theo slept together. Sleeping in separate bedrooms served to increased their desire for each other.

Rebecca held up a Vera Wang gown of luxurious off-white satin. Long-sleeved, cut on a bias with a squared neckline, it was a rhapsody of romance and modern grace. Instead of a veil, Hope had chosen to wear tiny white rosebuds and a feathered flower in her upswept hairdo.

"I can't believe you've gained that much weight

in two weeks," Rebecca remarked as she zipped up the back of the dress.

"Is it too tight?" Hope asked.

"No. In fact, it fits better now than it did before. All you need is your shoes, and you're ready to meet your groom."

Bobby's wife handed her a pair of off-white satin pumps, while Junior's wife dabbed her face with a powder puff. Marissa touched up her lipstick. Rebecca handed her a bouquet of burgundy and white roses with white velvet ribbons as streamers.

Hope peered into the full-length mirror. "Am I ready?"

Rebecca's reflection appeared in the mirror. "Are you, girlfriend?"

She turned and smiled at the four women. "Yes, I am. Lil Sis, go get Daddy."

A minute later Patrick Sutton walked into the bedroom, his mouth gaping. "Oh, baby, you look beautiful."

Hope's chin quivered. "Daddy, please don't make me cry."

Patrick offered his arm, and she placed her hand on his sleeve. "Let's go get you married."

Rebecca preceded them as they made their way down to the beach, where a small crowd had gathered to witness the marriage of Hope Sutton to Theodore Howell. Theo and Christian stood off to the side, watching and waiting for the bride.

Hope smiled at Janie and Thomas Smith, Charlotte Field, who refused to throw away her tobacco chew, even for the wedding of Queenie Robinson's grandbaby girl, Lee, Ashlee and Kyle Owens, Brandon and Noelle Anderson; her brothers, their wives, children, and Trey Baker and her twin nephews. Trey had resigned himself to his wife's going back to school once she'd proven to him that earning a degree would give them greater earning power.

Jeffrey Helfrick had flown in for the wedding. The agent was scheduled to spend the holidays with his children in Puerto Rico with the second of four ex-wives.

After Otis Pratt's article recanting his ménage à trois hoax, Derrick Landry had contacted Hope about the position at WLKV, but she had declined. She would continue her "Straight Talk" column for William Cullen and write books whenever the spirit hit her.

The minister from the only church on McKinnon Island stood ready to begin the ceremony. He pulled himself up to his full five-three height and smiled at Hope. "Who gives this woman in marriage?" His voice was unusually deep for a man of his diminutive height.

"I do," said Patrick in a strong voice. He placed Hope's hand in Theo's, then stepped back to sit beside his wife.

Theo smiled at Hope, mouthing, "Beautiful."

She returned his smile, nodding.

The afternoon was perfect for a wedding. The sun was shining, the temperature was in the low seventies. Hope and Theo repeated their vows, exchanged rings, then sealed their troth with a chaste kiss.

Everyone stood and applauded as Hope tightened her grip on her husband's neck.

"I have some good news," she whispered against his lips.

"What?"

"We're pregnant."

Theo went completely still. Eyes wide, he stared at her as if he'd never seen her before. "Are you sure?"

She nodded. "Very sure."

He swept her up in his arms, threw back his head, and bellowed like someone possessed. "Yes! Yes! Yes!"

Hope threw her bouquet over her head, and it landed in Ashlee Owens's lap. The young girl waved it above her head while smiling at Brandon.

Christian whispered in his brother's ear. The Anderson young men gave each other high fives, then winked at their older brother.

The minister's voice echoed above the sound of the waves crashing up on the beach. "Ladies and gentlemen, the ancestors and the descendants of McKinnon Island, South Carolina, congratulate Mr. and Mrs. Theodore Howell on their marriage. May you live a long and happy life together."

Theo placed his hand over his wife's belly. They shared a secret smile before turning to receive best wishes from those who had returned to a place that seemingly had stopped in time—a place where another generation of Gullahs would come to know their unique culture.